The Killing Jar

E. M. BEEKMAN

The Killing Jar

Houghton Mifflin Company Boston
1976

20493

Library of Congress Cataloging in Publication Data
Beekman, E   M   date
The killing jar.   I. Title.
PZ4.B4136Ki   [PS3552.E34]   813'.5'4   76-20542
ISBN 0-395-24763-2
Printed in the United States of America

C   10   9   8   7   6   5   4   3   2   1

For William F. Coughlin, Jr.

Wenn jedes Ich sein eigner Vater und Schöpfer ist,
warum kann es nicht auch sein eigner Würgengel sein?

Jean Paul

Yet a road must be chosen, a path must be trodden
which is not the easiest to go, nor is it the worst:
you must run a distance on the points of women's needles,
a second you must walk on the points of men's swords,
a third you must stride on the edges of heroes' blades.

The Kalevala

I

1

AN OFFICIAL GENIUS! Unaccustomed flattery seduced Toivo to accept the invitation of the U.S. Information Agency to go abroad on a lecture tour. After years of neglect and poverty his latest novel had suddenly given him fame, money and security.

He spent weeks writing, polishing and translating the lecture into the languages he knew or at least could fake. No problem in England, France, Germany or Finland. In Holland he could deliver in English, something he could also do in the Scandinavian countries. His agent, newly inspired like a test frog wired to a higher voltage, had placed several of his stories for astonishing fees, which would serve as security money on his trip. He had always dreamed of having a wad of crisp bills in his pocket to peel off like the skins of a green onion. Yet it was strange after all those years of saving on gas to pay the electricity, switching off the lights to save for the heating bill, cutting off the heat to pay for the car, scrimping on car repairs to pay for the electricity — strange after all those years of worry to have a surfeit of money at his disposal.

While he was preparing for his trip he received a letter from Blaise asking Toivo to meet him in Boston for a chat. After so many years of Christmas cards it was puzzling to have Mohammed come to the mountain. Toivo was curious to see again the man who had been the closest thing to family he'd had — someone who had acted like an uncle and even presumed the role of his dead father. He could ask Blaise to check on the young beggar he kept seeing wherever he went in Cambridge. Perhaps there was a plague of blind banjomen.

*

Passing the energetic young beggar again on his way home with a bottle of claret for Clara, his latest cockatrice, Toivo felt the eyes of the man use his face, prying for the coin of mercy. There were many people he let pass but he plucked at his banjo at some with a demanding air and the crass cord and stiff face, thrust upward, left no doubt as to his confidence in judging the select among the crowd whom he was pleased to have support him. When one of these didn't agree with him and hurried by without paying his dues, Toivo was sure he could hear the beggar yell, "Hey, you, you there, you cheap bastard, didn't you forget something?" If it was a recalcitrant woman of childbearing age he would remind her that fate could easily have put one of her sons where he sat now, on an assembly-line rug that he had lifted from the Woolworth's behind him, the limp beret in front of him begging to swell with lucre. It certainly looked that way, but it was impossible because the muscular mendicant was blind.

Toivo spied on him from behind a pile of bicycles thrown against a lamppost, waiting for a telling focusing or a turn of the head. Surely the man couldn't smell him out no matter how fine his nose, across the stream of human and dog bodies, babies, shopping bags and the unwrapped, unbagged groceries of the ecologically minded. Plus the groundfog of exhaust which never lifted in Cambridge, that citadel of humane learning in the land of the exterminated Algonquins.

The beggar was young, no more than midtwenties, and his rolled shirt sleeves displayed the mechanics of muscle while he tore out a vigorous banjo barrage. His thighs bulged eliptically in the tight jeans — none of that fake firmness which is no more than a hefty mass stuffed into a trouser leg, attribute of women and fat men. A smooth, tanned chest showed from his unbuttoned shirt. Glib American face: prefab good looks unimpeded by character, with whitewashed teeth and modish ear-lobe-length, shampooed hair.

If beggars too come sanitized now, there is no hope left for the heresy of city life. The down-and-outers have always shown an obstreperous nobility, born from a disgust with mankind and with life, both of which had brought them to that depth of existence where there's a true democracy of anthropophobes. A true beggar, crazy, filthy, snarling a mockery of good manners, such a beggar puts one's life on edge and it's fear that spares the change, not compassion. But with specimens like this one you could only feel like handing him a shovel and ordering him to dig for a buck and a quarter an hour. Fit to kick the legs from under a horse. Or kill a man.

"Cambridge is becoming impossible," Toivo said to Clara, who lay splashed on his bed, heavy braless breasts straining against gravity, her sloppy mouth open with concentration from reading one of the countless social purgatives the country was drowning in. When they reached paperback status Clara bought them from a friendly druggist who let her have them for a dime apiece without the cover since the paperback companies found it more trouble to reclaim unsold stock than to tear the covers off and take just those back to the home office for inventory. Clara studied history at Boston University. That is to say, exclusively American and then only after the Second World War. Anything before 1945 was ancient irrelevancy and Toivo made it for her simply because he was a writer — albeit one whose works she would never read.

"Why's that?" she mumbled, trying to be polite while she took a swig from the bottle of claret, ignoring the glass Toivo had fastidiously put next to her on a coaster.

"With the weekend influx of acned avatars, students, townies, local and out-of-town freaks, a man simply can't move around Harvard Square anymore without being hustled for money every inch of the way. It's a battlefield. Have you seen a young, good-looking beggar in front of Woolworth's? He's blind and plays the banjo."

"No, but I saw one like him the other day down here on Ash Street."

"Clara, stop reading that junk. Where and when?"

"Hell, I don't remember. Maybe it was another guy. And this stuff isn't junk, mister."

"This is important. What did he look like?"

"Just like you said. Young, good-looking and in terrific shape. Glad to give him a place to sleep any day of the week. What's going on?"

"Nothing. I just thought that he looked at me and recognized me. But that's impossible of course. Still, I wonder."

"Seriously, Toivo," said Clara, gathering herself into a shape that was still attractive but that would not wear the years well, "seriously, you should be more tolerant of what our generation reads and thinks. These books are important, have positive things to say even if they are negative."

He let go of her and watched her breasts while he drank from the glass she thought of as bourgeois. Why was it his luck to be constantly lectured by neophiliac women and children? After the divorce from chaste-chested Barb he had taken only full-bosomed females to bed. And wished he could attain complete misogyny. Yet had gotten no further than loneliness. He was tired of having others try to program his life with slogans and issues, all the more devilish because most of them were coated with a film of truth. Tired of being politicized. And politics knows no honest judgment except a selfish one. Often he had wondered, when he looked at his students, how they managed to keep all those hundreds of causes straight, each screeching as loud as the other for unconditional attention of your body and soul or else off with your head. Lewis Carroll's Red Queen would have loved this hydra era, these idealists of the literal. He was surrounded by indefatigable vocal chords in a rush-hour humanity and he now often dreamed of sparse Finland and its ancient heroes who were not demagogues but singers.

Barb had done one good thing for him. He had learned not to listen anymore but simply take what he was after. All that could happen was refusal. And for that too Barb had steeled him. Rolling the green T-shirt up and over her breasts he stopped Clara's mouth, took the bottle from her hand and pressed his luck. On the nipples. Which she couldn't resist. Yet the blind beggar would not stop worrying him.

2

HE WENT FOR A WALK in a night of bud-balmed sweetness with just enough of a chill in the wind to remember the winter past and to make him all the more happy about this night in May, fragrant with the uncommon sweetness of knowing people in bed reading his book. Most of the reviews had been glowing and he had even read the interviews to see if he had said anything of value.

— Tall, taciturn Toivo (sounds like *Teufel*, the German word for devil) Syystalvi (rhymes with *The Duchess of Malfi*) has caught the imagination of the jaded public perhaps precisely because he does not belong to any literary or intellectual clique. In fact, Mr. Syystalvi is not even an American by birth. He was born in Helsinki.

That night the magnolias by the Longy School of Music hinted their scent from huge fleshy bulbs curling back on themselves like savagely happy grins. The brick walks of Cambridge made sure he knew he was walking, forcing the toe of his shoes down while his heel was still slipping for balance on the uneven surface. Early bird bugs were dancing their halos around the streetlamps and he suddenly realized that there was no one around. He shivered a little. The banjoman still troubled him, and he could not forget the experience of a couple of nights before when he had gone to Boston to meet his ex-wife, Barbara, at the Auditorium.

She had gone to hear the latest guru promising solace, and he'd been told to look for her during intermission. He finally found her, standing on a flight of stairs leading down from the balcony into the foyer. She was talking to a young man in a polo shirt, his face hidden behind sunglasses. He was saying something to her while she looked over the flood of heads below for the pate of her former spouse. The man had looked vaguely familiar to Toivo. Where had he seen him before? Now, on his way to the Charles River, it occurred to Toivo that the man had looked a little like the banjoman. But when he had tried to get a closer look and had gone up a few steps, the man was gone. Barbara met him before he could get to the landing.

"I'm glad you came," Barb had said, pressing close to him in the crowd.

"What do you want?"

"Let's go outside and talk," she said. "It's more private there."

But under the marquee a large crowd was packing the sidewalk. With her long blond hair and the long blouse over pants which slopped over her sandaled feet, Barbara looked like a Visigoth, lacking only the droopy mustache and long sword. Under the tight-fitting jeans he could see the ribbed outline of her panties between the globes of faded material where friction had rubbed out the color. As if her ass was being held by two open hands. He really had never known this woman who had been his wife, never known her because there had been nothing to know. The feeling had been mutual.

They turned into a long narrow alley formed by one side of the Auditorium and the windowless wall of a warehouse. Far off in the tunneled darkness Toivo could see a faint, low-wattage bulb on an iron hook over a recessed doorway.

"Toivo, I didn't want to ask but could you give me some money? I wouldn't have asked if you'd still been poor. But that book of yours must be selling well and making you a lot of money. I am really flat broke. You know I've never asked you for money before but the course with the Master has taken all the dough I had saved from my job as a waitress in New York"

"You certainly get around. How much do you want?"

"Can I come by your place tomorrow? Okay? I've got to get back now because the service must have started again."

He watched her run to the lit sidewalk, the two white ovals on her ass bobbing like those of a deer.

Because his head was drooping from a sad thought the blow did not hit him at the base of the skull but was blunted by the length of his neck and the top of his shoulders. Going down toward the asphalt he tried to spin around and grab the ankles of the person behind him, but he couldn't finish the movement and slabbed heavily to the ground. Way in the distance of his ears he heard a sharp whistle and the foot in his ribs stopped kicking him. Then he was being dragged to where light could be splashed on his face. Someone was pinching at his flesh down the endless length of his leg and he felt rough and cold on his skin.

"Your wallet was found a few yards from where you were lying against the wall," the policeman told him in the station. "There was no money in it. Did you have any on you?"

Toivo nodded.

"Obviously a mugging."

The Irish cop was tired. He was sucking on the rim of his coffee cup as if he could draw enough strength for the remainder of his beat from the hot liquid.

"The cops will take you home," said the doctor in the emergency room of Massachusetts General Hospital. "Those pills I gave you will give you a good night's sleep. Here is a prescription for something else when you wake tomorrow with a hell of a headache. You should be all right day after tomorrow."

— If you have read *Past Reason Hunted,* the angriest, most honest novel of the year, then you should also read this author's previous work which is, if anything, more honest in its anger at a world he has refused to yield to.

Agreed. Even gibberish: agreed. If it's favorable it can't be all bad. Make absolutely sure you read the others. Yes, sir, yes indeed.

The sycamore trees on Memorial Drive shook their filigrain wigs like rows of green barristers politely shocked by a mischievous client. A few cars sped by and every so often bars of music would slip from an open window in one of the Harvard houses, slide along on a float of air and rock with the slap of the river on the stones a few feet below.

— I have noticed, Mr. Syystalvi, that you mention *The Kalevala* a lot. Is it important to you?
— Yes.
— What is it?
— It is a collection of traditional poems from a district in Finland called Karelia. They were written down in the field by Elias Lönnrot, an amazing Finnish scholar of the last century. I'll write it out for you. Though the poems were recorded in the nineteenth century they contain echoes of the Viking Age. This oral poetry was sung by pairs of singers who joined hands and sometimes accompanied themselves with the simple strumming of a small harp. What I love most about it is that the heroes are magicians. There's relatively little bloodshed in these poems. The weapons are song, incantation and magic. It is the most civilized national poem I know of. Poets win. Singers transform the world. My favorite character, for example, is a magician who was old at birth and cannot get older or younger. He sings a young upstart magician into a bog. *The Kalevala* is such a wonderful world, a world I have always been writing toward.
— I see. Obviously it means a lot to you. Do you use it in any particular manner?
— The heroes. Väinämöinen, who is the eternally old sage I just mentioned. Lemminkäinen, prototype of the recklessly charming ladykiller; Ilmarinen, the Finnish Hephaestus; and Kullervo who is a somewhat modern hero. He is sad and tragic and mentally befuddled from too much rocking when he was a baby. And at times I try to duplicate that wonderfully insistent rhythm of parallel repetitions.
— ?
— Well, I'll tell you. Something like,
  the snow blew in the night
  cold ashes whirled in the dark.
— Is there any other reason for your fascination?
— Yes. My father loved it and used to read it to me.

— I see. Your father seems to be important to you. Where is he now?

— Dead.

Would he, would Kall have enjoyed this triumph?

Toivo shivered on the bench by the Charles as he watched the moon traveling down the stream in an elastic silver boat which snapped only to form again. He ached. A man in pain on such a joyous night was out of order. He had wanted a son to give exactly what he had hoped for from his father. To travel, just the two of them. The embrace only a child can give which restores the most downtrodden outcast to life and mettle. In his own childhood he'd had so little of it himself. Maybe a couple of months, a paltry sliver of his youth, out of all those years of childhood. To have his son next to him in his car talking of trees, cars and numnums. Silences between father and son bursting with speech. Each completely trusting the other. To be willing, no, simply to give your life when harm comes in the way. Just the two of them against the world. With his father. With a woman. Against loneliness. Against a rapacious world choked by people. Twins, steady as a constellation. Kall had seemed to know so much. He loved *The Kalevala,* had it memorize him through hells erected by his peers. Would he have been proud of a wordsmith, of his son, a magician of words?

He got up from the bench by the river heavy with ghosts. A dead father. A son not born. Walked to Hayes-Bickford, a greasy spoon that was open all night. Where only the night crew from the streets slouch over the plastic tables cupping the heat of their coffee to get through the wee hours. Also thieves: bullies for a handful of dollars. Right then a fight would have been welcome but he found a cafeteria, empty except for the daughter of a dead philosopher, with a damaged brain, feeding cupcakes to a brace of parrots on her shoulder.

3

HE LADLED BUTTER and jam on the scone and ate the miniature three-decker sandwich.

"You'll be much safer here," his father said.

Toivo ate a marzipan cake and slurped some murky brew from the porcelain teacup with a gold rim.

"Is there also a low tea, Father?"

He was embarrassed to speak Finnish aloud, as if it were an unclean tongue amidst aliens. The boy was trying very hard to put his father at ease. He had great trouble not letting tears get into his voice and had to force down the sumptuous high tea past the rushes of fear which started in his stomach. Kall knew what his boy was doing and felt in at ease.

"Did you like the Gwynns, Toivo?"

"Yes. Could I have more tea?"

The father poured him some. Ordered more scones.

"I'm glad you like them. You can help Mr. Gwynn with his study of the sagas because you know Finnish better than he does, and he can help you with English. He will give you a weekly allowance and if there's anything else, you write to me in Helsinki."

"What if something happens, Father?" Toivo finally dared ask, building yet another three-decker scone with sweet butter and boysenberry jam. Each layer had to be meticulously even and he was afraid that if his hand trembled too much and bungled it he would throw the thing in his cup and climb into his father's lap and cling to him as he had seen monkeys do in the zoo.

"But nothing will happen, Toivo," said the father. Kall had given in and ordered a bottle of whiskey to keep the waiter from going back and forth to fill his glass, then changed his mind because the interruptions were welcome despite the man's obvious annoyance.

"But if?"

"Nothing will happen, but I'll think of something, just in case. I'll let you know."

He was still asleep when he felt his father's face on his head. Desperately he tried to struggle toward mindfulness but, at the same time, he was pulled back into sleep.

"Good morning, my boy," a woman said when he woke up. "I think we'd better get up. We've got a long journey ahead of us and you haven't even had breakfast yet."

It was very strange to hurt so much physically when no one had done him bodily harm. Crying made it worse since his sobs were closer to retching than tears. By the time he finally left the hotel with Mrs. Gwynn he hated his father. For three days he was sick in bed. But broken places mend, though they do not heal.

Soon Toivo knew the Gwynns' house better than its owners. He could lead the professor and his wife through the darkened rooms when the air-raid alarm sounded, lead them as well as a dog for the blind. Or grope around for Mrs. Gwynn's knitting when the electricity had again failed because a burning house had toppled on the lines. It often happens that a stranger is better acquainted with the city in which you make your home. He needs to be. Otherwise he might get lost.

They were kind to him, the professor of Scandinavian literatures and his proper wife who knitted socks and scarfs for their son who had been shot down over France. But Toivo never became a member of the family. He went to school, was an attentive student at the private tutorials given by his host, read at night in *The Kalevala*. Kall had left a specially bound edition with the Gwynns as a present for his son. And now he was trapped in a war, a fleshed-out memory for strangers who feasted on him with sadness because he was not the one they wanted him to be. *The Kalevala* became a refuge which did not shift and turn on him, did not desert or frighten him. A steady world. Books do not betray.

They are more faithful than people. *The Kalevala* became a magic book which, opened at a random page, nestled him back in his language, in his country, in his father.

After school Toivo began to roam with a gang of rubble rats and surprised them with his cunning and cool despite his heavy accent. Took lessons in judo, as his father had wanted him to, from an arthritic athlete with a drinking problem who only had the job at the Boy's Gym because the better-equipped instructors were in the armed forces. But the boy never did get very good at shuddering in air-raid shelters with frightened neighbors. After a few weeks Professor Gwynn refused to go down anymore, thinking the time would be better spent in saving his precious manuscripts if a bomb were to blow him to bits, while his wife saw no reason whatsoever for putting several feet of concrete between her curses and the enemy in the sky. At first she had to be forcibly restrained from going to nearby antiaircraft batteries so she could cheer them on, not understanding that her enthusiastic hatred would be a bother. She was only persuaded when someone pointed out that the gunners were unable to hear her because of the noise of their weapons. Still, it took Toivo considerable trouble to persuade them to let him stay upstairs too. Somehow, being a foreign charge made him more eligible for protection. But by appealing to their claustrophobia and faith in fair play he was allowed to stay with them, and Toivo, like a young sad Nero, watched the burning of London.

4

On his way to clean out his locker in the YMCA, Toivo saw the young blind beggar again at the end of his street, going toward Harvard Square. Without a stick, banjo on his back, the man walked briskly with a half step of caution feeling his way. Toivo wondered if he lived in one of the small basement apartments on Ash Street.

Toivo was a regular member of an Exercise for Your Life class during the lunch hour. His fellow teammates were a banker, two salesmen, a high school principal, two teachers, a fat Harvard graduate student, a waiter and a silversmith. Toivo had joined because it broke the monotony of his usual day. Woke him up and hypnotized him to a state of rhythmic motion. Like a ponderous, flat-footed herd they jogged the circumference of the gym, sweating, grinning, racing cardiac arrests. The rhythm of his piston legs, when he finally found the beat his muscles felt easy with, could keep him going for miles and miles, like a squirrel in a treadmill, never minding anything.

The others had gotten used to his taciturnity and did not bother to include him in conversation or force him into the horseplay of snapping towels to nude buttocks and restorated bellies. Gray-haired schoolboys savoring the rancid smell of sweaty bodies, soiled feet, drenched jockstraps and genital grease, romping around the locker room of their youth. But by ten minutes after one, the place was empty and the last of the reluctantly dressed men had suited himself for duty and stepped from the fond stale air into the foul exhaust of congested Central Square.

One night a week he went back to the Y for a class in judo. It had been part of Kall's survival kit.

"It is a sport which understands the nature of man," his father had told him in London. "It teaches you to use to a maximum the equipment you were born with. It's cunning, and cunning is what you need most. These days the majority of people believe in the superiority of numbers, and firearms have given imbeciles a chance to kill. In judo, however, you use your opponent to disable him. With a minimum of effort you get the maximum of effect."

Throughout his youth he hadn't doubted his father, but later on he began to question the motive for despair which spurred his father's eccentric educational theories. Then, when he got older, it was sad to acknowledge that the man's suspicions were correct. The world proved it everyday.

Another reason for physical exertion was to counteract writing. After endless nighthours of battling with words which would not surrender the images in his mind but, like root vegetables, show only the useless tops and leave the fruit underground, after the mental agony, it was invigorating to feel the body again.

The black belt who was his instructor at the Y had taught French paratroops and was now a student in a hotel management school. He was clearly bored with teaching his martial profession to eager overweights flatfooting it to their partners with the hustling ponderousness of hippos. The instructor liked Toivo a little more than the others only because he could speak French, and sometimes he would talk to his student about his love for France, a country not kind enough to be as lucrative as the States. With the typical paunch of judo masters — who have to force their center of gravity as low as possible for better balance and solidity of stance — and an otherwise smoothly toned muscle armor, the nude, aspiring maitre d'hotel would lean against his metal locker after a shower and survey the poundage lumbering by with a glint of danger in his normally flat eyes. As if at any moment he would jump away from the painted metal cubicle and start hurtling bodies through the air or dash them against the slippery concrete floor with the same mad urgency of a fighting bull in a corrida. After many months of cajoling, the Frenchman agreed to teach Toivo some illegal tricks, lethal wiles learned on the sly.

— Do you write easily, Mr. Syystalvi?
— No.
— What does it feel like when it doesn't go well?
— The need to smash somebody's face in.
— Why do you write if it is so difficult?
— Because to create an autonomous world is a miracle. A book is a defiance. A subversion.
— Then you don't believe in committed literature?
— No. The imagination is a warren of spies. It goes against the grain. To begin with a dictated subject, no matter how flattering it might be morally, is to deny the work of art its dictatorial power. And since it is a tyrant, the imagination will then fail to stir genius but let it rot in the prison of fact. For that matter, philosophical and scientific systems are the most wonderful fantasies. Who can prove that quasars aren't cosmic juggler's balls or that radio telescopes aren't oneiric spyglasses? Don't forget that even proof only confirms a hypothesis as an agreed-upon fact. It's not irrefutably so. Reset the mind and a line is the longest distance between two points and the squaring of a circle becomes an axiom of mathematics. It is said in *The Kalevala* that the world was created from the Virgin of Air impregnated by the Wind. Now, is that necessarily less right than our idea, our fiction, of protoplasmic stirring? Art makes people less sure.
— One last question. Every writer is born in his youth, as it were. Do you consider yours of particular importance?

5

FROM HIS MOTHER Toivo retained a fascination for the Virgin, but it was his father who came to lord his memory more and more during the years of his marriage to Barbara, while the mother faded into a hazy memory of a rather giddy icon. To the grown man childhood and youth were a crossword puzzle of fearful design and it appeared to him that there were times when he did not want the pieces to fit because the fragments warned they were best left alone.

"The reason you're an only child," his father once told him in London during the war, "is that your mother and history made it impossible for me to care for more than one. As it was, you were already one too many. Still, you were the happiest accident I ever had."

And accident, or fate, had not been very kind to the man.

Kall Syystalvi was a Finnish Swede (a decided minority in Finland), a Communist and a Lutheran. Toivo's mother, Ella, who was from East Karelia and considered herself more of a Finn than her husband, was anti-Communist, i.e., a White, and a member of the Orthodox Church. It has been said over and over again that the Finns are closed, silent, taciturn people who rarely jest. They are independent by nature (in this case a very true saying indeed) and through historical circumstances adept at the game of brinkmanship. This stubborn individuality and cunning realism created a proud people of amazing tenacity forced by geography and political reality to make a fine art of survival. Looking back he could say that as a child he was very much like Finland: caught between two powers tugging at him and with no

Solomon in sight. Since neither could prevail on him to take sides he became a precocious existential autodidact, just as the friction of two steadily rubbed sticks sets a spark and forces it to nurture itself into flame. Naturally the mother had more opportunity to politick for his affections. But a child soon learns that a solicitation to join one or the other of the armed parental camps is not the same thing as love, not quite an expression of affection. It took Toivo until he was an adolescent to know that his father's love for him, though marred by mystery and long absences, was unconditional and genuine. By that time his mother had disappeared into voluntary exile in Soviet-occupied Karelia.

A university graduate, a journalist, from a monied family with a military background, Kall Syystalvi honored the cause of the Red Guard in the 1918 war for independence, despite the fact that he remained loyal to an ideological affection for Trotsky. Stalin, he felt, was an intrepid kulak to be feared and hated. Mediocrity always breeds the best butchers, he believed, because stunted cerebral growth finds great comfort in utilitarian efficiency. Sometimes, he would say, the only way to stop butchers from slaughtering is to kill them — and he would smile at the brute irony of the statement.

In January 1918, when Germany and Russia were talking peace, Finland declared herself independent and immediately had to face grave danger. On her soil were 40,000 Russian troops with their discipline in bad disrepair, while a predominantly leftist mood was being fanned into violence and hatred by the "proletarian czar" in Moscow. What had started as a struggle for independence soon turned into a savage civil war which left gaping wounds in the nation and in Toivo's family itself. His mother remained in Helsinki, which was occupied by the Reds, and was several times spared imprisonment because Kall was a Communist leader. Kall himself fought in the battle of Tampere and was imprisoned rather than shot since his wife came from a well-known White family. These mutual debts became ammunition for marital battles when the war was over. Kall survived the hell of the government detention camps to come home and father his only child.

In the camps he learned the politics of hunger: a doctrine

which erases ideologies. He remembered a man getting killed for a handful of grass and another choking to death on a piece of leather he had ripped off the bellyband of a guard's horse which had slipped on a frozen puddle. The only allegiance he could afford was to his stomach. To keep his mind from running off with him he recited all the passages he could remember from Finland's traditional epos, *The Kalevala.*

"I stood in the middle of the compound yelling as loud as I could the charms against winter and the lines on the origin of beer, yelling to keep from eating a brick. You see, it had a satanic resemblance to a ham-loaf and one prisoner had just been dragged away by the guards while shouting that he recommended it highly to us but please to leave him some. Which was only fair because he was the one who had found it. Except that he had ripped his mouth open when he tried to tear a piece out of it."

To be saved by *The Kalevala* and blades of grass! Kall had often desired to be shot, seduced by the thought that if he caught the bullet with his mouth — which he had no doubt he could do because hallucinations from hunger are the authors of more miracles than Lourdes — he would have gotten hold of a powerfully concentrated sausage which would last him for weeks. The experience of the camps had removed any political creed. Kall came back to life with just himself and with a strange private code of conduct no one understood.

Least of all his wife. A handsome, flirtatious and gay woman, she was an inevitable antithesis to her husband. Whereas Kall liked the austere sobriety of the Lutherans, Ella found that the pomp and ritual of the Orthodox Church suited the mysteries of God better. That a mystery can be lean as well as opulent did not occur to her since she lived in an either/or world where both alternatives were constantly berated by her boorish husband whose duty in life, obviously, was to crush her spirit and fun. She had contrived to have a replica of a salon and was tutored in her beliefs by a bevy of mediocre middle-aged intellectuals who could only agree on being hysterically patriotic and anti-Communist. She upbraided her husband for being more Swedish than Finn, for having the wrong political coloring, for not being a poet, for making fun of her attempts "at raising the intellectual level of Helsinki, that poor relation of Paris and Berlin," for being more swinish than fun.

Ella had envisioned a life of parties, balls, official banquets with a brilliant young husband who, in her mind, ought to be something of a Richelieu in the body of Valentino. A journalist, no matter how well respected, an official whose job was difficult to define, a prisoner, not of Chillon but a real one with all the uncompromising marks of hardship and pain — such things were impossible, simply not to be tolerated in a husband of hers. One of the failings she could not forgive the man was his not being sufficiently romantic in his sufferings. He would not robe himself in the fineries of illusion but brought the stench of reality home, an odor she could not perfume or prattle away.

O how she loved to dance, how she loved to be dejected by woodwinds and strings or, later, in the thirties, by that "slightly seedy music called jazz." She spent an inordinate amount of time and money on clothes, rustling, swishing, clacking heels. Adangle with accessories. The child Toivo was lavishly kissed and hugged, assured he was "mama's boy" and he could still hear, years later, the sound of faintly clicking beads and pearls muted by soft skin and cloth. But beyond these dutiful tempests of affection there was little else to rely on and her son withdrew more and more from her and slowly began to veer toward the man she despised.

In winter, more than half the year in Finland, Ella would consent to travel only in the city of Helsinki itself unless it was for a short trip into the country in a horse-drawn sled so that she, dressed in furs, could dream of being Anna Karenina, to the point of shuddering fearfully in train stations. Her husband's typically Finnish love for outdoor sports such as skiing and hiking she observed with the same bemused condescension as she did Toivo's childhood games.

"Having no intention to become either a pioneer or a Lapp, I see no need to exert a lot of wasted energy in the pursuit of fatigue and perspiration." Meaning that she found such things common and participation in them unbecoming a lady. Saunas were never mentioned in her presence — they were vulgar beyond belief. For Ella, though she worshiped the game of attraction, was terror-stricken by the idea of sex and nakedness. Her body was an object to be polished to perfection so that it could entice members of the opposite sex in the safeguard of fashion. Kall had found this out very early in their marriage and the few times he bedded her he had had to seduce her with champagne and contest endless yards of wraps, robes and night-gowns. He once confessed to never having seen her naked and was surprised that she allowed her body to form a child inside her, a repulsive animality she only consented to because having offspring was de rigueur.

"It's really strange that your mother didn't like winter," Kall once told his son, "because she was eminently suitable to that season. After all, icebergs, even well-dressed ones, melt in summer — a fate worse than death for my wintry spouse."

Toivo was not astonished to remember his popular mother (since her vices appeared like eccentric virtues to outsiders) as an overpowering flourish at teatime (Ella adored the British for their reticence and implored her son to become a consul in London) and a dimly lit icon at night. His mother worshiped, both literally and figuratively, the Virgin Mary, whose magical parturition untouched by human hand or penis she felt to be the acme of human endeavor. Fancied herself a fallen replica of this inhuman motherhood and cajoled Toivo into primeval awe for the absent-minded lady with a sexagenarian baby floating above the palm of her hand. To the point that he had nightmares about his mother wishing him on the cross so she could stand at his feet and weep in the Italian mode and be transfigured into heaven smiling benignly down at her son as she rose, oblivious to his excruciating pain.

His father's trips within Finland and abroad became longer and longer. And he paid little attention to gossip about his wife's more than social interest in an etymologist, because he well knew that it would never get beyond the platonic stage: the friction of rubbery minds vainly attempting to produce a spark. But he did take his son away to the country whenever he was home and taught him how to ski, to use the sauna, to hike across miles of forest with just compass and map.

When Finland was invaded by Russia in 1939, Toivo was about fourteen and the marriage of his parents a caricature of custom. Ella refused to follow her husband up north despite the constant threat of air attacks in Helsinki. She insisted that her parents in Karelia needed her more than her husband did. Kall, who had volunteered for service on the northeastern front, told her he had little stomach for bringing up the rear of his wife's mad escapades when Finland was being overrun. When she persisted in her folly and wanted to take the boy with her, the father lost patience. If the creature was determined to get herself killed for reasons beyond his comprehension, well and good. But at least she was not going to have a hand in the murder of his only child.

"I can see you now, blundering through front lines in a limousine driven by one of your feeble-minded monkeys, sending Toivo out to get soap and hot towels to wash the dust from your precious complexion. I can't force you to move to the country up north, nor am I going to play your guardian. This is simply not the time to quibble whether Finland or you needs me more. No other woman is asking herself that. And a mother who wants to drag her child into what I know to be the most dangerous section of the country, such a mother is not fit to be a parent and I'll make sure that she'll never lay a hand on my son. The boy is going with me and that's the end of that. My wife can do what she likes."

The November morning his mother left, Toivo watched the car move out of the street from a window of the apartment. The fact that he had told her he preferred his father's company (and the thrill of the military) earned him a mere handshake of farewell. She said she wasn't crying because the biting frost would freeze her tears to her skin. He never saw her again.

Afraid of the unpredictable Russian air force, which would bomb the smallest hamlet for no apparent reason, Kall tried to keep his son with him as much as possible. Somehow, cajoling, pulling strings and promising that his son would make himself useful, he managed to keep Toivo at or near the front. His reasoning was that proximity to the enemy can be far safer than distance, something which can be observed in anyone's yard where a daring cat will sit quietly close to a dog and wash itself, though it would be in serious danger when further away or on the run. That fine, thin line which marks the boundary between unreasonable safety and certain danger is not found in manuals but learned only through experience. The guerrilla thrives on it. And what the Finns fought was essentially a guerrilla war. Their incredible success, particularly in Selkä-Suomi, the pinched waist of Finland where Kall was fighting, helped Toivo to remain with him. That and Sergeant Mikko, to whom Toivo was entrusted whenever his father was away. And so it happened that Toivo spent two months on the Arctic Circle, in the deep forest, learning the life of a winter guerrilla, learning how to survive and fight in extreme physical conditions, learning to be silent. Learning to learn in the safety of the front line.

This was also the beginning of Kall's quiet campaign to teach his son peculiar skills — skills which would save Toivo's life in later emergencies. His schooling was an odd mixture of training in small arms, hand-to-hand combat, languages, *The Kalevala*, the theory and practice of guerrilla warfare from the Old Testament Israelites to the British Commandos and cunning in every walk of life. Physical aspects the father left mostly to experts recruited either by himself or by emissaries such as Mikko or, in later years, Blaise. The intellectual education he provided himself by fits and starts over the next four years with a quiet urgency which foreboded his sudden disappearance in 1944.

In essence the father taught his son survival skill both mental and physical. It was all he had to give and he had become more and more convinced that they were more valuable than gold. It was a strange curriculum by most standards, except that the state of the world made it eminently sane. While most children were still being dyed in the vat of morals, Toivo learned to protect whatever constituted his private self. And when he found himself in exile, perpetually crossing the foreign borders of a geographic or mental country, he profited from the foresight of his peculiar parent who, out of love, had taught him the subversive tactics to maintain oneself in a slipcase of flesh lost in a hostile world.

And the Winter War in Finland was an excellent basis for such training. Unaided by stalling though sympathetic nations, the Finns were taught to rely on themselves and make the best use of their resources of cunning, necessity and hostile terrain to outwit an enemy far superior in manpower and materiel. Their secret weapons were mobility, invisibility, severe minus forty temperatures and hunger. Ruthless pragmatists, they showed neither mercy nor viciousness, for the extremity of their condition allowed for neither.

Clad in white hooded coveralls over winter uniforms Kall, Toivo and Mikko were lying prone behind some frozen firs on a slight rise. Their skis were lying next to them and both Captain Syystalvi and Sergeant Mikko were armed with Suomi automatic pistols.

About half a mile in front of them was the highway bottled up with stalled convoys. They were watching a Russian patrol picking its way gingerly through the gelid silence. Toivo was trying to find the Finnish patrol, which was in hiding. But he could not see it. Everything was white, lined with haphazard streaks of grayish brown and green, and the Russian soldiers were very noticeable as dark moving slugs, their boots crunching in the frozen crust of snow decked by freshly fallen powder. The boy was terrified by the silence, which magnified the hostile sounds as if it were an auditory microscope, and by the tension which lay coiled in the movement of the figures below him. Unwittingly he saw the economics of fear in the simplicity of sparse movement on a vast yet choked terrain. He reached for his father and the man gently pushed him down, laying the reassuring weight of an arm over his shoulder.

Behind the five enemy soldiers a mount rose up and two Russian corpses were lowered to the snow, their throats cut by a *puukko,* a Finnish type of hunting knife. No sound. No struggle. Just the fading thunder of three pairs of boots. Toivo bit his lips to keep from crying out, obeying his father's strict command never to make a sound in the field unless ordered to do so. The remaining three Russians jostled to a stop, calf-deep in snow, and turned around. When they saw their dead, a very brief rattle of sound came from the ground and they dropped where they stood, flapped down like figures in a shooting gallery. Mikko whistled piercingly and three white shapes seemed reluctant to cut motion. As if splinters of terrain were experimenting with locomotion. An arm was raised in response and then the figures bent down and got on their skis. Within minutes they had disappeared.

The three observers slid their feet into the toepieces of their skis and went silently back to their base. (Even Toivo had laughed at the senselessness of a pair of captured Russian skis which had both toepiece and heelstrap. Every Finnish fighting man knew he should be able to free himself of his skis as quickly as possible. Undoing the heelstraps could cost him his life.) Back in the dugout, three yards beneath snow and ice, heated by a stove which gave off neither smoke nor sparks, Kall answered his son's questions in a comfortable seventy-five degrees while above their heads a lifeless, soundless, moonlit waste betrayed no form of life.

"We fight on the principle of conservation. Conservation of energy and materials. We are a beggar's army. When a knife will do we don't waste bullets. We're too poor to be extravagant."

"But why can't we attack the entire Russian force on the highway and simply wipe them out?"

"Because we can't and don't need to. Always remember that pummeling your opponent's chest or thighs is useless. You go for the vital parts or you use your opponent's weight. As in judo, which I hope to have someone teach you someday, you defeat your opponent by preserving your own strength and by using his bulk as a lever. It's like a snake's poison, Toivo. An effective poison doesn't attack the entire system but goes directly for the brain or the spinal column. We are too small and too weak to attack the division on the highway with brute force. But we *can* attack their communications and command posts. Without their brains and voice they are helpless."

"Then what?"

Mikko answered: "They starve to death or they freeze to death. Or both. It's cheaper that way."

"And more effective," his father joined in. "Besides, we don't have to waste any of our men. The whole point of this war is to waste as little as possible in men, ammo and energy. Not only in this war, but in life as well. If you can kick and run fast it's better to do that and return for another kick than to stand there and slug it out bravely like a hero. The latter is just foolish theatricals, the former is street fighting."

But Toivo, drugged by the heat, was falling asleep. His father led him to the bed and stroked his hair with a gentleness which seemed to fit the absurd softness of the patrol actions in the forest. The cozy underground lair had nothing whatsoever to do with the surface war. He could stay there and hibernate until soggy with spring rains and come up to a flower-decked forest meadow to hike with his father to Lapland, to Norway, anywhere, as long as the man was with him, because he loved and trusted him. Because the man could look into the future and tell him things now which he forgot or didn't hear because he was tired and sleepy but which, many years later, would come back to him, perhaps save him. In his dreams his father became Väinämöinen, the sagacious magician of *The Kalevala* who can do everything and overcome anyone. Never growing older than old, Väinämöinen can hide you under his beard and sing all enemies away, sing you all of the earth's wisdom while accompanying himself on the harp he carved out of a pike's jawbone and strung with hair of the Demon's gelding.

"Maybe I'll be sorry, son. But right now I don't see any use in teaching you soccer," he heard his father say at the doorsill of sleep.

In Cambridge, Toivo sometimes longed for Kall, at night when the moon over Ash Street hung suspended between heaven and earth like the copper boat where Väinämöinen waits, knowing that he will be needed again someday. Needed by his son, Toivo, who knew him as the only ally he'd ever had, the only sage whose wisdom he welcomed. Why was it that he could not remember his face?

Sergeant Mikko taught Toivo how to use the Suomi automatic pistol. Mikko was a short, squat man without a waist. His torso was a square rock lowered gingerly on short legs which strained outward under the pressure. Kall had met him in a government detention camp after the civil war where Mikko shared a slice of bread he had stolen from the guards' kitchen with him. Such a gesture was nothing short of miraculous in that hell where want had made shades of men so that when it rained one could barely distinguish flesh from water. Kall never forgot and he sought out Mikko after his release. During the war against Russia he made him his aide and entrusted Toivo to his care.

A peasant, Mikko had spent most of his life in the woods trying to scratch a living from the unyielding forest floor. He was glad when Kall relieved him of that duty and wished never to see a cow again. Kind and straightforward he could not hide his love for violence and adventure. As a guerrilla fighter he was not easy to surpass simply because he liked danger too much and because he knew the forest better than a logger. Given the limited world Toivo was living in, Mikko seemed a genius to him: one who could make his skis find paths in the forest where there were none, knew how to cut a Russian throat with his puukko knife or whittle trolls out of pine, could field-strip a Suomi in minutes, could make bread out of bark, knew just how many birch twigs were needed to make a pleasant whisk to "tickle your back" in the sauna, knew why a horse would refuse a saddle and could build a dugout in a week.

Mikko's craftsmanship and his ill luck with women reminded Toivo of *The Kalevala's* smith, Ilmarinen, who made a girl out of gold and silver to lie with him in the long winter nights. But the side that touched the metal woman got as cold as sea ice and so Ilmarinen took his handiwork to Väinämöinen as a gift. His friend refused it and told him to throw her in the fire or take her to Russia or Germany, for it was not for him "to woo a gold woman, to try and please one of silver." Yes, Mikko would have been capable of doing that and Toivo told his father of his comparison. Kall laughed and agreed with his son.

"But don't be fooled by him. What he's really complaining about is that every female he gets his hands on wants to marry him. And Mikko is convinced that a wife will send him right back to the farm which, he feels, is a fate worse than death. The other day he told me he was mad at the Russians for not having female troops. Then, you see, he could take them prisoner, have his fun with them and send them back to the Urals."

Mikko's favorite weapon was the Suomi automatic pistol. And he taught Toivo all he knew about it, wasted no time in explaining his affection.

"Rifles are ridiculous in the woods. Just go outside and take a look at those idiotic Russians dragging them around. Only if I am standing in the middle of a frozen lake with a full moon on me could one of those nuts use one on me. What you really want in our thick forests is something that will fire a lot of ammo rapidly. Now you think of course that any old fool can do this. Just press the trigger and five hundred rounds per minute come out. Sure. You'll hit a lot of trees. But you don't want trees, you want bodies, right? So, only when they are coming at you in groups should you make our friend here automatic. But if you're on patrol and you're after two or three of them you should have a single-shot weapon. Well, you get that by simply flicking on this catch here by the trigger guard. This beauty is a real woods pistol.

"The other nice thing is its caliber. Nine mm. Know why? Because the Russians have lots of nine mm ammo for their Mauser Colts and all we have to do is capture some supply convoys and we can give every Finn as many bullets as he'd like. I bet you think that my friend here is not accurate, right? Wrong. The drum, you see, is directly under the barrel so that when the seventy rounds in it are being fired the nose of the barrel doesn't kick up. Let me tell you, at short distances it is just as accurate as any fancy rifle, but, at the same time, when a herd of drunken reindeer are coming after you you've got all the firepower you need to stop them."

"Reindeer?"

"Sure. Don't tell me you didn't know that they get drunk on the Arctic berries that they make this stuff out of."

Mikko held a bottle up to the light half full with Mesimarja, a liquor distilled from fermented Arctic berries.

"I tell you, they nibble at those berries by the ton and their stomachs ferment it and they get stinking drunk. And when they're stinko they'll run here all the way from Lapland. Back at my father's farm I caught many of them simply by putting raisins in the palm of my hand. The stupid bastards are so far gone and so hooked on the stuff they'll gobble up anything that looks like those berries. I had them eating out of my hand. Then, while they're eating, you grab them by the antlers and you've got yourself a genuine Lappish reindeer. Of course when they find out you've been cheating them they run off to tell their buddies and they'll come after you. And there's nothing worse than a herd of mad reindeer looking for booze coming after you. And that's the time when your automatic comes in pretty handy."

Mikko imitated a drunken reindeer and the laughing soldiers in the dugout tried to shoot him from their beds of furs. Just when the reindeer was begging his hunters for one more swig of Mesimarja before he was smoked and exported as a delicacy, a guard pushed the heavy door-curtain aside and told them that an enemy patrol was coming right at them.

"I bet they're from that so-called crack Siberian Brigade," grunted Mikko while pulling his boots on. "Those monkeys think they're really something. But they're just a bunch of Tartars shuffling around on the lids of garbage cans. We'll fix them."

"Four of them," the guard said.

"Four? At night? They got to be drunk. Hell, at night they only go out in their tanks, if they can move them. I tell you, I bet they're those drunken reindeer I was telling you about. Come on, boy. I'll show you what I mean about our automatic friend here."

Because Mikko was just drunk enough to be incautious he took Toivo with him with the casual good humor of a father showing off to his son.

Only a few feet away and Toivo couldn't see the dugout anymore. He wondered if he'd ever find its cozy, fur-lined warmth and brightly lit safety again if Mikko and the two soldiers were killed in this frozen night sporadically illuminated by a half-moon. Only details are smoothed by ice in a winter forest. Generally the ground and surroundings are rough as frostbitten skin and, where trees have been cleared, there is an eruption of blisters frozen solid on the skin of the earth. A sameness of chaos. The men had disappeared, just as the dugout had, among the iced trees. Even their noise was camouflaged since a thick forest is never silent in winter but creaks and crunches like an arthritic skeleton. Toivo was no longer sure at all that he had ever been in a fur-lined underground lair with joking men. The drunken reindeer were only a memory; now he was on an endless hike with blind shapes on wooden slats for feet and wooden sticks for arms pursuing blind brown shades. He bumped the tips of his skis against Mikko's to make sure he still had company. Wanted to yell and hear curses answering him: only voices are not native to ice and snow. But these shapes were silent and suddenly he was absolutely certain that his tongue would never move again and he would gradually stiffen in a deep deep freeze which would capture him in the series of strides he had taken since he had left the lair. His father would go look for him and pass by the stilled multiplication of sons, incapable of hearing ice scream. Toivo was trying to find the blanket on his bed so that he could at least be certain of a dream when Mikko whispered to him to get down and look directly ahead of him where the enemy had been spotted.

The Russian ski patrol was crossing a small lake like bumbling stumps in the pallid light.

"I think they've gotten lost," Mikko whispered in Toivo's ear, "because they must be a good two miles from their outposts. I bet they miscalculated the amount of daylight, thinking they were still strolling along a lit Moscow boulevard." Toivo could only see Mikko's nose outlined, although, when he moved, that too was swallowed by the dark. With their hooded white suits over thick clothing the three figures looked like large, armed snow hares waiting to trap wolves for provision. When the enemy troops began to scramble up the ragged shore of the lake, Mikko eased the safety of his weapon and, supporting his right elbow on a birch stump, steadied the automatic pistol by the drum and took aim very carefully. The brief burst of solid flame steadied on Toivo's retinas like an arrested rocket. It must have been the lash of sound that killed. The Finns put their skis back on and went down to the lakeshore.

Death was appropriate: a silent dispatch without the gore that would have been a reminder of living flesh. If anything there was a fearful loneliness about the four brown bulks sprawled on the ice. And when they returned, Toivo with one of the captured rifles slung across his back, it seemed they had merely gone out to catch some fresh air, to stretch their legs.

After he had pulled the blankets over his head Toivo felt he had done no more than take a stroll in his sleep. Except for a streak of lightning which bothered across his closed eyes like a tenacious will-o'-the-wisp.

6

THE WINTER of 1939–1940 was a time of patrols for Toivo. His life was measured by their length and the boredom of waiting. Being an unarmed messenger, there was little for him to do so he polished leather and cleaned furs and read in *The Kalevala*. He was surprised how little danger there was at the front. From the soldiers he heard of air-raid casualties in the cities and towns while here, where the actual fighting took place, there was only the absence of men who were only begrudgingly mentioned. He never forgot the irrational peace and security of those months. Something magical about them, like a mouse living under a lion's paw.

In January Kall was called to the front on the Karelian Isthmus because that section had become the most vulnerable position in Finland now that the Russians knew they were defeated in the north. Kall left the boy behind, arranging that he would be moved to some friends in a small town until the war was over. Mikko was to join Kall after Toivo had been safely lodged.

Tired of sitting around the quiet dugout all day, Toivo begged Mikko to let him go with him on one of his courier trips. Pestered so long that Mikko finally consented. By mere chance Mikko's orders were incorrectly assigned and after two hours of skiing they came upon a deserted battlefield where there was not a living soul to receive them. Mikko wished his superiors every torture hell could provide when he realized the mistake. He looked anxiously at Toivo, who was leaning on his sticks and gazing in amazement at the huge woodless space.

For miles around not a single tree was standing. The petrified Russians had used the trunks to build stockades and barricades and the branches had been chopped up for firewood. Despite these defensive precautions, they had died of cold and hunger. How desperate they had been could be surmised from dozens of heads of horses, their grins perfectly preserved by the severe frost, strewn over the campgrounds. The severed heads were all that was left of them.

The man and the boy slowly picked their way across the battlefield, through the litter of killing. The wind, unaccustomed to such a large space, whipped the snow in spindling drifts, erratically covering up piles of human and animal shit under the tiers of defensive stumps lashed together with barbed wire. Their skis crunched over tin cans and empty vodka bottles, over shredded helmets, packages of powdered soup and large piles of human shit and animal scraps. The massive evidence of life was all the more ghostly because neither animal nor humans were to be seen. Just severed horse heads like huge chess knights thrown violently around the board after a lost game.

The north wind scudded over the enormous waste and howled in the skeletons of burned-out bombers, wrecked tanks and shattered armored cars as through so many outrageous fossils. It also wrapped papers around the intruders' feet and Toivo bent down to look at them. Propaganda leaflets printed in Russian and Finnish, each country warning the other. Tattered copies of tactical articles on defense and antitank warfare, crudely drawn maps, brown wrapping paper, frozen stationery. The boy was depressed by the pointlessness of the debris. After months of scouting through dense forests it was so unreasonable to find this open space which had been hacked out of the woods simply to be a huge dumping ground. As if the sky had opened up and spewed out litter it had sucked up over continents. Slowly the two aliens left the paper noise behind and entered the forest again.

Setting a faster pace Mikko said: "It looked as if even weasels or martens didn't come there." They were checked almost immediately by several dozen corpses frozen in various attitudes of falling, running or kneeling. Life-size statues in a manic winter garden. Powdered snow had stuck to the ridges of their clothing and the terribly bare heads, making white outlines like those in overexposed negatives. They were forced to walk through a stilled motion picture. Death was simply immobility and silence. And outstretched arms. Faces could be avoided but not these exaggerated arms which grew longer and longer and never reached what they were grasping for.

Toivo had to squeeze by one who had never finished clutching his head and who had been stopped jumping for a tree, frozen solid on the support of one small branch. It really seemed as simple as setting the projector in motion again and the man would finish his leap and disappear among the trees muttering a sigh of relief from having had to keep his breath for weeks. This was the truth of death: rigor mortis. The paradox that it was so inhuman because so perfectly lifelike. All manner of death he had ever heard of now seemed a joyous occasion because there had been agony and blood. But here was true terror in the abrupt cessation, in the sudden stop from one second to the next. He could not move since fear was freezing him. Feel! Feel! Mikko hurried over and pulled at his arms and Toivo felt himself sliding on his skis as if on a sled until he had been tugged out of the gelid negative.

When again conscious of motion he tried to run. Not so much from fear as for a panic of joy to hear his breath and his heart and his blood pumping in his head. Mikko held him up when his long wooden feet tangled with hidden branches and embraced the boy. Toivo let his head dip away from the cold cheek and burrowed for the throat where the warmth of Mikko's body could be smelled. Mikko got them a ride back in the cab of a truck which was hauling frozen beef to headquarters.

The next few months Toivo stayed with a florist in a small town among the most northern of the Central Lakes. The florist was a stooped, bespectacled man with half a skullcap of hair and with long arms. Childless, his wife, a butterball woman, took to shadowing Toivo like a mother hen. The woman was upset by the boy's silence and cooked him all sorts of delectables in order to draw him out. It was a day like her confirmation when Toivo embraced and kissed her because she had given him a kitten. He called it Kantele.

Life was tranquil. Toivo tried to catch up on his studies with the local schoolmaster, who had been instructed by Kall in what he was to teach his son. Kall wanted his son to learn English, and since the schoolmaster didn't know that language Toivo was tutored by a former university student who had been forced to quit his studies because he was being strip-mined by consumption. Sitting next to the chaise longue where a shape of clothing lay stretched out, loosely attached to a long, osseous face, Toivo heard for the first time about Shakespeare, Byron, Keats and T. E. Lawrence. The sick student had a passion for Lawrence and most of what Toivo learned from him came from the prose of *The Seven Pillars of Wisdom.* Dying slowly in a frosty room scarcely a hundred miles from the Arctic Circle, the tutor roamed in his mind through the blazing desert toward Damascus. He had a prodigious thirst. Each time he reached for his glass of water he warned the boy not to drink too much or too fast because he would get severely ill.

The florist seemed to know his father well. It appeared that Kall came through the town fairly regularly on his way east. Before her husband could order her to keep her mouth shut, the wife had told Toivo that his father would come and stay for a few days, talk with her husband for hours in the greenhouse, then leave after having left instructions to send flowers to the strangest addresses in Finland and Sweden. Yellow tea roses, their specialty, were sent even as far as Russia. And she thought his father was responsible for these foreign sales. Trying to find out more, the boy helped the husband in his greenhouse and learned some rudimentary horticulture, but little else. The florist scorned chemical aids, relying mainly on natural aids and Mendel.

The planes had been over before en route to a nearby railroad complex. But that one morning they drew a circle and came in, one by one, to drop incendiary bombs on the town. There was not a single military installation in a fifty-mile radius. But then, that hadn't bothered the Russians before. The simplest explanation for the ruthless and pointless bombing was that a Russian officer had misread his map of Finland. Whatever the insane reason, they came back for four days in a row. There had been no preparation for this sort of thing; not a single air-raid shelter had been built. But in modern warfare one cannot claim innocence in a landscape which, for reasons beyond comprehension, has been designated hostile.

At the florist's the first victims were the glass greenhouse and Toivo's kitten who, while stalking a sparrow, was lanced by a large splinter of a cold frame where geraniums had been wintering. Because of Kantele, Toivo learned the hatred of impotence, the rage of those who are not even dots in the bombardier's sights. Nor did he forget the icy whistle of falling bombs, like a teakettle that won't let up and finally bursts in a smash of yellow that erases the light of day. He was like a water molecule in a monstrous boiler, where everything was seething and heaving, part of a worldwide screech that strips off the skin.

The harmless little town had been transformed into a scene of desolation where the game of technology's chance had come up with strange consequences. A bomb which had not detonated according to specifications had blasted three wooden houses and gutted them with fire. A fourth was demolished except for its front. The locked door guarded a pile of rubble and the debris of personal belongings. The house behind it had its front blown off, though the rest of it had been left intact, as if someone had taken a knife to a doll's house. An unmade bed testified to a hasty departure: in front of it a pair of slippers, a book on the nightstand and a chair, with clothes folded over its back and its end. The local cinema was untouched but the barbershop next to it had taken a hit. Through the holes where the windows had been, one could see the lathered brushes and the last customer's hair on the unswept floor.

When the snow covered it all up, only the tall chimneys were standing. Hardly any of these had been toppled and they stood, in the midst of burned-out houses, like accusing fingers pointed at the sky. The chimneys had that same lethal invulnerability as the frozen corpses at the edge of the battlefield and they stalked Toivo on his daily walk to the tutor who had lost his nursing mother in the raids yet continued the English lessons for fear of going mad. The planes never returned after the fourth day, but for the rest of his life Toivo did not trust the sky and was afraid to travel by air.

The florist survived his multiple lacerations from the flying glass of his greenhouse, where he had been trying to protect some valuable seedlings. But his wife had been shocked into regarding Toivo as her body's child pursued by sky machines plotting his death. She knitted caps and scarfs the color of the snow for him so that It up there would not be able to spot him so easily. No matter where he went she went with him, holding on to his sleeve so she could drag him into the nearest ditch at the first sign of danger. Instead of stuffing the boy she now nearly starved him, convinced she could diet him invisible.

When Kall came to get his son after the peace had been negotiated in March of 1940, she would only let Toivo go when the father told her he would buy sunglasses for his child. After he had explained to her what they were she grew calm enough to cry at his departure, satisfied that dark glasses would hide the only child she would ever have from that which killed from above. Kall left with Toivo for England in April of 1940.

A quarter of a million Russians and eighteen thousand Finns had died in the war. The Finns had fought for their lives, but what had the Russians died for? Sorry creatures, in a physical condition hardly fit for a barroom, they were led to their death by a trick of stupid fantasy. Told that they were to set Finland free they only liberated themselves from life. Where nature had been the ally of the defenders, as on the northeastern front, Russian peasants died in strongholds of stalled tanks and staggered tree trunks which were not tomb enough to hold them. On the Karelian Isthmus the Russians finally won by sheer number of corpses. Men such as Kall, who got back from that front, were close to insanity from the horror of slaughtering thousands upon thousands of bodies. The Russian command took it literally when they ordered the Finnish positions overrun. The Russians also had the distinction of being the first to use aerial bombardment as a means not only of demolishing military targets but also of shattering civilian morale. The Germans learned the lesson and perfected it. And the British thereafter. And the Americans.

And . . . again: for what? It was called Molotov's War. A quarter of a million lives to back up a murky foreign policy? The demands before (or after) the war were never made clear. What reason lurked that could dispatch a quarter of a million lives, bomb innocents and force another people to kill to keep its life? A border dispute?

It does not matter. Nothing is enough. When there's enough of nothing men will march off to capture it, as insensitive as a mobilized toy store. There is no nation, no home, no flag. Only borders. To be crossed. Only exile. Into loneliness. No allegiances. Except for hugging one's own flesh and holding on to the head of yourself. There's no more to be gotten. That's all you're likely to get. And if there's more it's either madness or a lie, since nothing gives of itself for nothing. Thus Toivo went into exile. For his natural life. It is a sentence one should be thankful for, and you don't have to travel far to enjoy it. Chroniclers of this age have made one error: survivors are not meek, they are ruthless. A quarter of a million Russians and eighteen thousand Finns died in five months of battle. The Finns had fought for their lives. But what had the Russians died for?

7

"I HOPE, Mr. Syystalvi, that you don't mind all the publicity you're getting," his publisher told him over the phone the week before he was to leave. "But *Past Reason Hunted* is doing so well that it would be foolish not to go along with the free exposure the interviews are giving us. After all these years of neglect it must be sweet revenge for you and, believe me, we're very proud to have published your book. Sales are so good that I predict your book will be on the best-seller list by next month. You must have seen the papers lately. Could I ask you to be a little more cooperative? Anyway, I called to ask if you could come to a party next Tuesday. Some of the most prominent reviewers and critics have accepted our invitation and it would be a good opportunity for you to get to know them."

Most of the editorial staff of Pembroke Press was there that night, congratulating him on his success as if a recalcitrant prodigal had made good: a sobering indication of the fragile margin of fame. Only a few months ago he could wander through the building and no one would pay any attention to him unless he made himself a nuisance and had to be reprimanded and sent back to his editor through the chain of telephone command. But now there were handshakes, whispering behind his back, smiles up front, requests for his signature. The Pembroke executives were constantly asking him if he was working on something new. He could dip in the till of his unpublished manuscripts and have them printed and in the store before Christmas. Before, they had made the dreary round of offices, gathering reams of rejection slips. There was something sinister about this sudden turnabout of fortune, like the false light that sheets down on a landscape before a storm. Seldom did someone pass him without looking up and smiling. Success is a dental triumph.

"Really, I finished the book at one sitting lying in bed. My husband kept waking up from the light of the bed lamp. He doesn't read, you know. Doesn't have the time. The poor dear has to work too hard to keep me in books and in bed."

Toivo excused himself from a circle of bodies and moved away, staggering a little and aware of it. He had drunk too much too fast on an empty stomach. But in the other room it was no different. Outrageous dresses were packed around a punch bowl ladling rapid speech to turtlenecked males, mostly with glasses. Long dresses bared cleavages, short ones gave a lot of leg. He was a little incredulous such succulence could go with so much tripe. The conversation rolled on like a player piano with the same flat topics out of trade papers and literary magazines. He found it difficult to converse, his tongue seemingly unwilling to shape words, dragging them as grating as a finger drawn slowly over rough sandpaper.

"There's much to be admired in his work, but the social issue is not fully developed and these days writers have no right to a private vision. The world is doomed. How can they go on telling us silly tales of suburbia?"

"With thirty thousand titles how can you expect anything from the *Times?* It isn't fair."

"Besides the novel is dead anyway. I only read nonfiction."

Across the heavily draped and carpeted room a well-known literary critic from New York stood slightly back from some sycophants, his head thrown back as if an iron rod had been drilled at a slant through his skull into his bunched shoulders so that his eyes had difficulty sloping down his swollen cheeks laced with alcoholic veins. He used his deep voice sparingly, bored by the pariahs of readers and writers alike. He was only interested in ideas. When a meeting between him and Toivo was arranged he gave Toivo a limp hand and withdrew it before any pressure could be applied. Languidly trekking his eyes down he studied the writer's face with the boredom of an expert entomologist forced to look at a familiar species handed him by eager students. Like his ilk, he was engaged in combating systems of thought and it was an intrusion of macular reality to have a book identified with a breathing corpus delicti. The genius had brought his Pygmalion wife: a young, chesty female, half his age, in a very short piece of material that looked like a flour sack. Toivo felt a crazy desire to lean her against her husband's back and screw her with all his might.

Alcohol drowned the voices more and more until Toivo had trouble hearing them and had to tune himself like a radio. Sex came increasingly to mind and he began shuffling around the crowded rooms looking down dresses and bumping against promising hips.

"Oh, you're Mr. Syystalvi, rhymes with *The Duchess of Malfi*. So pleased to meet you," said a woman near the entrance of the room. She had huge eyes and fleshly lips red from natural circulation and not from a perfumed stick of coloring.

"Can I get you something? Anyway, you really have a knack for death. One of the most marvelous pieces I've ever read about pain. I didn't cry, mind you. No. Not at all. It sent shivers up and down my spine. You've certainly got a way with death."

"Glad you liked it."

"Did you ever experience death? Oh, you must have in order to be able to write so movingly about it."

Hyde Park whispering with trees around a bench a stone's throw from Speakers' Corner. The park had been his secret Finland in the limestone desert of London. He went there often when his father wouldn't come back from the Continent to visit him. A robin led him to the whooshing whirling cove of thick-leafed branches. Past the trunks stretched a large sheet of green where a solitary man walked away from him into the blue sky, a rolled umbrella pricking for gravitational support in the rich sod. In that lost hour after lunch there was no one else in the park, most Londoners apparently engaged in clearing up Göring's rubble. He ducked behind a tree when he saw the man standing in front of him, his profile clearly etched against the patches of blue sky dabbling through the thickly grown branches which swept the ground. A pergola of diffuse green like watered silk.

The long drooping branches gave Toivo cover and the man was unaware of him. He was neatly dressed in a light summer suit with a freshly laundered shirt of tinted rose and a bright red tie. Looking back at him again Toivo knew the man had been young, no more than in his late twenties. Suddenly the man's left arm came up with tense jerking gestures so that it was at a right angle to his body as if he were going to give the stiff, snappy salute of the British army. A sharp, loud noise cracked through the arboreal pagoda and the head seemed to be shoved outward toward Toivo with an enormous pressure which the skin and muscle could barely manage to contain. An implosion struggling to explode. Almost simultaneously there was a hole in the cheek and a bullet sucked into a tree. The man fell on his side, his pistol-arm flung wide, the other side of his face up and smashed. His temple was gone. Just as the arm had gone up the sound had flashed and there was death on the ground with flecks of light over it in a sweet breeze, the lowest tip of branches brushing the body gently like a duster dusting valuables. No reason. None at all. And something was put into gear inside Toivo and began whining like an air-raid siren. A corkscrew of sound that lifted through his head and drowned the noise of his body. It was a cutting away from the tree where his nails were buried in the bark, and it was quite literally a cutting of steps across the grass and the gravel of the walk, cutting a space to place his feet in step by step. Motion had to be carved. Now he knew again what he had then been close to: it was the utter loneliness of the event which terrified him. The mechanical snapping to a salute which finished in a pistol and the face bulging out without giving. A silent suicide in time of war. Why hadn't he screamed? It would have been better. It would have been human.

He wanted to rush his hands down her dress and hold on to her breasts. Try to wrap himself in her body even if he didn't know her. Barbara had never understood that and he had never been able to tell her. That he wanted to hold on to her because it gave him a life, a simple brute existence.

He sat down on a bed of coats. The vice president of Pembroke Press sat next to him and talked about his book and about Washington, where he had met Blaise, who had commended him on a job well done.

"Who?" asked Toivo, still deafened by the silence of leaves sweeping the dead man's body. "Who's that again?"

"Mr. Donner," answered the vice president. "He knows you quite well."

"Mr. Donner. Yes. Well. What does he want with me?"

"Perhaps you're a little drunk, Mr. Syystalvi?"

"So what? That's quite all right. Don't pay any attention to him," said the woman who thought he had a way with death. She leaned over him and laughed for his eyes, her breasts falling, then caught by the safety of her dress. If a body were insubstantial, Toivo thought, her breasts would swing a full arc.

"After all," she said, well aware he was looking since, being drunk, he did so with precision and a great deal of concentration, "poets are supposed to be drunk. Aren't they? Particularly at literary parties."

An editor leaned over and whispered in his ear: "Remember that he was the one who pushed your book and fought with the upstairs to get a large advertising campaign going. He kinda made you, if you see what I mean."

The first thing Blaise had said to him in London was, "Your father has enemies, you know." An accusation, as if the boy was an irritating reminder of an imperfection.

"Have you noticed two men following you? You know, just walking behind you no matter where you go?"

Blaise's hand tripped over the coffee table imitating a pursuit. A very bald man. So bald in fact that the skin over his skull seemed to have strangled all hair forever. Eyebrows taut as tugged springs pulling from their point of anchorage at the bridge of the nose. Underneath these thin-haired arches were green round eyes which had a lighter green aperture in their middle leading away to where his thoughts had to be hiding. Everything about the face and what little of his body dared peep out of his clothes was round, tight and shiny. A glossy healthy skin. Effective hands. Like loyal supporting actors, they drew attention away from or directed it to the eyes which were the star performers. When he pushed his arms forward and his hands mimed italics to a sentence, Toivo could see where the white cuffs with their beetle cuff links of hammered gold had been drawn up under the invariable tweed jacket. Could see the reddish blond hair bulge into a bracelet where the joint of wrist and hand puffed up the flesh into a bank of fat.

"Of course you noticed them. You're just afraid to tell me. But believe me, your father told me last fall to keep an eye on you so that no harm could come to you. That's precisely what I'm doing. To make sure you will let me carry out your father's wishes I'm asking you to come here every third day and report to me where they have followed you. Besides that, I'll put one of my men on your track." Satisfied, the man nodded at his glass of port and sipped it as if he were sucking on a stick of licorice.

The boy was ill at ease. Had he missed seeing the men Mr. Donner had mentioned? But he didn't want this man's help. He wanted his father to come back and take care of whoever was trying to frighten him. Strong arms around him and a chest to bury his head in. This man's chest didn't seem capable of hiding anyone. Toivo felt that if he pushed it Mr. Donner's head would bounce off his shoulders like a ball.

"Just call me Blaise, my boy. In my country, the United States, we're not so formal as they are here. Even your father had caught the politeness bug from the British. He refuses to call me by my first name. But certainly you can. Fathers aren't always right you know."

"Yes, Mr. Donner."

A pilfered light fell into the room. Winter had little use for exuberance. The room was sparsely furnished with gleaming, waxed pieces on curved legs.

"Sir, do you know when my father will be back again?"

The man looked at him slowly, taking his raised glass of brown liquid shot through with pale light away from his eyes.

"Well now, why should I know that?"

"You said, sir, that my father talks to you. Maybe he told you when he'd be back."

"You know something," said the portly man laughing, showing a very fine set of even white teeth, "I bet you're absolutely right. Why wouldn't he tell me?"

Blaise kept trying to gain the boy's confidence. Once when

Toivo had to come up with a biology project for school, Blaise had suggested whirligig beetles because he thought the boy would like the patterns they made on the surface of water and if you picked them up they gave off a smell like pineapples. He had even asked Toivo to come to his apartment so that he could get some firsthand information from his collection.

When the boy walked in, long cables of winterlight were tugging at a room of Blaise's apartment in London. The light swayed over rows and rows of glass cases filled with carefully tagged insects on pins and slides, or preserved in envelopes and fluids. Blaise looked very much like a scarab himself, one who was calmly and dexterously classifying his own kind with hypertrophied prehensile tools. He had the casual air of the expert, picking his way among the killing jars of carbon tetrachloride and chloroform, all the while talking in a scholar's monotone about the relative merits of each agent. He demonstrated to Toivo where to place the pin to fasten the insect to the mount: either through the wing in such a way that when the pin emerges from the soft underside of the body it does not damage a leg, or in the thorax, behind the head, always making sure not to damage the corpses. Techniques for spreading butterflies. How to mount small insects or individual organs such as genitalia, wings, parts of the mouth, legs or claws for easier and detailed study. Blaise mumming Linnaeus, labeling his vast collection according to genus, species, subspecies, the name of the man who discovered the animal — all in scientific, Latin nomenclature, with the vernacular name (if there was one) printed underneath. And his huge bulk would shrink to delicate touch in order to glue a tiny beetle on a triangular cardboard "point," then push a pin through the point and a tiny printed label and place it in the neat rows of miniature weathervanes in the airtight Riker mounts.

The remnant of the party had left for a more intimate apartment on Beacon Hill. Too drunk to care where he was taken and apprehensive about going home, Toivo tagged along. A stack of records on an automatic spindle slurred soft music with a gentle bump as if a well-oiled peanut had fallen between the rotating rubber table and the circles of pressed sound. He was lying on a bed of coats, no longer visited by a stream of admirers like a drunk pasha giving audience. At the foot end of the bed two welterweights were sizing each other up with much movement and exposed anatomy. Toivo had his head crunched in a pillow with the young woman who had felt he had a way with death overlapping his right side, his hand trying to reach around her back to her unbuckled bosom. Human use of human beings. His hand had found her breast, like a smooth pate with a pliant little cue.

The two men held him captive in the doorway. Wide-brimmed hats seldom seen in London threw a surgical mask of shadow over their faces. Remember, Toivo, he heard his father say, remember to be cunning and silent and don't make a move until it's worth your while. Look, Toivo, look at those men and tell me what they look like, intoned Blaise like a monk chanting.

Almost seventeen now and tall for his age, Toivo looked directly in the men's eyes. He held his schoolbag full of books and papers against his chest with both hands. He was nervous but not scared. When you start being afraid, get mad, Kall had told him. Anger is a fine weapon.

"You better let me go," he said to them. "My foster mother is coming very soon and she'll call the police."

"When is your father coming back?"

"I don't know."

"When will he be back?"

The man closest to him put a foot on his shoes and tried to press his weight down on the bridges of Toivo's feet. His breath stank as if he hadn't had a chance in days to scrub his teeth or scrape the coat of sleep from his tongue. Large nose with black hairs spurting out. Brown eyes. Chin and Adam's apple one and the same. Blackened collar and raffled tie. The man tried to shove an elbow in his side but Toivo lowered his bag of books.

"What do you want from him?"

"Just tell us where he is. Where do you meet him?"

"What do you want with him?"

"You'll find out, boy. Now hurry up or I'll hurt you."

Suddenly the man scraped his wrist over Toivo's cheek and

the boy thought it was odd until he felt pain from a long, deep cut. He never figured out whether it was chance or whether the man had deliberately roughened the case of his watch for just such emergencies.

"You want to kill him, don't you?"

And though hysteria was edging up from his stomach he was made brave by the thought that they would kill Kall so that he would never see him again, not even occasionally. The youth jammed his schoolbag up against the chin of his tormentor, jerked his foot back from under the man's shoe and kneed him as hard he could in the groin. Toivo paid no attention to the other one but shoved past him on to the sidewalk into paradoxical solidarity with a crowd of people who didn't know what had happened.

Mrs. Gwynn came out of a shop and saw him. He yelled to her and pointed at the two men. The slight woman dropped her packages and ran toward him, looking for the enemy. She placed herself in front of the boy and raised her voice with eerie calm, inviting the two running men to come back and try to put one hand, just one finger on her boy and she'd make them very sorry indeed. Toivo looked down at the slender woman as eager to draw blood as a fighting bird.

"Are you all right, my boy? My god, those bandits hurt your face. Let's go home and see to it."

Toivo never asked anyone to call the police.

"Yes, Blaise told me all about it. I guess you would have to say that he was right."

"Do you like him, Father?"

Kall was silent. They had been to a movie together and were sitting on a bench in the park feeding the swans the toast they had sneaked out of the cafeteria where they had had tea. He looks tired, thought Toivo; he is really old but not an old man. Just as youthfully old as Väinämöinen. I wish he could charm all his enemies away and teach me to play the harp and we could travel together all through England chanting charms from *The Kalevala* and amaze people by making them come true when they didn't believe us.

Slowly Kall took his eyes off the narcotic swans borne on an invisible current and looked at the strip of adhesive on his son's face. As if he had cut himself shaving. Yes, it was possible. He had begun a few months ago. But the plaster was to help heal the deepest part of the cut made by the man's watch.

"Blaise? No. I don't like him," he said carefully, trying to gauge what his words would convey. "But he is useful. Remember that you can always depend on him for your material needs. He owes me quite a lot. And if he ever puts a finger on you, you let me know. All right?"

"Yes, Father."

"He is useful, so use him."

"Do you ever call him Blaise? He asked me to call him that."

"Did you?"

"No."

"Neither do I. I call him Donner."

"He's American, isn't he?"

"Yes," Kall said impatiently, "but let's not talk any more about it. Let's try instead to decide what we're going to do tonight."

Whenever his father came back to England to see him it was awkward trying to imagine what they could do together. Toivo was too old now to dare let himself go to his father and curl up in his lap. A strange, odd couple, they roamed around London day after day until, when Kall had to leave again, reams of questions and desires rushed Toivo's mind. But he never spoke them. A familiar tearing pain would make him almost ill; a nauseous pain which he rarely felt again in his adult life. Father and son skirmished with each other, not daring to confront one another with their true feelings, speaking the parts of actors in a brave show of maturity. The child spoke the lines of Toivo the maturing youth, while his father pretended to be a happy parent showing his son a good time, not daring to speak the words which would betray his love and misery.

It was Kall who noticed that they were being followed and who asked Toivo to look at the men in the glass of a shop window.

"Yes. That's them."

"All right. You just keep on walking, and don't look back."
His father's face had become smooth. Wrinkles and lines had
been ironed out and Toivo thought there was a glint of relief in
his eyes. From satisfaction that something decisive had charged
the unsettling boredom, or was it from the pleasure of a quarry
outfoxing the hunters? When he reached the end of the narrow
street and couldn't decide which direction to take, the boy
looked back and saw one man lying on the sidewalk in that
strangely limp heap which makes wounded humans kin to tossed
marionettes. The other one was in a portico being hit by the man
who was his father. Who was hitting his adversary with pleasure,
with gusto, with the precision of delight. The hands of his parent
were expert and merciless.

But on the bed of coats in Boston the son did not know if the
man who was his father had defended himself or his son, whether
it had been the instinctual courage of the species or the acquired
skill of a professional. Hit him, hit him, Father. Please hit him so
he will never shadow me anymore, ever shadow at all.

"What?" asked the woman over his shoulder. "Why would
you want to do that?"

Toivo forced his bleary eyes to the light and slowly circled his
consciousness back to his present situation.

"Nothing. Nothing. I was thinking of something in my youth.
About my father. My farewell father."

8

THAT LAST SUMMER they made three trips into the country in an automobile requisitioned by Blaise. For years Toivo had ransacked his memory to provide that summer with dramatic incidents which he could cherish and use to fortify the memory of his father. To be worn smooth as finely tooled cameo portraits. But all that was left were vague pleasant times — sightseeing, towns, rivers, castles, battlefields. Though one left the war in London when one went into the countryside, there were still times when Kall's foreign accent inspired a feverish rural suspicion of foreign agents. Still, nothing remarkable happened. Only suffering, pain or disaster would have left an imprint, which he could have reissued to himself again and again.

For years Toivo had tried to infuse that summer with lethal forebodings, with a finality which no other summer could ever have again. But his memory refused to comply. Sweet summer oil embalmed those hours which could never be anything else than peaceful and beautiful and insignificant. Each present moment was fulfilled, yet as infinitely unsatisfying as a recollection. He could recite the map names like beads on a rosary, but they would not release anything beyond the smooth roundness of contentment.

They had motored through the lovely Cotswolds with its yellow cottages, through Cheltenham, Broadway, Mickleton, along the River Stour to Stratford-on-Avon. There they visited Shakespeare's birthplace and Nash's House, Harvard House and Holy Trinity Church where the poet was buried. To Anne Hathaway's Cottage and Mary Arden's House. In Warwickshire they saw Kenilworth Castle and listened to a guide relating the boring details of the battle at Edge Hill between the Parliamentarians and Royalists, which only became interesting when it was said that nothing had come of the death of 1500 men except that every year on the twenty-third of October one can hear and see the ghost armies battle each other.

They went on to the Lake District where a friend of Kall's had a summer house. From Windermere along Lake Windermere to Ambleside and Grasmere (where Wordsworth lived), along Lake Grasmere and Lake Thrilmere to Keswick, then through Whinlatter Pass to Cockermouth. The most dramatic scene from that trip was the goats, high up in the pass, bodily stopping the cars for handouts.

Back to London along the east coast through Northumberland and Yorkshire. From the town of Flodden, famous for its battle slaughter, to Holy Island with its priority of Lindisfarne, to Bamburgh Castle where King Arthur was reputed to have lived. They walked several miles on top of Hadrian's Wall, that miniature Great Wall of China, and went further south to Durham Castle where his father visited the tomb of the Venerable Bede:

> Your Majesty, when we compare the present life of man with that time of which we have no knowledge, it seems to me like the swift flight of a lone sparrow through the banqueting hall where you sit in the winter months to dine with your thanes and counselors. Inside there is a comforting fire to warm the room; outside, the wintry storms of snow and rain are raging. This sparrow flies swiftly in through one door of the hall, and out through another. While he is inside, he is safe from the winter storms; but after a few moments of comfort, he vanishes from sight into the darkness whence he came. Similarly, man appears on earth for a little while, but we know nothing of what went before this life, and what follows.

They lodged in Newcastle upon Tyne and then drove through the North York Moors where they stopped briefly to walk through the walls of Rievaulx Abbey, which had been built by Saint Bernard.

Yorkshire, Northumbria, the Lake District, Shakespeare Country — somewhere his father must have dropped a hint, must have suddenly hugged him, must have received a message. Sometime during that summer he must have said farewell. After those few moments of comfort he went and vanished. Up into the airplane, a RAF transport, having kissed his son goodby. A father defined by his absence, by war, by the promise of return. Like Väinämöinen. The farewell father who left his son with the task to search for a paternal shadow in his flesh.

Toivo forced his body off the bed and lurched upright. More guests from his publication party had come to the apartment, stuffing its small rooms like chokecherries. Faces bobbed on a stream of dimmed light. Teeth, glasses, jewelry tinkled against bodies. What did it matter that he had written a book? Or ten books? Had carved palimpsests under his skin? Stood on his head and written graffiti on the ceiling? Come and gone? He was invisible now. Loneliness leaves a smell of danger. Great effort to focus his eyes back down again on the bed to look for his coat. Found it. Dragging it along behind him he stumbled through the trampoline floor, his head sick with weightlessness. Bumped into flesh and walls and banisters going down the stairs. Cobbles and city air fresh as a deodorizer after the rooms stuffed with party. Head up now, my friend. Dejection is an ode not a hangdog ditty. Classic pose: drunkard with one arm around lamppost trying to get coat on. Grinning. Remembering that he always grinned a lot to himself when he was drunk.

For fun and laughter he reeled off the names Cheltenham, Broadway, Mickleton to weekend couples passing in natty suits. Nash, Harvard, Arden House. Trinity Church. Winder, Gras, Thrilmere. The narrow streets like Hadrian's Wall, teetering and tottering, ribboning through the heath of Boston holding off barbarians from the north. South. East. And west. Profusely apologetic when he nearly collided with a dressed lady, coifed and primed for fun. A low bow, dusting the sidewalk bricks with his sleeve, and the sudden tripod of his body, supported by his hands and feet, on the street. Best position for push-ups. Two. Three. Four. People going out of their way to avoid him. Must be something wrong with them. Famous authors have a right to eccentricity. The woman from the bed of coats helped him stand straight. That's not necessary, O Guinevere. Stick to Lancelot 'cause Arthur's a sad monkey. He knew from the beginning the Round Table was bound to fail. The sadness of Camelot: a wishful Eden with a built-in serpent ready to poison. But thanks anyway.

"Why did you run out?"

Well, what shall we answer the lady? Too much to drink? That wasn't it really. Too many people? True. Too little space? True. And him. The farewell father.

"I have to catch the last train back to Cambridge. Ah yes. That's the reason. That's the reason I left." Hate that slurring. Hate alcohol when it Novocains your tongue.

"I'll take you home."

"But why, my lady of the turnips? I am a danger to society."

And he went forth bravely up the crooked cobbled streets of Beacon Hill toward the golden dome of the house of state, missing taxis, people, dogturds and stoops, chanting: "Leper coming. Leper coming."

Clacking the wooden sticks of the disease between his imaginary fingers.

Since he hated roller coasters, since he hated the world careening away from him into the infinity of blackness behind his closed lids, he forced himself awake out of reflex conditioned by fear. Never had he been able to drink himself unconscious as people are ready to swear they can. Got out of his bed and walked around his apartment from chair to chair. Turned on the TV but couldn't keep the picture focused. Opened a window to shower in the colder air. Took his pants off too because they constricted his stomach. In the kitchen he chewed coffee beans and swallowed them down with water from the tap. Instant coffee. Let the water run over his face and splashed it on his chest. He had called him Blaise from that noon hour on. Never again, Mr. Donner. Kall had told him the address. For emergencies. Though you're not supposed to know it. He owes me. And debts, as a matter of law, are handed down from father to son.

"Blaise! BLAISE! What have you done with my father?"

Trying to shove the polite letter of condolences down the man's throat. But someone is always stronger than a boy of seventeen. Even one who already shaved regularly.

"Where is my father?"

"As I stated in my letter . . . That's all right now. Let him go. He'll behave, won't you, son? . . . missing and assumed dead. Since we don't have the body we can't state it legally for sure. But from other sources at our disposal we know your father is dead."

He ran his hand over the typewriter as if it would sound a perfect run, a toneless ladder. Switched the machine on and, steadied by the hum of his most precious piece of machinery, tried the TV again.

"You will pay. You owe me."

"I know. Did you think I would leave you stranded here, alone in a strange country? First of all you need money. Here. Now, I want you to go back to the Gwynns, they're waiting for you. I phoned them." My farewell father. Gone. He promised. Late maybe. Very often late, you damn bastard. But you came. You said you would always be back. But you're a man now. From sources at our disposal we know that your father is dead. He slept in the train, shocked by the motion of the wagon into the corner by the window. A heap stuffed in the corner with cheeks wet from crying. In the town where he got off the train nothing wanted to attack him. Nor in Beaconsfield, in High Wycombe, in Bicester. Nor on country roads. On macadam roads. On bicycles. In cars. Stole a topcoat from a restaurant rack. Washed his face in a puddle. Didn't know what change he got from the fistful of bills he shoved at the waitress. Didn't thank truck drivers for rides. In the bathroom again for a long piss. In the shower to try it alternating hot and cold. Should have a sauna in my place. I think I'll buy out the apartment below me and have one built. Got the money now. You famous author you and socked himself in his stomach. Naked and shivering he went back to the TV. Good thing there wasn't a woman to go to and explain how he felt and have to listen to remonstrations and, after all the effort, still get dunked headlong into that endless dark where, even when he opened his eyes, it took minutes to hide behind familiarly lit objects. Better to walk around some more.

Back to London. Through streets at night. Slept during the day in Lyons Tea Shops, on benches, in buses, in the underground. Didn't dare go to a whore, the police, the Gwynns or Hyde Park. Took him two days of going from bookshop to bookshop to find an edition of *The Kalevala*. He tried reading it in a library but the silence drove him crazy, didn't allow him to read even a single line. He spent a day in a cafeteria where he kept buying coffee and cakes to prevent the waitress from cleaning his table and throwing him out. He gave the cakes to old wrecks, remnants of fathers or sons, and poured the coffee in the large potted plants which couldn't make up their minds whether they were rubber or real. He read in particular poems fifteen and thirty-one.

Fifteen. Where the mother of Lemminkäinen goes to Death's domain after her son has been killed by Soppy Hat. Goes to the icy river where she rakes the water to find the bits and pieces of her son. It takes her a long time. Always "a little something was lacking, one hand, half his head, a lot of other bits and pieces, his life to boot." Patiently she keeps on raking and patiently she reassembles her child. Fitting bone to fractured bone, matching flesh to bit of flesh, knotting veins to arteries, stroking the body, assembling from death's junk, with a honey salve. Smearing it on all the cracks, seams, all the junctures of her tireless labor. And makes him speak again. But he couldn't do that because they wouldn't even tell him where his father's body was. Perhaps he wasn't dead. For only Väinämöinen managed to get out of Death's Domain, managed to slip through the nets after having charmed himself into a snake.

Thirty-one. For the first time Toivo felt a close kinship to Kullervo. That hero crazed from excessive rocking in his cradle, who rapes his sister, whose father doesn't care whether he lives or dies, who roams the forests asking his sword if it would care to kill him. Alone, thinking he's an orphan, he roams Finland's woods, a huge crazed giant of a man, pushed inexorably to his tragic fate. Told with utter sobriety. A dry accounting of inevitability.

It never failed. Whenever he was drunk and had finally been granted some sleep without that dreadful bobsled ride through space, he would wake up at some ungodly hour. At 5:00 A.M. he got up from the couch where he'd fallen asleep to go to the bathroom. He had to sit down to urinate because he was too tired to stand straight and aim true. In the middle of the afternoon the boy stood in Piccadilly Circus and looked at a map of Britain he had bought in a secondhand bookshop. The huge island lay in the sea like a tottering nightmare animal, rampant on a field of blue, head drawn back for a feeble strike at the Continent. On that queer animal spread a huge net of red trunk, train and motor roads like the bloodweb of an inverted eyeball. Dusted with hundreds of thousands of cities, towns, villages and hamlets. With lakes, rivers, hills, mountains, valleys, meadows, moors, forests, minefields. And like the weight at the bottom of a toy to steady it there was London, at the lowest point of gravity in the Island of Angels. Millions and millions of people lived, ate, slept, loved there. Around him milled the traffic, a constant tire of noise and metal circling the hub of Eros with grave purpose.

The map had fallen to the ground and pigeons swooped down briefly to forage the nation for food. But the bright colors were only imaginary and the birds tripped away to scour the cracks in the pavement for the meager offal of the wartime lunch hour. He had no more money. The book in his left hand was slippery in his sweaty palm. It was hot, August. And there was no one he could call his own. In this entire island choked with people not a single person was his. It was terribly frightening to be so utterly alone among a surfeit of people. His heart sank and for the first time during those days he felt that astringent, sour taste of utter separation like a mouthful of spoiled milk. To be back in the forests with Mikko, in the dugout under the frozen steel of winter. There was no other place to go than the Gwynns'. Mrs. Gwynn, who loved the ghost of her dead son in him. Mr. Gwynn, who liked his command of Finnish. Blaise, a mere deputy of his father. The sky was hazy with heat and exhaust. The sun shimmered through like troubled copper. The copper boat suspended in the sky where the wizard sage who can never grow older than old stopped the trail of his vessel because he was tired. You will be back. Yes, you must be back. One day. There's nothing else you can do. You're all I've got. I don't even have a photograph of you, not even a snapshot. I wish I could remember your face.

Toivo went to his bed and found the woman who thought he had a way with death sleeping in it. When he was crawling in next to her he wondered how she had gotten in. Had he opened the door for her or did she have a skeleton key? He was too tired to ask.

9

HE WOKE UP LATE in a day warm but kept cool by a steady breeze which rippled the curtains out from the windows like the colorful cloth fishes the Japanese suspend at the birth of sons. The muscles and tissues of his body felt like the beaches of Normandy on D–Day, so he had to move gingerly. The one aspect he did enjoy of these alcoholic aftermaths was the calm they gave him; they reimbursed him with a resigned clarity of mind. It seemed that with the lengthy brushing of his teeth he had restored his smell because there was an odor of brewed coffee in the air. When he stepped toward the living room he heard someone slurping daintily, so he went back and put on his pyjama pants.

The woman who had praised him for his way with death was sitting in a wicker chair by the open window in his terrycloth robe, legs tucked under, hands around a mug on top of her knees. She smiled at him and wished him a good morning. Deferential to his touchy stomach Toivo nibbled daintily on a piece of toast she gave him and sipped from the coffee she had made from the same brand he always bought but which was infinitely better than what he could ever have managed himself. Both of them sat quietly looking out of the window at the trees which were in constant motion. She smiled at him. Not teeth ripping but the smile of an intelligent creature: a kind cast in the eyes and a contraction of the seams of the lids. A subtle change of face.

She had thick blond hair with deep waves falling no further than her shoulders and around her wide face. A face that invited intimacy. All of her features were firmly pronounced and genetics had not been niggardly in cushioning the bones of her head and frame. Her molded face was a pleasant alternative to the common one where the features are skimpily drawn on a billiard-ball skin and wiped off with a wet towel. There had been times that Toivo had been apprehensive, when American females dove into a pool for fear they would surface featureless. She sat there poised in ease as if concealing a secret, that angle of repose painters are so fond of, perhaps because they know something valuable is hidden in that charged relaxation of unconscious mystery. A sybilline noon hour with coffee and toast.

"I probably said some stupid things last night to you. A few drinks make me say the obvious."

"I'm sure it was the other way around."

She stood up to get the empty cups. When she was in front of him Toivo put his arms around her and leaned his face against her stomach. Her hands full of the cups clanked a bit behind his head and the calm rising and falling of her breathing and the warmth of her body which came through the fussy cloth of the robe coddled him as if in a hammock.

"I am glad you saw me home. I'm not so sure I could have made it alone in the MTA."

"Please yourself. I came because I thought you wanted to sleep with me."

"I wasn't much good at that last night."

"You had too much on your mind."

They had some breakfast. After that Toivo lay on the floor and let the breeze suit his torso like cooling silk woven from the feathers of hummingbirds. Immobile motion. He fell asleep with the fine feeling of weariness that reminds you of the crisp heels of fresh home-baked loaves of bread.

Dressed, they sat and talked lazily as if resting in sunmeadows. The nap had done him good.

"No, there's little drama to my life even though my books might make you think so. After you've gone through the details of experience they all cohere into sheets of samenesses and you say, 'When I was shot during the war' and you've quite forgotten the insensate terror of the pile of dirt your face was pressed into. To relive something you've got to catch the details. So I build my books from details and from shamefully brief generalizations."

"Still, when did you come to the States?"

"All right. Put it like this. I was born in Finland. My mother left one morning in a limousine when I was still quite young. I spent part of the war in Finland on the front, and the rest of it in England. My father took me there. He disappeared and presumably died in nineteen forty-four, and I came to the States as an immigrant sponsored by a man in the State Department. I worked at all sorts of jobs. Went to college. Got a B.A. and an M.A. Taught in small colleges, got married, got divorced. I wrote for many years and now, finally, seem to have made it. That's all of it really."

"That sounds very lonesome."

"How about you?"

She laughed. Her throat, a pliable cylinder rising out of the whimsical blouse, vibrated with the sound. Her firm jaw suited her broad, full-lipped mouth, red from blood natural — not a synthetic dye had touched her.

"I? Well, let's see now. I was plucking flowers when my husband gathered me. Or, if you like, I was working in the garden when a man with many names came and took me. They used to call it rape."

"You are married then?"

"In a manner of speaking. But what difference is that to you?"

None, he had to admit. He put his mouth on her lips and roamed with his right hand through her abundant, pale blond hair soft as corn tassels and just as resilient.

"Was I trouble for you in the MTA? The underground can be pretty rough at night."

"No. The underground, as you call it — I can see you learned the language in England — the underground does not bother me so much. I am used to it."

Toivo felt light in her arms, felt that he could be hidden there, be carried by her as a child would be in her womb. Heracles with one sip from Hera's breast became immortal. Why not him? Indeed, why finally not him? All of his life weighed down on him and he had had little to do with it. Like a shuttlecock he wove but had no idea of the weaving. Most of the events in his life were so much accident, as static in their development as figures in a frieze. There was movement when one passed but not standing still in front of it. Then it had a gelid severity where everything fitted but in a design he had not grasped. He was tired of being fitted. His mother had used him for social games. His father had been prevented from knowing him by history. War and death had been forced on him. But he had not acted, had been an instrument. Let me play for once. But he had been taken to the States by chance in the shape of rotund Blaise, the man with fat of steel. What else could he have done except go to school, get degrees, get married and be betrayed by a woman? Only writing had been his and his alone. A forging of fragments — testaments of a unity which surprised him on occasion.

"Why that look of surprise on your face?"

"Because I seldom have seen a woman so fully naked on my bed."

"And your wife?"

"Always covered."

"Maybe she had nothing to hide."

The woman combined the robustness and curving grace the Greeks admired in their statuary. She lay back on his bed, assured of her beauty, without modesty and without vulgarity. A rhythm of spheres, globing from the chest to the broad hips and belly down to the curved cushion, sloping into a small delta of fair hair. Blond on blond. She could be called abundance. And his passing into her was somewhat like the stirring of a bowl of rich cream. Violent movement ebbed out, smoothed into her. He never would have enough strength to exhaust her. She took him and held him firmly down and he forgot himself in that delicious death so rightly punned by the Elizabethans.

Spent, he lay next to her while she appeared hardly ruffled. Except for the glow marks of friction and a sheen of sweat which faded as they were cooled by the breeze from the open window. He was amazed by the robust softness of her flesh, that resilience which is stronger than force. She picked up an orange from a bowl by the bed and balanced the fruit on her belly. It became a violently lit color there and he looked silently at the burning.

"Why so solemn? Does making love make you sad?"

"In a way. I understand that old saw better now. What I like about it is the mindlessness, meaning that quite literally. Without a head. And when I say I lost myself in you it is dispiriting when it is over, because then I've found myself again. There's sadness in that."

He shoved his face down her body toward the orange and was wanting a bite when she laughed and said: "If you eat from it you'll never be able to forget me. You'd better think twice about it."

He looked up in her smiling eyes which mocked him and he bent back down and bit the fruit, sinking it in the soft mass of her belly and felt his mouth light up from the tang of the taste and fill it with spittle. Then she peeled it and fed him the parts. The rind was scattered on top of her as brightly as fall leaves on a stream. The strong perfume of the fruit was on the bed and tiny jets from the crushed flesh pricked their eyes and blinded them for a wink.

"I bet you didn't know that the tree is an evergreen."

"No."

"Just wonderful. It never dies and produces fruits like these. It is a miracle tree and it would be the best reason I can think of to move south."

The room had gathered the dusk while they had been eating and, after she had rubbed their bodies with the skin of the orange, she took him once again and he drove in as deep, as deep as he could and wanted to follow himself in and stay there. Not like Barb who reached for the Kleenex as soon as she considered him finished, making him feel as if he were in a public rest room.

With her clothes on again she pushed him back on the bed and kissed him lightly on the mouth. A mother comforting her child when she's leaving for an evening of fun without him.

"Maybe we'll see each other again."

"But what is your name?"

"Come on, what difference would it make now?"

"Your phone number then?"

"I don't know.. I think I left it on the kitchen table. Be good and keep up the good work."

Looking at her he noticed that she had put up her hair, which stood like a crenelated city wall on her head. From his prone perspective she looked uncommonly tall, filling his room with her person.

He went to the window and saw her help the young blind beggar across the street, the one he had seen before. He quickly threw on a robe and ran downstairs. But she was gone and in the street filled with the shadows of night he heard nothing but the tapping of the blind man's stick on the stones.

10

THE LAST TIME he had walked at leisure through the Boston Common was during Christmas of the year before when the park had been tinseled and lit with the flat light of electricity illuminating acrylic paint. Now the illumination was warm sun, bucking and babbling like a vivacious urchin among the colors of growth and sap and chlorophyll-craving summer. The swanboats were out in the shallow pond, baglunches papered the lawns, derelicts curled on the public grounds in endless naps like recessive children and insects had whirled wormed wrested their way off the pages of handbooks into a short, spun reality. Sallow, saffron-robed and shaven Krishna youths hoped to transmogrify themselves from ugly proselytes chanting by the Park Street Subway Station to suppliant souls in Nirvana. But the competition was tough, what with itinerant Paddies bellowing blarney with a lilt, an accordion man in a wheelchair, an apoplectic little man dervishing for Christ, drunk bums interrupting everybody in their capacity as bumptious Bostonian Sophists, newshawkers, paper flower merchants and an inexplicable swarthy mother with two children selling unseasonable gardenias from a wicker basket, their wilt-edged perfume kept frantically moist by the little boy's handfuls of water from the public fountain. The mother tagged along wide-eyed with her children laughing at a private joke, all three graced with a sprig of innocence and good humor. A true Common place for everyone and everything in this happy summer sunhour. A confusion of smells and sounds and colors cunningly orchestrated in a polysensate clavecin played by a devilish buffoon. A day which inspires tenderhearted democratic feelings in even the worst of snobbish tyrants. Dictators only enjoy public summers behind bulletproof glass on wheels.

Toivo felt apprehensive walking into a tearoom on Arlington Street facing the Public Garden. In the air-conditioned chill of the place he hesitated among the curlicued iron furniture that belonged out on a green lawn, wondering if he had gone through the wrong plate-glass mirror. Once he had waited here for Barb. They were supposed to meet each other but she had never shown up. She had been listening to a labor organizer belaboring Washington and had completely forgotten about her husband. This happened some time after they had committed domesticity. That crime had its flair in the beginning when a typical student existence stalled the attrition of more mundane familial life.

Barbara had admired Toivo's ease with languages and was fascinated by rows of books in foreign print she could not decipher. But she did not share his devotion or interest. Her higher education was cultured skim milk with all the nourishment taken out, fit only to whitewash the chambers of intellect. Disinterested passion for a subject not relevant to the present was a mystery, if not an absurdity, to her. For Barbara breathlessness could only result from too much exercise. Though she had done French in high school and college, French had done little for her since she was constitutionally unable to hazard a peek beyond regulated levels of minimal competence. When Toivo came to her with his enthusiasm for authors such as Diderot or Baudelaire she asked, after having listened to him for a while, "Why?" When he told her that such knowledge is not easy to acquire but that routine is, that it does not go to waste, she refuted him by pointing to her own inability to speak French anymore after a good four years of study.

Many evenings she heard no sounds of activity coming from the little alcove her husband had turned into a study. It was more reassuring when he was typing, so much more human than his silence and blank stares as if he had been drugged with thought. Toivo sensed her restlessness and felt responsible for the time she was spending with him, even if she denied complicity in his concern. She would lie on the couch-cum-bed correcting homework from the students she taught social studies as a permanent substitute teacher. Finished with that chore she'd turn the little portable TV on, put earplugs in her ears and open a book. He could never understand the purpose of the book until he noticed that she read during commercials. The slump of her back accused him and he got furious at the debility of that body wired to a flickering box because of his incompetence. He'd kiss the back of her thighs, stroke her buttocks, wait for her body to tense, to be there as flesh alive, no longer the extension of a vacuum tube. Never did he rip the plugs out of her head. His hand had to win. Up her back, the sharp blade of her shoulders, into the shrub of her cropped hair. Back down again under her clothing to her skin. Until she'd slowly roll over onto her back and put her hand on his body. He refused to hurry and waited until she had his pants off, until she had disconnected herself in order to make contact with him. Many times there was intercourse with a gray alien face in boxframe, discorporated sound coming faintly from the two white plugs on the floor, a deathly pallor illuminating heaving flesh. A lively anatomy lesson.

Blaise beckoned to him from the back of the shop, shook hands vigorously, beamed and asked if he'd care for a tall drink to kill the heat. But Toivo felt the sun being blotted from his clothes and thought a cup of hot tea would warm his bones a bit, keep arthritis at bay. With his chin in his fist as if he were holding the stiff beard of a pharaoh, Toivo studied the man opposite him and sniffed the ozone nestling in the pores of his skin, just as his mother used to sustain herself on a handkerchief steeped in eau de cologne.

Age, a rich diet and the sun lamp of a health club had sclerotized Blaise until he shone like a polished beetle. As usual he was so clean shaven that it seemed he plucked his beard with tweezers and his pate was as hairless and pink as a lovingly waxed rosewood table. Perhaps his fondness for rough tweeds was a conscious antithesis to his depilated condition. Toivo had never seen him wear anything else. A grotesque combination, as if a seal were hiding in the fur of a bear.

"Well, my boy, though you're hardly that anymore, does my appearance come as a surprise to you?"

Still as observant as always. The eyes still as green as jade and about as committal. Hands always scrubbed, manicured, gleamingly taut with flesh straining the skin like well-stuffed sausage. Fingers stoppered into the metacarpus with the same expensively discreet rings Toivo remembered from London.

"Let me tell you then. You look as good as I do. Success becomes you. Yes, sir, a handsome man you are. Tall, good-looking and silent. The European ladies will be delighted."

Incredible how he doesn't show his age at all. Like an ivory Buddha he could be centuries old.

"Sorry. I just can't get over the fact that you don't seem to look one year older than when I last saw you at the wedding."

Alas, poor Barb. They had honed each other to find happiness without the other. But why the whetstone of marriage to begin with? The best Toivo could muster in his defense was the admission of needing shelter, trust and confirmation of self. Barbara had vowed curiosity and her assurance that this was a man not to be gotten.

Which brought them to awesome vows on a muggy June afternoon in West Virginia, with costumes, posies, Handel organ, a small chorale mustered by Mrs. Clapp, the mother, and a fracas at the chapel door where rented ushers had to corner and disarm the lover who had been a close second and who was, quite literally, mad about Barbara.

"Who the hell is he anyway?" screamed poor Roger, struggling against the tuxedo which was serving as a maladroit strait jacket. "Barbara, tell me, what does that foreign bastard have that I ain't got?"

Everyone looked at Toivo, while the ontological loser was hustled away, begging the ushers to give him back the gun he had borrowed from his father, who was a marksman member of the local chapter of the American Rifle Association. Toivo almost told the inquisitional assembly that he agreed with their doubt. The question was a good one and had injected that metaphysical consternation so painful at festive rituals. The culprit, he, in top hat and tails, unable to answer for his presence. His dead father gently laughing at his son, who had suddenly been confronted with the dubious nature of loyalty.

Mr. and Mrs. Robert Clapp were hard-pressed to shroud their ignorance of the brand-new son-by-law.

"Well, you see, his father is Lutheran and his mother is a Catholic. Both of them dead, the poor dears. From Finland. Yes, that's right. Works for the government now, and teaches. He also writes, I believe."

"What I like so much about him," his mother-by-law confided to an aunt, "is his reserve. He's a true gentleman. Probably that European blood, you know."

Which meant that Mrs. Clapp was disturbed by her daughter's choice and was pretending to be delighted with her anger at not having a lawyer or a doctor in the family.

Blaise came to the reception all bubbly and roguish, like a jovial bumblebee. Mr. Clapp, an undersecretary in the Office for Economic Opportunity, was impressed by Blaise's intimated credentials and hurried over to his wife and her company to revenge himself on his mate's venomous aspersions on his character which he had had to endure every night for the past six months like a vile purgative before sleep.

"He's in the Pentagon. I've heard about him. Been told he's the man to watch. Has a lot of power."

"So?" snorted his wife willing, in order to be right, to give Jesus the lie.

"He's an old friend of Toivo's father and sort of an uncle to your son-in-law."

"Pentagon, you said? Did you hear that, Clarence?"

True. Blaise saved him that day by giving hysterical Roger the lie with his customary vagueries, so smooth and so untelling, perfect for the occasion and for the parents' peace of mind. Hugging the mystified bride like an affectionate teddy-bear uncle.

Quick change of costume. Barbara as Demeter on the landing, casting her contagious bouquet. Rice pelting. Kisses. Tears. Handshakes. Blaise greased Toivo's palm with a hefty check redeemable at any bank. Then the nerve-jangling cacophony of tin cans tied to the bumper of the new car which Daddy Clapp had gifted them with like a blessed chariot. In front of the police station, where Roger was held in protective custody, Toivo attacked the empty soup, peas and tomato cans with a savagery that shocked Barbara and left a dent in the shiny new chrome. Off to honeymoon on Chesapeake Bay with a cheery bride. Roger became Barb's lawyer for their divorce.

Flesh unto flesh it was on the wedding night and, truth to tell, for some eight months after. Until his desire became, overnight, a burden to her. But for that ozone epithalamium clothes were shed, juices fermented, coquetry was for his cock, and he could still refer to her "pretty little cunt" with its hairs almost the color of skin without being relegated to the company of the infamous Marquis. Fascination with details: how she combed her short blond hair backward and fluffed it with the edge of her palm, how she cracked the lining of books to stop the pages from falling closed, how she cleaned her teeth with a strand of hair. Beach, body, bedfun. Yet Toivo could still remember a peculiar sensation when they left for Washington to set up house. A sudden terror. Was this what it was all about? And what was that "it"? Excuse me, sir, but could you please introduce me to my wife?

Toivo was trying to scratch the inside of his thigh as unobtrusively as possible. A minor skin irritation there had been bothering him intermittently.

"I had to be in Boston for a conference and I figured I could let you know in advance and see you again in the flesh, as it were. I'm lucky to have caught you, two days before you're leaving. But, seriously, I'm very happy with your success. I knew it was going to happen one of these days. And you deserve it. Don't get me wrong. I've followed your career closely and I've often been disappointed when I've seen you by-passed time and again while one of those faddish snotnoses hits the jackpot. But I must admit, the book about your father is still my favorite."

"It wasn't really him. I never knew him well enough to do an accurate job. I fabricated what I thought could have been an episode in his life."

"You're right, of course. He was a spy in a manner of

speaking, but not quite as daring as you would like him to be. He did his job and did it well, but then, you don't know all the details."

"You never told me much."

"Oh, but I know very little myself. I was his chief, of course, but only on an operative basis. The bigger picture I never saw. Look, I'm not denigrating Kall. He made me, in a sense. What's the matter, your thigh bothering you?"

"Yes. There's a spot there that has been bugging me. The doctor says it's just a minor dermal thing. That it will go away when the weather gets cold again."

"I'm sure it will go away. Heat rashes are common. Let's have some pastry."

Toivo lit a cigarette and thought about this man who could give him tons of material for stories if only it were possible to squeeze it out of him. Yet all he could get was about as much as the amount of oil from a single lemon. Blaise nibbled at the pastry with dainty gusto. Then he leaned back in his chair and lit a cigarette after tapping it first on the nail of his thumb. Toivo watched for a moment, hoping the chair would give way and simply melt from the strain: an elephant reclining on a paper clip. Blaise observed him through the smoke of his Abdullah cigarette.

"So you're all set for your trip. Two more days and you're off, sailing for Europe. Got your lecture all written? Your readings all organized? Good. I told them it was a wise choice. Though there were doubts to be sure."

"What doubts? What are you talking about?"

"Come, come, Toivo. I was the natural man they would check with as a reference. They check everybody. And you're old enough to realize that they wouldn't just okay a person like you."

"What the hell are you talking about? I have been quiet most of my life. I've never participated in anything political. The only subversive acts I have committed are my books."

"Perhaps so. But don't forget that your father was a Communist who fought for the Reds in Finland and that later on he could slip in and out of Russia without ever being caught."

"You mean to tell me that if he'd been caught and killed it would have been better for him, better for his memory in the States, a place he'd never been to?"

"Remember where you are, don't shout. All these things are facts you can't deny so the obvious conclusion that his son might be writing propaganda for the wrong side can be easily believed. By a large number of people in fact. You see, it's not that difficult."

"Well, why don't we let that pass. I know that it can be easily done. But I still don't — tell me, what position do you hold these days?"

"Let's not start that again, all right? I was just thinking about that time in London when those two men almost kidnapped you. Your father should never have given in to their provocation. I had both of you under surveillance and nothing would have happened. But he made a dangerous move and almost blew the cover off the operation. Their game was so obvious: to get him by harming you, and I would have had it too. They were from a Slavic refugee organization playing at being operatives. An amateur outfit. But such types can be very dangerous, precisely because they don't know what they're doing. Ignorance is a deadly weapon. And a useful one. By his act of violence your father told them they were right. You see, perfectly simple. Thank God you knew nothing. And thank the Lord I was around. Now if your father had killed them and gotten rid of the bodies it would have been a different story. Unfortunately unconscious men come to their senses again and can still walk and talk. But anyway, let's not discuss silly things on such a beautiful day. Have some more tea and another pastry. They're really not bad, not bad at all."

Blaise smiled and rubbed some nicotine from his index finger. "Let's face it, you and I live in two different worlds, except that I know a lot about yours and you know very little about mine."

"That's true. You've got everybody covered."

"Ah yes, it's a pity that we have so many machines these days. Now don't misunderstand me, I think they're wonderful, but only for certain things. But it does take some of the romance out of intelligence. A little cold and harsh if you ask me. Being the kind of writer you are, the old ways should fascinate you and give you loads of material."

Toivo had to admit that Blaise had a point there. He was interested and would have liked to take notes if it hadn't interfered with his indignation.

"Now I'm going to give you an even better chance at some firsthand experience. Rarely do writers get that kind of opportunity unless they're leftovers from the war. I want you to check up on someone. A scientist. I believe he's hiding out in Amsterdam at the present. Find him, have a talk with him, see what he's up to."

"What did the poor man do? Declare the arms race a farce?" I know what I would like: I wish he were pudgy. Flabby, with a truck tire around his middle. With jowls. Soft. When you'd push him he'd give. But the damned man is solid, absolutely tight fat, stainless-steel obesity. Would also have to get rid of the eyes. They make him distinctive and individual. Without them and with some natural flab he would be colorless: a vagary slightly human. An erased outline in a dense drizzle. His mouth doesn't exist except as a slight swelling of the flesh above the chin, and the rest of the head, bald as it is and uniformly hairless, would tuck down like a ball bearing into the mass of his torso.

"Let's say that he's a brilliant mind who disapproves of his native country and has been shopping around for 'saner governments,' as he calls them. Although he apparently hasn't found any yet, he could be of use to the other side. We would simply like to have him back."

"I see. I suppose artists are dispensable."

"From our side of the fence, yes, they are."

"And what if I refuse?"

"We wouldn't clear you."

"That's blackmail."

"Of course not. After all, you're already cleared."

"So how can you prevent me from going?"

"By not clearing you."

"If I agree, my clearance will stand, and I can go abroad as a cultural ambassador for the United States. If I don't agree to do this job I won't be cleared, even though this has already been done. That's neat."

"Well, it's all a formality. Everything has been arranged. Reservations have been made, money's been spent, you've written your lecture and I'm sure you've sublet your apartment. It would be very inconvenient, don't you think? Besides, as I said, I'm giving you the rare chance to sniff around the otherwise strongly odorless body of Information. I've made sure certain amenities will be allotted to you."

"Such as?"

"Access to embassies. Contact with professional personnel overseas. Things like that."

"Is there anything I should know about how to behave?"

"Don't mock me, Toivo. Just the usual. Don't say what you think and don't act hastily. Be familiar with him and with others but don't be vulgar about your dislike for the States. He wouldn't fall for it. Listen but don't let anybody speak through you. In order words, be yourself."

Kall speaking, inflated in a taut skin, at a tearoom in Boston. Cunning, silent and artifice. "Just be yourself." How easy it is to say but how difficult to attain. It would never stop being a struggle.

After Toivo had completed his studies they moved to a suburban house. He worked in the State Department translating miscellany to inform the Security of the Nation and taught part-time in a junior college. In the evenings he wrote for himself. Blaise had procured him the job at the State Department.

Methodically Toivo Anglicized handbills, newspaper clippings, broadsides, magazine articles, and wrote abstracts of political articles that had been published in foreign intellectual magazines. Snippets from both official and unofficial presses in countries behind and facing the Iron Curtain. After a few months he was mildly surprised at the similarity of rhetoric no matter what tongue shaped it, and soon he wrote his own versions without bothering to read beyond the headlines. No one noticed. Everything was filed and stamped classified.

At home a similar irking tedium. The costumes changed but

the play remained the same. His wife's hair grew longer over the years and her clothing became simpler. Yet it still took her just as long to select a pair of blue jeans as it had to choose a dress. From ladies' boutiques to bogus military surplus stores. From J. D. Salinger to nonfiction.

Where he had hoped for help he had found coexistence. And when one is living with a roommate one has the choice of removing the person, especially when it is the enemy. Barbara sued for divorce on grounds of incompatibility.

"Well, I think we had a nice talk. Everything seems to be fine. You'll have fun there, believe me, traipsing around the fleshpots of Europe. Well, I really have to go now. Take care. And remember, I can always be reached. Enjoy yourself. Perhaps all this success will finally scrape some of that gloom off. You've got to forget your youth and the war sometime, you know. Your father, for example, was far from gloomy. Well. Bon voyage. Look me up when you get back." Pressure from the cool, solid palm, a smile, payment of the bill and he was gone.

It had become a little warmer in the tearoom. Toivo supposed it was because they couldn't condition the windows. Everything was set. Packed, ticketed, arranged. He felt a sudden urge to go to his place, break the lease permanently, pack one suitcase with one copy each of his books plus his most enigmatic stones, get a sheaf of bank drafts and disappear abroad. Light luggage. What was overweight was his head, crammed with words. The lightest baggage of all. He watched the leaves swirl around the spoon when he stirred the cold tea, a funnel of fall leaves in a tiny whirlpool. Blaise. Yes, Blaise. The man he could neither get rid of nor like. A man utterly incapable of eliciting affection, not even for a price. Yet he was for Toivo something like a paternal uncle, might as well have married his mother. It was strange he should have such a place in his life. It seemed illegal, a travesty of chance. Blaise had always helped him but had there been a design? I bet he doesn't have innards, a gut, intestines. What he consumes spreads in semiliquidity under his skin like an oil slick. In ancient times he would have been a disaster because a priest would not have been able to predict the future from that belly.

Toivo got up and left, walked through the lulled Common and took the subway home. He had a need to see his stones.

Chance miracles were lying on strips of velvet in his bedroom. Exquisite Cubist paintings, petrified jungles growing into polished deserts endlessly ending on ten inches of stone, gas jets writing a secret calligraphy on the softest black no night could equal. Nature dashed these miracles off with an abundance of creativity only the most blessed of artists can muster. Glowing mystic eyes bedded there in velvet. The stones lay there in their dead beauty, still lives, nothing but themselves. Blaise, you would not understand, except for a passing fascination, would not understand their hypnotism nor why they mesmerize me because in them I see a code of life far beyond mine. Your insects are merely stunted perfection. But here I have a row of philosophers' stones which by their beauty can petrify. A perfection which is true because it menaces. A perfection finished in infinity.

II

11

"ONLY NUTS. They can't do anything to nuts, now can they? Or can they? I only eat imported ones, but they have fine walnuts here in Holland. Have one."

Toivo took some of the wrinkled seeds, which reminded him of atrophied nicotine brains. He missed the shell which, if pressure is carefully applied to the seam, breaks into two tubs. With a toothpick and a snippet of paper you'd sail it down a puddle as vast as the Atlantic.

"Thank you. I like nuts. To get back to my article. Then you feel that there's a conspiracy afoot in the States to kill all of us?"

"Yes, I do. And subtle, yes, I must say, for such a vast operation, quite subtle. A metabolic poisoning which starts at birth. A mother refuses to suckle her child, as mine did and she told me so with pride, and starts it out on formulas. Chemicals, my man, chemicals. No one simply tells them that what the body produces is better than anything else. Even diseases? Perhaps. So: bottled babies. Jars of baby foods with salt added to satisfy Mom's taste buds even though it's bad for the kid. But then, you see, baby doesn't fork out the dough. On to beef riddled with stilbestrol, stuff that chemically castrates cattle to fatten them. And then vegetables, grown in soil contaminated by fertilizers and pesticides and transported over great distances and kept fresh artifically—if you can call it that. Fruits dyed to attract the consumer. Bread not fit to wash your windows with."

"So it's the food that made you leave?"

"Don't be silly."

The man looked at Toivo without seeing him. The smoke from

his cigarette bandaged his index finger and he shook his hand as if to get it off. A tall, bony man with a pinched frame holding on to a large head for dear life. It would balloon off and float around the room, absorbed in itself and decidedly against its omphalic point of gravity. Dr. Russell de Bruce was only in his thirties but he had a ring of light fuzzy hair which gave him the appearance that age couldn't make up its mind to state a number. Fine silky wool of a blond close to white sand, it stood straight up around his skull as if electrified. His occasional grin put him back in his crumpled suit on his chair—gave substance to his person.

"You wouldn't be another one of those embassy clowns? They keep offering me tickets back to the States and dangle promises of superlabs in front of my nose."

"No, I'm just doing an article on you. I don't know a thing about you, except that you're a well-known scientist who left the States in disgust."

"Famous scientist, my man, famous. That's why they want me to come home. But I've gone a bit soft in the head. Things won't fit. There are all those pieces floating around. Not much is making sense to me anymore. 'Course, could be from having been a child prodigy or something like that."

He folded up out of his chair and paced the room, fishing for cigarettes in his pockets. Toivo gave him a pack and de Bruce promptly shook it empty in his right coat pocket and threw the container on the floor.

"Should be smoking a pipe, right? More the image. The government doesn't care a damn whether its population eats, breathes or drinks death. Money talks. It's all for the money. Can't live without it, can you? O, I tell you, I love old Ezra Pound and his hatred of the moneychangers. The root of all evil. Yes. Quite so. They locked him up too. No, my mind is unhinged. It won't slam shut on facts and keep just one under observation. Worked on molecular structures and the journals were breathless. Messed around with physics and watch it, Niels Bohr, you're gonna have to move over. Biochemistry and pure physics. They don't mix. Want to know why? Write it down. You don't write much. Ever done any writing?"

"As a matter of fact I have."

"Name."

"What?"

"Your name."

"Syystalvi. Toivo Syystalvi."

"Never heard of it."

De Bruce went to the window of the room and shoved it open.

"Here, have some walnuts," he said to some pigeons. "Better for you than bread. Doesn't mix, you see, because with the one you explore life at its most minute and with the other you're blinking at the utter vastness of the universe."

Toivo had to get up and walk over to him in order to hear because de Bruce kept his head out of the room.

"Seriously," he said, turning to Toivo again, "you see what I mean? In biochemistry we're dealing with substances under our noses and hope to decipher the stuff. And the more we decipher the more we don't know. Oops. The more we know for sure. The test tube tells all. Sure. Aunt June in Watertown: my foot. But all right. There's stuff, it's there, and it's decipherable. In principle. But the other, the universe. We don't know anything. All theories. Microscope and telescope. What we do is turn the first to the stars and use the second on organic tissue. That's one hell of a bad pair of glasses."

"And the food, how does that fit in?"

Toivo wasn't really concerned with logical progression but he had chosen to play the role of the journalist so he felt he had to be confused and demand some sort of order in the argument.

"What food? O, I see."

Dr. de Bruce folded down in his chair and sniffed the vault of his fingers. He was trying to cooperate.

"Well, I found it difficult to find private funds to finance my research. As a matter of fact, impossible. I, like everybody else, even Chomsky, had to turn to federal money. There's one thing wrong with that: they always want a piece of the action. Let me put it another way: they will always find something to use for purposes I didn't have in mind. See what I mean? I say that a lot, don't I? Now, I am not in the public interest, or in the private one or in the federal one. Damnit, I am my own ally."

He was banging his fists on the armrests of the cheap easy chair of the rented room. Toivo watched him with sympathetic interest. But he was his own man now. Only needed the equipment of words and, when you got down to it, didn't have to ask anyone for material. Just listen and look and you've got all you need. Toivo watched the man struggle with composure and made notes in his head. De Bruce got up, rubbing his face with his hands. The face was white from the pressure when he took his hands away and let them drop by his side. He looked at Toivo and smiled.

"Let's get out of here. Amsterdam is a good place to walk in. Nice bars too. Bars where you can sit and sip and there's light. Our dark American bars always make me feel I'm hiding in myself."

Down the stairs he kept on talking, throwing words back over his shoulder and up at Toivo. His long body stooped over his chest, dragged down by the weight of his head, making it difficult for him to find his feet. Outside on the street he straightened up somewhat and stared at the bicycles rushing by.

"Circles," he mumbled, "circles. There's another side to everything. The trouble with science is that, once you're in it, you can't get out." He grabbed Toivo by the arm and tugged at him for emphasis. His face smiled, frowned, thought, spoke. It was never still. Even when he didn't say anything.

"See, as a writer, if you choose to stop, you stop, and no one can write your books for you. Correct? Right. Not with a scientist. Some investigation is started and if you don't follow it all the way to the end someone else will. It's inherent in the method. I was with antimatter and now that I've quit for a while, someone else will go on with what I already started. See what I mean? And another thing. People think that scientists are all alike: quiet, studious, composed. But hell, we're just like other people. Screwballs, weirdos, losers, and the real failures go into technology and make the money."

He started laughing and had to be prodded to notice that people were staring at him.

"Okay, all right. I'll be quiet. Don't want to embarrass you. I knew a fellow once, a brilliant guy, almost beat Watson-Crick to DNA, he was doped on pills all the time. Prescribed them to himself since he also held an M.D. Grants up the ass, if you know what I mean. One afternoon he got in his Stingray and went to a rifle range and killed himself. Couldn't apply a method to his own life, see."

De Bruce ordered another round of jenever and settled back in the wicker chair of the outdoor café. There was enough traffic going by to make his voice harder to hear.

"It's difficult to explain. It's such a mess up here. My head's just flitting about trying to find a shape. No matter, one must try. Scientists, even when they're off their rockers, must go methodically insane. Fine. Specific problems, how shall I say it, of a particular utilitarian value, I am not interested in. Yet that's what they wanted. And they're patient. They sit around like vultures waiting for offal. It's more of a game with me. One day I noticed a dog sniffing another's ass. I said to myself, we must have done that once. We know of some sort of flying hormones called pheromones which have an effect on the species. In fact, our noses are facial genitals. There's erectile tissue in the mucosae which increase the sense of smell when they're swollen. All to do with sex. We know that. But when we say that we can smell fear, or smell hostility, we're talking about sniffing concepts." He gulped his glass empty and leaned over to Toivo and sniffed his face.

"You smell quite friendly to me. Quite friendly. I think I rather like you. That's good. What did you write again.?"

"Novels and other things."

"What's the latest?"

"*Past Reason Hunted.*"

"Umm, yes. Sounds like something I might like. We'll buy it on the way back to my place."

The sun was moving over where they were sitting and de Bruce pushed his face up and closed his eyes. His Adam's apple bobbed like a float the length of his throat. When he shrugged his jacket off he proved himself even skinnier than Toivo had imagined. His torso was the hanger for his clothes.

"Why did you come to Amsterdam, any particular reason?" Toivo finally asked.

"Yes. Street organs." De Bruce sat up straight and his eyes were glistening.

"I love them. When you think of them in comparison to recordings and sound tapes, or the real thing like orchestras, they're so woefully off the mark. So imperfect. But there's something in that kettle-pot sound that is incredibly beautiful. Nostalgia and melancholy as if the big box on wheels is trying its best to sing with a perforated larynx. They quiet me and let me cry a little if I listen too long. Nothing else can. They're good things, those wonderfully gaudy contraptions. But you must hear them on the street. They need the noise of a busy street. Then they're at their best, like forlorn accordions with bronchial trouble. I can't take them by themselves. The other night I went by one very early in the morning. The guy who owned it was drunk, dead drunk, and turning the wheel in the middle of an absolutely sleeping street. It sent shivers up my spine. The longing it sings is too strong. Like a mermaid singing. Definitely a seaman's instrument. Got to be."

"How about women?"

"What? Ah yes, the human angle, or whatever you call it. No, don't care too much for them. Got enough with myself. All the female I need. No. Seriously. The females don't realize that they're 'it.' They're the basis, even genetically. They win, buddy. Always will. Let's say human life is basically an X matter—the female chromosome. Just pure chance we got a little tiny Y to make us so-called males. And let me tell you it's tough going to stay male when you're being shaped in there, in the womb. Any little nudge in the chemistry of formation and the maleness returns to its home base: femaleness. See how I talk laymanese? I'm a nice guy. It takes very little to push the penis and scrotum back into the body again. It was Diderot who first wrote that down, I believe. That the only difference between man and woman is, and I quote as we say in the biz, that between a bag hanging down outside and an inverted bag inside, unquote. He even talked about the dark line that goes from your scrotum to the glans as a sewn-up vulva."

"Yes, I remember. So he was right after all."

"Quite so."

"You remember d'Alembert saying to Doctor Bordeu that, when he was talking about these matters, he was talking filth?"

"Yup, sure do. And also Bordeu's superb reply: 'When one talks about science one has to use technical terms.'"

"Women have got it all the way, don't they?"

"They sure do. It's unfair that we are trifles of chance in the chromosomal game, and they hold all the cards. Why should I give myself to the cardsharp too?"

"Makes men look ridiculous when they rant and rave against them. Because they will always lose. The female principle always wins."

"Absolutely. Primitive peoples knew that and so did the ancients. But we love to forget it. The one thing I am interested in is whether there's a genetic codification linking sex to killing. The female has a decidedly lesser impulse. At least in humans. But that's all adaption of course. Society and all that. Yet who knows? The female spider kills her mate because he happens to be handy for dinner that night. He's meat. She doesn't do it out of malice or anger. With us though, the intraspecies killing seems always to be done by the males. But I could be wrong."

"What else have you got up your sleeve? You're wonderful."

"Thank you. I am so glad you said that. I mean it. I've been against myself too long now, but I haven't gotten anywhere yet. Little pats help, don't they? What else you say? O, I don't know. Insects maybe. They scare me. I looked into them a little. They've got a somatic morphology which makes individual particularities disappear, you follow me? Good. Those distinctive particularities are absorbed by function. Which is to say, insects have perfected themselves for their role in nature and that's that. Everything else has not only been subordinated but also eliminated. Limitation by perfection! That's scary. See, that's what I could have become, perhaps am. Looking at one damn nucleus and forgetting the body. Just a prier with brains, and brains whittled down for that purpose only. That's the bureaucrat working only for his next promotion, the politician for election, the whore who becomes just snatch, the man who's just a trigger finger. Stay diversified, remain a spectrum. You can't let them isolate you to a tiny particle of single use. Don't do it. Of course writers have less trouble."

"Possibly, but writers are tough though. They can watch anything and judge it for material."

It was a mistake and Toivo knew it as soon as he had said it. Suspicion flickered in the doctor's eyes and he straightened up from his slouch where he had seemed so comfortably letting his thoughts trickle free.

"Yes, well, that sounds like our embassy men again. Maybe all of you want a formula from me which will perfect men into insects. It's been done already, so why go after me?"

"Come on. I didn't mean it that way. I have nothing to do with the embassy. I'm a writer traveling around hoping some experiences will stick to him so he can go back home and turn them into fiction."

Toivo put his hand on the other man and shook him a little. He'd never had any intention of hurting him. How could he have known that de Bruce was that suspicious? But you should listen to yourself, my friend, he thought. Your intuition has been right more often than not. Except that it comes faintly, gains in intensity when you speak, and you're left with the certainty that you were right before you spoke, when it's too late. Remember what Kall said: Be silent. Arm yourself with silence.

"As a matter of fact I'm in total agreement with you."

"Well, good then. But you shouldn't say things like that. I'm a suspicious individual. But you know what? I really don't know why you guys want me. I'm not important at all. Did you know that? Perhaps I've neglected to tell you. I never discovered anything of value. Or perhaps the ammonium chloride thing? Couldn't be. There's no future in that. Tell you what, let's walk back to my place and buy a bottle. You're all right. The only reason I'm going on with this interview is that I haven't had anyone to talk to for quite some time now. I don't speak Dutch and if I singled out scientists here they'd be too busy with their projects. Besides, their knowledge of English isn't sufficient for my crazy jumps and Hula Hoops. And trying to converse the way I do in mathematical language is only fit for a loony bin. So come on, let's do that. You pay. You've earned it."

*

Toivo and de Bruce looked for *Past Reason Hunted* in several bookstores, but all of them had only the Dutch edition. Finally, on the Damrak, not far from the Central Station, they found copies of the original American edition.

"Tell me," the tipsy doctor asked a tall salesclerk with a face as morose as if he'd been scrubbing his paralyzed grandmother, "is that any good?"

"I wouldn't know. I didn't read it. I never read best sellers."

"Best seller?"

"Yes. In the States, and in Germany and in France. The Dutch will follow too, they always do."

"You think it's bad then?"

"I don't think. I read. Books. Not best sellers."

Toivo had been browsing head down in the back of the store with the air of devoted single-mindedness one can expect from a cow just brought in from a stint in the desert and let loose in a lush Dutch meadow. Afraid someone would recognize him and hoping they would do so and please embarrass him.

"You never told me you were famous."

"I'm not. It'll pass."

"What's it about?" de Bruce asked and handed Toivo the two brown crocks of jenever while he flipped through the book in the middle of the busiest afternoon hour in one of the busiest streets of Amsterdam as if he were in bed or invisible.

"I don't know. I hate to say."

"The jacket here says that it is about an aging master spy who disappeared one morning because the light of a standing lamp threw a question mark on the glass of a radio. Boy, that's cryptic."

"It kinda goes on from there," Toivo said lamely.

"Of course it does. Otherwise the jacket wouldn't fit."

While they were waiting for the jenever to get good and chilled in the miniature refrigerator, de Bruce said cheerfully: "Why bother to do an interview with me? A famous writer should be interviewing luminaries, heads of culture."

"Don't like them. I like heads with something in them."

"Okay, that's good. No, let's not sit down. I feel like moving."

So the two men walked around the little apartment on one of

Amsterdam's quiet canals, giggling, talking, doing a skip and hop every so often, as if a farmers' band was brassing polkas. The uninhibited mood switches of the scientist ex officio were catching and Toivo felt like a boy again, arm around a friend's shoulder, doing just those sudden crazy things grownups dislike because they fail to follow a pattern. By the time the sun went down they were drunk enough not to care about properly chilled liquor and, dumped on the bed, they passed the jenever and the cigarettes back and forth and talked. Toivo mostly listened and tried to take mental notes while de Bruce threaded ideas on a string of words only he knew the sequence of.

"There I sat in my pyjamas in my apartment back on Elm Street, U.S.A., listening to a perfect stranger in black who wasn't saying anything. He just looked at me and I was hearing him say that my research in antimatter was disturbing him because I was getting close to a source he didn't think humans should know about. Believe me, all this was deadly serious. I couldn't move. Have you ever had that, when you lie in bed and you know something's wrong and you want to get up and can't? I forced my mind to go to my muscles and lift my legs, but my mind wouldn't budge from my visitor. I'll even accept you're saying it was hypnopompic but only in the sense that the messenger came from my sleep, so I was telling myself something. Except that he sat there clear and true, with the face of an Oriental angel, dressed in a neat, black business suit. I hadn't been asleep because I wanted to try out a series of equations that night. He said, well, communicated to me, that my equations were child's play, and he showed me one so astonishing and so true and so impossible that I asked him to repeat it so I could write it down. But he laughed and vanished. Right in front of my nose. That's crazy, isn't it?"

De Bruce sat up and bottomed his glass. He looked moodily at Toivo and shook his head. His eyes which had been bluish when he had been having fun now stared an impassive gray. He began to shiver and rubbed his head ring of hair flat. Toivo got up and put his arm around the shaken man, took him to the bathroom and wetted a towel. After de Bruce had drunk the glass of water Toivo handed him he began to regain control again.

"It's ridiculous that a scientifically trained mind should come up with such nonsense, isn't it? And what worries me is that I couldn't smell him. Now if he were part of myself, wouldn't you say that there should have been olfactory recognition? I mean, Jesus, I should be able to smell myself." All Toivo could suggest was another drink in the living room.

"I've got it," de Bruce suddenly said very loud after an uneasy silence. "It's what I've always thought. Too formulated. Too abstract. We've got to flesh out our abstractions with symbols again. Someone said that before. Who was that? The hell with it. Laymanese right? Nonsense. It's right, very right. In layman's terms it means putting the abstractions back into circulation again. That's what my night visitor was all about."

He looked expectantly in Toivo's face, his eyes rekindling some of their blue again, then he dropped his face and mumbled "but he was damn real" and recouped his depression with a cheerful hosanna voice.

"We deal in symbols, but they're empty and cold comfort to a mind made of flesh. I know, I know. We want to reach beyond. But that's nonsense. It all started with physical objects which could be observed and tasted and touched. Also measured: held in hand. We've abstracted from the basic pebble to the square root of abstraction."

"You mean that we should clothe our ideas in fictions again?"

"Right. Fine. That's the spirit, if not the flesh."

De Bruce was drinking now not for the euphoria but to quench his thirst. His face was gaining color, red spreading along the cheekbones like a dyemaker dropped in the ocean to spot submarines.

"I've been after nothingness all my life. As a kid I wanted to invalidate my kid sister. That's what I called it. I meant, of course, insubstantiate her. Plato or Democritus. Those are the two spools science is wound up around. What the atom smasher smashes are the traveling salesmen of fundamentally stable ideas, says Plato. That is: ideal forms are put to torture. But Democritus talks about boxes within boxes within boxes within. Keep on splitting and splitting and you'll come to fundamental matter, the basic stuff. Planck and Bohr and Heisenberg proved that energy comes in packages, in boxes: quanta. Always those damn sets of boxes. And Democritus says that all particles, atoms, the indivisibles, move around at random, bump into each other by chance and form something. He's scary, you know, old Democritus. On the one hand total confusion and pure accidental chance? Perhaps chance made into a chanceless norm? And then also the tunneling of big to small, to smaller, to smaller, to smaller — never reaching the superlative of smallest. For, once we've said that atoms can be divided into nuclei with electrons, which can be divided into protons and neutrons, which can be divided into quarks, which can be divided into snarks, into who knows what — well, then, there's no end to it. Doesn't that make you dizzy, doesn't that drive you crazy?"

He was stomping around the room, hopping and skipping, bumping into things, disheveling the place. There was no gaiety in it. More like a man trying to get at an intolerable metaphysical itch.

"I keep on staring into particles and see doors opening to more particles, to more, and more, down an endless corridor. Chinese boxes. And try to imagine, damnit, you're a writer, you're supposed to imagine, imagine all those infinite boxes floating around in infinite multitudes, subject to nothing but infinite chance."

Someone above them started banging on their ceiling and Toivo got up to quiet de Bruce down. De Bruce nodded all right, all right, and licked his fingers, which were stuck with tobacco particles from the lint in his pockets. The bitter taste stung him and stole his mind away for a moment.

"You got anything to eat here?" Toivo asked.

He was concerned that if he left the doctor in his present condition he might do something unforeseen, start counting boxes, for example. But he didn't want him to stop either. Just as you hate to put a ladybug outside because its movements and body fascinate you, yet at the same time you're afraid it might dash itself to pieces on something if you don't. Toivo found a link of sausage. He cut it in half and the two men munched on it while they looked out over the canal from the window.

"I wish I could smell particles," said de Bruce, "like I smell this sausage. I wish I were a metaphysical hound. Without an abstracting brain. Plato or Democritus. Maybe it doesn't matter. I wish I were a street organ." Even the upright head ring of hair seemed despondent. But what do you do with a drunken scientist who's blue? Console him with a hug and the assurance that life will go on despite the peeping Toms peering into its pores? De Bruce rubbed his face. The pressure of his greasy hands left dark half-moons under his eyes and a sheen on his face.

"There's more to this whole business than we can ever dream of. But you see, I can't publish dreams, they have to be proven. I thought I would have one over on Plato and Democritus both. If you got past quarks and whatnot, you must reach a final point. Not necessarily an end. There can be no 'end' to matter in that sense. But at the edge, where you fold the paper, the other half looks exactly like the one in front of you even though you've bent it backward and out of sight. Antimatter. In nineteen sixty-five in Brookhaven they combined antiprotons and anti-neutrons. So antiatoms can make up antimatter. That's where the whole business might be laid to rest. In order words, our earth is made up of matter and antimatter in balanced proportions. But then, if this were true, and I do think it is, then we have the other side of the mirror all around us. Then, and this is where I go crazy again, we have the possibility which can be entertained in all seriousness, that there is an antilife as flourishing as ours. And if in that realm there is also an antideath then, well, logically, it would cancel itself out and death would not exist. Also, if the inhabitants of that realm have an intelligence like ours say, that doesn't mean it need be as restrictive as ours. They could be much further advanced than we are and know the way to make matter, our so-called matter, materialize. At will. Whenever they want to. There you have the answer to invisible men and doubles, to mirror images and even to my own night visitor. That's what I was after. A dangerous journey you see, because the snark might be a boogum after all."

He was speaking in a monotone, his head pressed against the pane of the window, breathing the glass dense and watching it emerge transparent again.

"Maybe that's what the government was interested in, and the other ones too. If I could formulate how to slip into that realm and back again, they really would have something, wouldn't they? But Christ, I am like a drunk trying to find a keyhole to open the door. And I don't even have the key."

De Bruce began softly to snore leaning forward as if he were going to be frisked, settling a slight reverberation in the glass. Toivo took a lit cigarette from the slack hand that hung by his side and eased the man away from the window to get him into bed. He told him to get undressed while he straightened the bed and smoothed the sheets. Toivo also took the empty crocks off the bed and placed them gently on the floor so no noise would rouse the irate upstairs neighbor again.

"You know," de Bruce mumbled while fumbling with the cord of his pyjamas, "the antipeople, because they don't know death, would be as old as matter has existed. They would have been there with the pharaohs and all and they would know it now, this minute, the way you remember yesterday."

He yawned but his mouth wouldn't shut because he suddenly remembered: "But then there would also be an anti-Plato and an anti-Democritus, and the whole damn tunnel of Chinese boxes would start all over again. No, there's got to be an end, an end."

For once that evening Toivo had a brilliant stop-gag idea. He forced the man on the bed and said as calmly as he could: "No, that's all right. Because when they reach their end they'll have found matter. And the twain would meet, shake hands and start a series of conferences."

De Bruce smiled at that, satisfied. His eyes were closed already while he was still drawing the blanket up. But when Toivo turned off the light he heard him mutter: "I hope I never get boxed. Disperse me but don't let them box me."

"Okay, okay," Toivo soothed, and left the room.

Toivo thought of cleaning up the apartment but he felt too tired. He had spent over twelve hours with a shrapneled intellect and he felt something like shell shock. Bits and pieces were still floating through his mind. They would all make sense somewhere, at a distance perhaps, as a pointillist painting does when you back away from it. He recalled seeing a series of photographs once which stilled a bullet hitting an orange. A series of stills in slow motion shot with an incredibly fast camera.

The man was not mad at all, he thought while he fumbled at the door for the lock. He had shut off all the lights so de Bruce wouldn't wake up anymore. Softly closing the door behind him until he heard the click of the safety lock, Toivo thought of de Bruce as someone who had been mustered for the expedition that hunted for the snark. He made as much sense as did that fabulous crew — as much sense as sense makes. Which was not enough in his world of proof.

12

TOIVO WOKE LATE in the day, past the noon hour. He ordered a large breakfast by phone from his bed. He was hungry. While he showered and shaved de Bruce came to mind again and he resolved to talk to the embassy people and tell them to lay off the man. He was as useful to a government as a sieve would be, and only a genius to himself. A bellhop wheeled the food in and Toivo tipped him generously, pleased that he could enjoy the luxury of service.

While he was eating he looked out over the Dam Square toward Amsterdam's Royal Palace. Children were clinging to their mothers in front of a Punch and Judy show. Pigeons were swooping like fat gliders around an old woman with a bagful of bread. The lecture in Amsterdam had gone well. His Dutch publisher had made promotional hay out of his visit as a "cultural ambassador" from the States, and he had fulfilled Blaise's request to see the scientist. All he had to do now was make sure the embassy people would get the news to Washington, get them to leave de Bruce alone, and he would be on his merry way. Next stop Paris.

But the man from the consulate in Amsterdam couldn't promise him anything about de Bruce. He said that he couldn't because there were no regulations he could go by, and without having been briefed he couldn't do a thing. He was only doing his duty. No matter how much Toivo pleaded, the man refused profusely, though sprinkling amply with sirs, to state anything definite. Upon demand it appeared that the superiors were either lunching or in conference. Furious by then, Toivo threatened the man with using his connections in the State Department. Pure bluff, though he was thinking of Blaise. The man's potato face blanched as if he had been peeled, and he finally agreed to go with Toivo to de Bruce to at least explain to him that Toivo had nothing to do with officialdom, to show him a press authorization which had been hastily produced by potato's secretary and to tell the suspicious scientist there was nothing to worry about. Toivo felt he owed de Bruce as much, hoping that, even with such vague assurances, he would not wake up to a wicked attack of paranoia when (and if) he remembered that he had spilled his innermost secrets to a stranger.

While they drove to de Bruce's address the Class 4 Foreign Service officer belabored Toivo's ear with reasons for his caution.

"It's a hierarchy, sir, believe me. I'm bound by it. I'm up for promotion to Class three and any little thing that could make a wave, even the teeny-weeniest, please understand that, can wreck my career at this point. You simply don't know what we in the Foreign Service have to go through. Out of the three thousand officers about a hundred are weeded out each year. My superior is reviewing my case for promotion this week, and his report goes to the departmental reviewing officer who doesn't know me very well, except my file, my file he knows, you understand me, and he recommends his decision to the reviewing board. It is a very delicate business, sir, I assure you. Anything at all, any little thing out of the ordinary, something that is not covered by the rules, will upset that delicate balance of my file's contents and I am out of a job. My superior is not overly fond of me, not because of my work, oh no, my work is very satisfactory indeed, precisely because I go by the rules and do not make the mistake of overstepping them, nor do I make waves, but he dislikes me somewhat, but please don't tell anyone, you promise me, sir, don't you, because, well, he likes my secretary. And Miss Clarence and I are planning to be engaged and he doesn't want to lose her. So you see, sir, I'm in a ticklish position. I have to go by the rules. I'm sorry." Toivo didn't answer but sat grimly next to the Cassandra'd fool, hoping to be rid of him as quickly as possible.

"It's a nightmare, sir. Once you're fired it's very difficult to get another job. I would be overqualified and there's the matter of recommendations, you understand. A colleague killed himself because of all this, that's how bad the system is."

"Could you please shut up," Toivo finally growled. "Just do what I told you."

The door of the apartment was ajar.

"I wouldn't go in without his permission, sir, preferably in writing. The rules state so. Legally I am not even here, if you see my meaning."

"I see nothing. The man has a hangover. Maybe he went for a walk to get some air and went back to bed again."

The living room was in the same mess as he had left it in the night.

"Come on, Russell," Toivo said cheerfully while walking to the bedroom. "Get up, man. It's a beautiful day out."

There was no answer. Class 4 was nervously looking to the hall door, his hands fingering the linings of his jacket pockets as if he were plucking at his body.

"I'll wake him," Toivo said, "and you say your piece and then you can go back to your precious file."

De Bruce was still in bed. His head was snapped back and his skull was cracked open at the temple. Blood and matter pulped out. He had been brained with a jenever crock. Brown shards lay scattered on his pillow with other segments of his head. Class 4 saved Toivo from his deadlock of decision both physical and moral. The nervous man yelled, stuffed a fist in his mouth and fell against Toivo. Toivo turned to catch him, thinking he was going to faint, but when he saw the man's stomach muscles beginning to contract he shoved him toward the door and out of the apartment. When they were outside, on the landing of the staircase, the dead man was a problem of the room and didn't ask for their action anymore.

"We've gotta get back to the consulate. Gotta get back to the consulate," Class 4 whispered over and over again like a child, who, despite the trouble he's in, looks at his home as a heaven where things will get sorted out. Even if there's pain and punishment.

"The consulate, we've gotta get to the consulate."

Toivo went quickly down the stairs with the official holding on to the collar of his jacket as if he were reining in a horse. At the street door he wanted to run but Toivo threw him back and peered out. No one was particularly near so he stepped out on the sidewalk and began to walk toward the car, controlling his companion by pulling the man's wrist down with his fist. Scuffling along, the little potato man suddenly realized.

"What will they do to me? My god, my promotion! They'll fry me for this. O my god, why did you get me into this?" He wrenched himself free from Toivo and faced him. But before he could speak Toivo told him coldly: "You are attracting attention now and you'll be in jail pretty soon. Just walk normally to the car and I'll drive you back home to big daddy."

"But I have diplomatic immunity," the terrified man whispered. "I didn't touch anything. Nothing, I didn't touch nothing. I'm immune here. They can't touch me."

And he repeated his hopeful litany all the way back to the consulate.

The consul made sure Toivo knew how annoyed he was at having to leave a luncheon in honor of a Dutch philanthropist whose gout prevented him from attending testimonial dinners. Murder did not faze him. Toivo doubted it would curl a hair of his barbered mustache if the victim were served up for dinner as long as it did not interfere with protocol and clean table linen. The consul had business of import to worry about which was clearly elevated above the mundane perplexities of violently diseased Americans.

"Murder is an annoying business. What's more, it's untidy. We're not equipped to deal with such matters, but we have been in touch with the embassy in The Hague and some points have been cleared up, points which concern you."

The consul was a six-footer, properly aged, with marcel waves in his faultless hair, attired in the demure distinction of grays and stripes and laundered linen suited to his office. Which he took very seriously in an august manner. Seated behind the dustless, polished desk, the bright sun of a happy day washing through the windows behind his back, he looked as completely in possession of clean power as was possible for a man who had been muddied in the traffic of tragedy. Toivo shrunk somewhat in the imitation leather chair, wondering what this Olympian had in store for him.

"You have put us in a very unpleasant position. First of all, you are at the moment a cultural representative of the United States government in Europe. We cannot deny that fact, and it merits careful consideration. We don't want to compromise the State Department with even the slightest suggestion of foul play, anywhere, at any time. God knows we don't need that."

The consul was nearsighted and had to purse his eyelids in order to see his unwelcome charge. The tone of his voice left no doubt that he was ill pleased with Toivo's distant official relationship to him. It shouldn't have been.

"Of course writers are woolly ones, aren't you now, and we have to make allowances for the antics of artists."

"I don't see any need for moralizing," Toivo said. "Just tell me what's what and I'll leave you to your luncheons."

With a voice like an iced martini glass the consul continued. "Very well. Secondly, we will for the present accept your remonstrations of innocence. The police will think different, of course. They always do. It will be difficult to match you to your fingerprints unless they care to go all the way and contact Interpol and the FBI. Until drastic measures need to be taken we think it advisable that you stay calmly in your hotel and then proceed to your next engagement in Paris. We simply cannot have such a, shall we say, unforeseen complication, derail a carefully planned lecture tour sponsored by the Information Agency. It would be an embarrassment and difficult to explain. I am sure you have had much less experience with the fourth estate than I have. Believe me, it would be awkward at best."

"In other words: go on as if nothing had happened."

But Toivo was relieved. He would not have known what to do and it was reassuring to have a power larger than he was tell him what to do. It took the moral edge off the dilemma, if not the practical one.

"No need to get sharp with me, mister, uh, well, no need to get fresh. I have been instructed to tell you that you should stay in touch with personnel of the Service in Paris and in the other cities you will visit. You don't seem to appreciate that we are trying to help you despite a very nasty set of circumstances. After all, and this is from our experts, you were the last one seen with this troublesome man, your fingerprints should be all over the place, at your own admission this, and there should be witnesses to prove that you were seen together for quite some time. Out of consideration for your position and because you are a naturalized citizen of the United States of America, we are choosing to help you despite the fact that this affair could become very unpleasant and cumbersome to us. What else do you expect? Surely not more. In fact, as someone from my staff pointed out, all you need to do is travel and present your talks or whatever. By crossing borders you are confusing matters for the local authorities, making yourself a complicated juridical case, and giving us time, when and if it becomes necessary, to find the right course to steer."

"I see no need to argue this at the moment. Very well, I will leave tonight."

"No, that would be precipitous. In order to reach Paris by train in due time for your appearance, there's no need to leave earlier than two days from now, or, at the earliest, by the night train tomorrow night. We don't want any added suspicion caused by your own behavior."

"All right."

Toivo stood up. His left leg was asleep. He wanted to get out of the carpeted and heavily draped consultation room with the limp flag on a stand and the eagle gripping arrows and looking fiercely disinterested. In the bright day outside he needed to be jostled by crowds and eat raw herring from a street stand to get the taste of pencil lead out of his mouth.

"Let me make one thing clear. We do not accuse you of a crime but neither are we insisting that you are totally without guilt. Only a court of law can decide that. If it came to a trial you would have to submit like any other ordinary citizen. Remember that, please. We are simply hoping that the police will clear up this matter in your favor without getting us involved until it is absolutely inevitable. We have to adopt a wait-and-see attitude. Is that clear?"

"I don't understand your position very well. Is it all for expedience's sake because things were arranged already, or is it because there might be a lot of publicity? Just think of the headlines: BEST-SELLING AMERICAN AUTHOR ON OFFICIAL LECTURE TOUR IMPLICATED IN MYSTERIOUS MURDER IN AMSTERDAM. Maybe that's simply all that's behind your concern."

It didn't bother the consul. He pulled the cuffs of his shirt down a little further and said: "Just do what I told you and you'll do just fine. Is there anything else?"

"Yes, there is. Would you make sure that Dr. de Bruce does not get buried in a coffin?

"I beg your pardon?"

"I am serious. He told me he hated the idea of being buried in a box. I sympathize. It was something of a last wish. Cremate him, throw him in the sea, make comestibles out of him, but don't box him. Will you promise that?"

The consul had risen. Anger had insinuated itself on his face.

"I most certainly will not make such a promise. Secondly, if you are trying to joke with me you are certainly in bad taste. I'd watch myself if I were you. You seem to be man who deliberately looks for trouble."

"Damn you, I am serious. I am not joking. To hell with it, I am sick and tired of your pompous attitude. It seems as if strange things don't happen to you unless they've been typed out on the proper forms. Just don't box him. He deserves as much."

Toivo came away from the interview with the consul feeling soiled, as if he had committed an indecent act. Had he been callous in his reaction to discovering the corpse of a man he had been drinking with for an entire night and who seemed to have spilled his private secrets to him? But what else could he do in such circumstances? Go to pieces, throw up, yell hysterically, go confess a cultural guilt to the police?

He was in a large pavilion in Amsterdam's Vondel Park. A warm summer's day, perfected by a steady breeze just strong enough to set curtains away from windows, had drawn people to the park. But it wasn't crowded because it was a business day. He

hoped that the whiskey would muffle his brain a little. Con-
sciously he loosened his muscles and slumped in the creaking
wicker chair, relishing the alternate washes of warm and cool.
An immersion in physical pleasure, a feeling good to be alive.
But the sun lit up patterns of arteries in his eyes and lids, febrile
patterns which reminded him of his septaria stones. He had to
open his eyes to cool them and saw a spider hanging from a
branch.

It was busily weaving from the liquid protein which solidifies
as soon as it leaves the spider's body. Strands stronger than steel
wire of the same diameter wove a dead-certain trap for insects of
the correct size. A tiny green bug bumbled into the web and the
spider raced across the dry strands of its device and paralyzed its
catch with a bite of poison. Eating was sucking the body dry of
nutritious fluids and discarding the dried remains.

Somewhat like de Bruce's scheme which had been mentioned
at some point during that night. Ammonium chloride, NH_4Cl,
effects a total loss of the body fluids. Only a mass of solids
remains — de Bruce had worked on it to find a way to dissolve
the body — which can only be recognized chemically as having
once been a human being. Tasteless, it dissolves in alcohol, and
its powder is water-soluble. If injected the compound will
activate in less than three minutes. Had de Bruce perfected the
idea he would have been wildly applauded and across the world
strange little piles of solid matter would have appeared in the
gutters of cities, to be swept away unnoticed with the dog turds.

The spider was binding the still insect with silk. Such fine
trappings for a dinner. Amazing creatures. Spiders are not
insects; they work alone and they're found everywhere on earth.
On his way to Europe he had seen a spider drifting over the
ocean suspended from a gossamer parachute. Toivo had wondered how it would feed there. Board a passing ship or suspend a
web from nothing and catch, yes, what would it trap there?

The sunned snugness of the park reminded him of the boat
trip. On the ship he had found an isolation devoutly to be wished.
A few days' suspended existence between continent and continent on a softly humming sliver of civilization loosed of its
moorings. Existence was messing somewhere beyond the hori-

zon front and aft, but it didn't really exist. On board one was reduced to living and the ship's voyage proved Bishop Berkeley right in that only perception verifies metropolitan madness. A reduction to details of one's own choosing. A nose here and a rope there, a sprig of spray on an oilcloth, latticed parallelograms of deck chairs. Or nothing — sponged by the spheric vastness of sky and water. As if he were on a dieseled speck inside a huge walnut. There one can concentrate on the most irrelevant thing possible and think it immortal since there's no constraint to act. Everything's there, and if it isn't it doesn't matter. One can only prepare for the voyage and trim necessities. Fellow travelers are chances you can take or leave. All that connects are invisible spider's threads in the air collected on radio and radar. They need not be seen or heard. Land is only for refueling and supplies.

The spider had finished hanging its prey in a suspended cocoon and was busy repairing the web. When it finished it retreated to a corner and waited for another tremor of food.

13

"THE NOVEL, MESSIEURS, DAMES, is like a stained-glass window. Different segments of artificially colored glass are fitted into lead and then welded together to form a larger picture. In other words, the sum of parts does make a whole. Certainly in the case of novelistic fiction. That is why the demand for story, the linear progression of events, is no longer a prerequisite of great texts. There are enough people writing that sort of thing to satisfy public demand. Not to mention TV, the movies and the magazines. Don't misunderstand me, I do ask for tension, and tension is suspense. The reader should not be bored. But that fact does not equate with the simple-minded, utilitarian plot I have just mentioned. For that a photograph would do as well as a stained-glass window. There is suspense in Plato and Wittgenstein, there is tension in your own great Marcel Proust."

Toivo was speaking in a hall in one of the buildings of the Sorbonne. Behind a lectern, on a raised platform, he looked down on completely filled, semicircular rows of seats. Even the small balcony was filled. The floor sloped up to two heavy doors which creaked open from time to time to let latecomers through. After the initial stomach fisting he felt good now, knowing his audience was all ears. The rest of them was immaterial. Like Orpheus you should be able to keep them eared for days with your words, charm them like a Väinämöinen.

He was beginning to find confidence in crowds as if he were a prodigal ant returning to its nest. And the French liked theories such as the one he was propounding — and believed in. They also liked to look at American best-selling authors. He poured some water in a glass from a pitcher on a table next to the lectern. Always sprinkle your deliveries with pregnant silences: they'll be fooled into thinking your next words to be brilliant. Until they hit the cooler air outside. He straightened up and brushed his hand over his forehead to wipe off the sweat. Then he pulled his tie further down and his shirt collar more open and coughed.

"No, the specific structures are built by the critics after the fact. A writer might, just might, have a design in mind. But it will be a general one, a vague shape, insubstantial as a ghost. That general feeling can be as little (or as much) as a single image or phrase, but it starts him off spinning, sets him to polish little stones and slowly fit them together in a necklace the mind can wear and call a book.

"Each novel makes a world specifically its own. Everything fits and echoes what went before or what will come after. It has its own logic. And that logic has no business being realistic. What, for that matter, is realistic about life? What actually is purposeful in real life? Most of our attempts at purposeful action never reach their goal. No, if you look around you don't see a unity of action but multiplicity, senselessness, confusion and distress. So the novel cannot objectively describe a nonexistent unity, but it records the vision of unity of a single consciousness: that of the author. The writer makes order but, unlike scientific empiricism, the novel he has written needs no proof for its order. And now, *messieurs, dames,* let me try to find a probable reason why our novels do not have the logical sequence of a ledger book.

"To say 'I'm an accident of birth' is stupid since all births are accidents. The particular chromosomal cocktail which I happen to be could have been poured into anyone else's skinglass. We have our start in chance and everything thereafter is necessity. Because, when I look back over my life I see a pattern — a pattern of chance. Chance made into a norm — and a norm is a fixed authority. Stern as hell too, and forbidding. Norm comes from "*norma,*" Latin for a carpenter's square. Wish I could square the carpenter."

Toivo stopped again. He was worried that he was sounding ridiculous. Don't show it, you damn fool, act cool and in control. As if all your actions are calculated and well rehearsed. Were they still ears or had they reassembled into bodies already? When he reached for the pitcher he tried to flap his shirt so he could dry his armpits a little. He lifted the glass and pitcher high as if he were pouring a rare wine. When he had filled it he held the glass in front of his face at arm's length and looked over his shoulder at the audience: "Here we have such an accidental miracle: a fusion of sand and ashes holding liquid." At that moment the glass shattered and when his hand had been flung back by force it stayed empty at the end of his rigid arm. Drops of water sprayed his face and body as well as the platform behind him. Tiny glass needles settled in his flesh as if in a pincushion. The glass seemed to have burst spontaneously in his hand, except that it hadn't.

Toivo cranked his face toward the audience and saw nothing but silence. Perhaps they don't realize he panicked, perhaps they will try again. So with great effort he unstuck his muscles and jumped from the platform into the middle aisle. All he could think of was gathering bodies between him and the weapon. His face was the color of thawing snow and stippled with blood. A large sliver above his eyebrows let out a red line down his cheek. With an unseemly smirk on his lips he hastened up the aisle in a crouch. Till he reached the far wall by the exit doors. By that time the audience had erupted into bodies rushing and tangling and shouting and Toivo had been hustled outside and into a room where he was pushed into a chair and talked to with hysterical speed.

A doctor treated him in the manner of a vet removing porcupine needles from a dog's nose. Only the cut on his forehead required adhesive tape. While the French were spinning theories Toivo himself deduced that the attack had been connected with the death of de Bruce and that they were out to kill him. There was no reason for it at all. He knew his life better than anyone else and saw no possible motive there. But the plain facts could not be denied existence and he caught himself looking for pistols under jackets or in waistbands, feared for silenced rifles aiming at him from behind panes of glass. When they admonished him to go to his hotel and rest, he refused and said he really would very much like to go a party at the apartment of an editor at Gallimard. He said he needed company now more than ever but he hoped they wouldn't ask him to be witty. The shock had impaired his French. Sure, sure, they patted him and crowded him in a Citroën and then into a smoke-filled room where he smiled a lot and drank a lot to steady himself. The verdict of the witnesses and, apparently, of the police too, was that a berserk, leftist, revolutionary student with decidedly antiimperialist, anti-American feelings had wanted to kill him in protest against Washington's foreign policy. By the end of the evening die-hard debaters muddled by alcohol were challenging the efficacy and efficiency of such a gesture. A man refilled his glass and reassured Toivo: "It wouldn't have made any difference my friend. None at all. You wouldn't have changed a thing. They can't even assassinate properly. What a bunch of shitheads."

Look, Toivo told himself, what are you going to do now? Because you are to some degree famous it's not so easy to hide or to cancel the rest of your tour. Besides, as long as you're with large crowds it will be more difficult to get at you. It won't stop them, obviously, but it will make it more difficult nevertheless. Imagine if you'd been alone, walking along the Seine or in the Jardin du Luxembourg! No, you've got to live from lecture to lecture and fill the time in between with as many people as possible. Volunteer for autograph parties, invite yourself to receptions. Get in touch with the embassy. Stir up the system until the reverberations reach Blaise. He said he would help. Or take a plane and go back. Sure. And sit in his apartment waiting for the door to creak open and for them to step inside when he had dozed off for a moment.

He was like a cornered badger he had once seen. A German shepherd had trapped it in a dense bramble bush. He had thought: why doesn't the dumb thing charge through and make a run for it? But the animal only attacked the dog when the latter got too close and then tunneled back into the tangle of protecting pain. The dog could not burrow after it for fear of having his muzzle ripped open by the bush. So they kept up a long series of sallies and retreats, with the badger safe as long as he didn't make a long, uncovered run for it. Only when the dog finally slackened his vigilance and began sniffing at a distraction did the badger sneak away, and when he was at a considerable distance ran quickly into the woods. Better badger wise than corpse foolish.

He asked if he could stay the night and the editor granted him hospitality and a locked door in a room next to his small son. Toivo felt safe sleeping a wall away from the child. Next morning's papers called his lecture a sensation.

14

Two afternoons later he spoke to a *cercle littéraire* about the writer's notebooks.

"Entries in a writer's notebook are promissory notes to himself. Authors, being proverbially bad accountants, either forget to pay them or, after their imagination has failed to rally, wish they had. Be that as it may, they are useful to the reader to get a more complete insight into the process of constructing a work of art. Note that the building materials are expensive. Sometimes a single entry, a phrase, even a word, are the only scraps that remain after long hours of forcing the issue of the imagination. Nor is it a novelty to observe that some bits can have an irritating profundity many a finished structure lacks." But his heart wasn't in it.

Shadows were aiming at him and he shivered at oblique angles of light. Men kept on reaching under their arms and women into handbags. Every so often he got down behind the lectern and gulped from a hip flask of whiskey. The words on the pages in front of him mattered little and he wouldn't have cared if he hadn't written them. Toivo stopped and on his way down for the flask stopped once more.

His words were being stricken and sucked lifeless. These ideograms were his very own, his very life. Whatever else had happened to him, they had been faithful. Difficult, yes, but also constant to their task of translating what was his into a communication with the world. An inviolate silence that hummed. Not wife not child not territory but all such passion of his was in those pages. Perhaps he was crazy by any normal standards, but according to his own he was clearly right and anger began to refuel him. They would not stop his mouth or his pen. That's what they were after. And when he started on the stained-glass novel the words were wishing for him again. But people had been leaving and only patches of ladies, hard of hearing, remained in their seats, unaware he was now speaking in English.

He had showered, shaved and changed into freshly laundered clothes. The hotel barber had shaped his hair into casual elegance. An expensive dinner in a three-star restaurant had smothered a few isolated nerves by soothing them into submission. Toivo had even dared himself to walk to a party of yet another littérateur where he had apologized for that afternoon's slovenly performance by blaming it on nervousness. The embassy had meanwhile reassured him that he was being taken care of, that he had no need to worry. Wheels had been set into motion and would he please continue and finish the tour. Appealed to his sense of duty. It would not, could not happen again. There was a faint glow under his skin when he went back to his hotel, resolved to sleep in his own room.

It was late and the corridors were deserted. Shaded little lamps on the pastel walls made the noiseless carpet under his feet even softer than it was. Several pairs of shoes were waiting outside doors for the bellhop and someone had lost a sweater: cable knit with horn buttons. Toivo opened the door to his room and switched on the light.

A man in a caramel overcoat was slumped on the bed, feet on the ground, but loosely, the rest of his body carelessly draped across the width like a half-filled bag of dirty laundry. Not again. He half turned to open the door but then anger and curiosity made him grin and he stepped to the bed. Kall was beginning to stir again as a ghost in his son's flesh. Toivo tipped the light of a desk lamp on his visitor. The head was broad and plain with bushy eyebrows. Blood came from one nostril as sluggishly as a nearly dried-out creek. Under the light caramel overcoat he wore a gabardine suit and a far from fresh shirt with buttons missing from rough handling. A floral tie had come undone and lay in limp loudness on the soberly dressed body which was still breathing. Tucked under the chin like a bib was a sheet of paper torn from a note paid. It said: "Don't worry. We're not as messy as our friends in Amsterdam. Delay unforeseen. Just take a walk for half an hour and you'll never know it happened." No signature. It had been typed on his portable lightweight travel typewriter. The curtains were too short to hide anyone. He shrugged his whole body as if he were settling his bristling fur and examined the man's pockets. Money, pen, handkerchief, atomizer and some scribblings in an incomprehensible language that looked Slavic. In an overcoat pocket was that day's copy of *Le Monde* and a French paperback edition of *Past Reason Hunted*. Nothing.

Toivo kicked the bed hard but the man only bounced slightly and a gun stuck its muzzle out from under his left set of ribs. It was a Luger and Toivo sniffed it to see if it had been fired recently. Well, Toivo thought, one part of him only mildly astonished at his increasing sang-froid, let's see if they are as neat as they say they are. He stuffed the pistol in the waistband of his trousers, in the declivity of his stomach just next to his hipbone, and went out of the hotel to walk the streets of a Paris by night.

The weather was deliciously cool, an ideal temperature mixing with the dayheat stuffed in stone. People were boulevarding it to their hearts' content and he hoped Europe would remain lucky in its meteorology for the rest of the summer — a lucre more valuable than dollars. The one brings the other; rain would keep people away and Toivo isolated.

It has the feeling that it isn't going to stop so you might as well adjust to it and see what's going on. But you need help because, despite your momentary courage and calm, your double is seeing otherwise. Armed trees tailing you, pissoirs with their motors idling ready to pursue you like awkward armored cars and rifles and pistols using shoppers for cover. Buildings perspiring with fear. There's nothing you can do about it. You can't just simply close the book and bottom a cognac to help you settle down. It's all over and all you can do is fight back.

Strange how undramatic this all was. Far from melodrama it was matter-of-fact, happenstance, evidence which could not be denied, made no sense, drew no picture. Except for the ubiquity, the feeling that they knew exactly where he was and were lying in wait for him.

Over a vin blanc in a packed sidewalk cafe Toivo wrote his thoughts down in his flat, leather-bound notebook and caressed his clothes unobtrusively for bugs. There were none. Surely they wouldn't waste a whole satellite on him alone. He grinned and the grin grew until he sat there almost in pain trying to stifle an onrush of roaring laughter, tears streaming down his face, one hand clamped over his mouth and one holding his stomach. People were staring at him and some passers-by glanced over their shoulders, perhaps to check. Could jump over the table and whip his pistol out. Eccentricity, my friends. Fiction can be troublesome like water on the knee. It's nothing: just that the whole world is after me. The city of light is lying in wait for me and god only knows how many other capitals are too. Toivo reassembled himself over a Pernod and checked his watch. It had been an hour.

He opened the door of his room with his right hand holding the left on the butt of the pistol under his jacket. The man on his bed had vanished, the bed looked as freshly made as that morning, the room was as clean as it is supposed to be in an expensive hotel. But he couldn't possibly sleep in that bed. Besides, he had suddenly decided to follow the example of the badger and go underground. He packed his belongings and noticed that even his typewriter case had been zipped up again. While a bellhop put his luggage in a taxi, Toivo checked out. It was too classy a place to ask questions.

15

FOR THE REMAINDER of his stay in France Toivo went to ground in a fleabag in the Quartier Latin where no questions were asked, not even of well-dressed gentlemen with expensive luggage. Questions rumored silently in the eyes of the desk clerk and in the glances of the guests who were a mixture of salesmen, unmarried workmen, luckless students and types who fit no-where, as anonymous as characters in a cartoon. For two days Toivo stayed in his room, not washing or changing his clothes, not even when he went to bed. The morning of the third day he reappeared properly shabby and smelly, with a solid black stubble on his face and red-rimmed eyes, looking modishly haggard. He asked the man who doubled as the only bellhop (when he felt like it or smelled money) and waiter (though none of the guests risked their lives in the four-table restaurant) to sell his typewriter and suitcase full of clothes. Toivo felt that with this action he had made a reasonable pretense of being a broke foreigner in some sort of personal trouble.

All he had left now was one suit, two shirts, two ties, two pairs of socks, a pair of shoes, two sets of underwear, his half-dozen stones, a folder with his lecture, his book and the Luger. It was all ready to go in a locked suitcase. The way Toivo looked now he easily disappeared in the general crowd of the Quartier, where grubbiness had always been common. There were lots of down-and-out students and many frayed fringes of humanity who acted compulsively strange. The newest occupation that season was writing "revolutionary" poems in white chalk on the sidewalk and then pestering money from passers-by.

With the proceeds from the sale of his belongings, minus a generous commission for the cutthroat's services, Toivo bought a good pair of sunglasses which hid his eyes completely. Then he walked casually down several blocks and crossed the Boul Mich'. He took his post on the Boulevard Saint-Germain in front of a brasserie and chalked some verses he had written during his cocoon days on the sidewalk. The first stanza was:

> l'argendarmerie nous dit merçi
> et nous casse la tête.
> c'est ainsi, ainsi
> l'éducation du peuple.

He had reached back into his youth to mimic a European handwriting which had more pronounced loops to the f and g and j, and slants more to the right like a windblown crest of a wave. American handwriting, more upright, rounded and open-lettered — a mixture of printing and writing — would have betrayed him immediately.

A rare person would stop and smile at the pun in the first five syllables which combined into a portmanteau word. One dapper gentleman with an heirloom of a white mustache, broad and curved as the flat looping horns of a water buffalo, inclined his head and said that Toivo's education had at least taught him a more advanced usage of words. He dropped some coins on the newspaper Toivo used as a collection plate and poked the coins around in a reflective manner with the end of his bamboo cane, as if he were playing checkers the way the aged Matisse used to paint murals.

"Some of your grievances are justified, understand me, but you've got to do something more than just sit around and write drip-dry verse on pavement. Why don't you get on your feet and sabotage something?"

Toivo nodded politely at the receding gentleman. Washable verse. As long as there's chalk there's hope. He was enjoying his slumming; he liked the role of the beggar who, though at the level of sewer grates, towers over his fellow men by having nothing more to lose.

The fairly steady trickle of coin assured Toivo he had bought himself a reprieve from being tagged and cornered again. Slumped against warm bricks he sunned and let himself drift, gently lapped by a puppy wind. The breeze also kept his own sour smell from him and as long as he wasn't walking he liked to lounge in his scruffiness. He snoozed a lot because during the night he did not go to his room until there was light somewhere in the sky. The nights were balmy and busy. The streets didn't sleep while his room had a door which could be opened in the dark.

Toivo felt strangely secure. He tried to reason a pattern out of the violent fragments which must, he felt sure, have a purpose and design. But they wouldn't fit and the obscurity of their source frightened him into scanning faces and legs and objects as they passed him. He had noticed that if he centered his attention on a detail and tried to see it as sharply as possible, parenthesize it, as it were, in its objectivity out of the larger context, he would grow calmer, then calm, etching a precise image against a void. Pant cuffs, scuffs on shoes, the paws of a dog sniffing his verse, and feet, thousands of cobbled feet. Until the flurry disoriented him and he would look up to assemble a person with his eyes: an imposing collection from his low angle. Yet, when he fixed on a nose, a mouth or eyes, and gathered a face together, and it scorned him, he could always look beyond it up into the sky and the person was lost again.

A stray cat came around every so often and rubbed against his thighs and purred. He bought it a saucer of milk and after a number of saucered bribes the cat would stay with him and sun itself by his side. Toivo could leave to drink some wine in a nearby café and the cat would stay, stretched out full-length above his poem, like a title.

Across the street from his post was the tall, stern building of the publishing company Librairie Hachette. There people bought the blue leather *Guides Bleus* ("the keys to the world") so they could document and verify their movements through capitals and countries, museums and cemeteries. A city all mapped out and described in a compact tome of 700 pages. Wouldn't it be smarter to buy it and take it home and dream your travels? The recollected Paris is not the real one on the Seine, and even there each person carries a different city around with him.

A man in an unbuttoned cream raincoat read his verse with the toe of his shoe. He nodded with approval, smiled at Toivo and then shook his head.

"Not quite up to your usual stuff, is it? But it's not bad. Why don't you write a novel on the installment plan? People would have to come and stop every day to know what's going to happen next."

"Thanks for the tip."

"Of course, there are hazards. Rain, wind or the municipal cleaning trucks. Might be too tricky. You'd never know if you could finish it."

"I am going now," Toivo said, getting to his feet. "I have forgotten to eat and there aren't many people around now anyway. It's dinnertime."

"That's all right," the man said, rocking slightly on the balls of his feet, his hands in the pockets of his coat. His sleek hair glistened and Toivo smelled a faint odor of brilliantine. He didn't like the tanned neck and the v of his chest in the open shirt collar. There was a dangerous pleasure in the man. An undercover cop after him for his bogus revolutionary zeal, or an Interpol agent with questions about the tiny finger-labyrinths he'd left around a corpse in Amsterdam?

"I'm sorry but I must be going. Some friends are waiting for me." Toivo could not move, held by the stare of the man and the mock of good will embroidered on the face.

"I have friends waiting too. I haven't eaten either. I never do a job on a full stomach. It impairs my aim."

His hand came in front of his belt holding a short-barreled revolver. Toivo saw the cylinder turn for as long as the earth's tour around the sun. The metal was very clean, polished and oiled. A man who took care of his tools. The hammer was cocked, the man's mouth had zippered up. Then he fell forward as if his feet had been swept from under him. Pitched forward without regard for injury and with a dull snap when his face hit the pavement. Lay there perfectly straight and stiff as if he were lying at attention. Blood came from a small hole at the base of his skull. Toivo didn't even look around, he just turned on his heels and walked off stiffly as if his limbs were controlled by strings. A lattice walk.

At the corner where the Boulevard Saint-Germain crosses the Boul Mich' he looked back. Two men had set the corpse on its feet and carry-walked it to a car, where they bagged it in the back seat. Then the old-fashioned, low-slung, black Citroën drove off down the boulevard leaving a flattening balloon of exhaust behind. Toivo had forgotten to pick up the money from the newspaper.

16

CUSTOMS FORCED all levels of society to stand in line in the long, shabby shack of the douaniers in Calais, the last checkpoint before leaving France. Though it was early morning a comfortably large throng of travelers wandered around the building, funneling slowly into lines as ragged as the columns of a retreating army. The streams of people inched forward with much grumbling, shoving of luggage and laughter, which came mostly from the young, hirsute travelers who were covering Europe that summer like a biblical plague of locusts in a demotic version of the nineteenth-century-Englishman's grand tour. There were enough scraggy types with beginning, intermediate or advanced beards, and with indifferent or outrageous clothes on, to make Toivo's appearance seem quite natural. He also checked for sunglasses and saw enough of them to allow him to keep his on, though it was an uncalled-for blustering day with rags of rain fluttering now and then in a sky which could not make up its mind whether to continue with summer or switch to fall.

The long hut was dimly lit, except for the counters where luggage was checked for contraband by a group of sour, bored, sallow men with unbarbered hair greasing out from under their kepis and coiling down over their still stained collars. They too were unshaven and looked as if they had been dawdling there for a year of night shifts. Toivo was angry with himself for being afraid of these shabby officials who control the crossing of borders and decide whether you are a legitimate citizen or not. Afraid of officials and afraid of his fellows.

This time he had taken subways around Paris, switched taxis

by the dozen and had finally jumped on a departing train for Calais without having bought a ticket. But they were watching him here too, though they wouldn't do anything in this crowded stockyard. They always knew the best moment to hit and they always knew where he was.

Toivo picked up his suitcase and left. In Calais he booked a room, explaining nervously that he had missed the morning ferry to England and that he was in great need of sleep. He slept into the afternoon, got up, took a long and thorough bath and put on his inconspicuous clothes. At the bottom of his suitcase was the Luger and he had to sit down when it suddenly came to him how narrowly he had escaped. Controlling himself he stuffed the Luger in his waistband, buttoned his jacket over it and went out. He left the weapon behind a toilet in a public lavatory. Then he went to a barber for a professional shave and to have his hair washed and trimmed. After a good meal of a simple cassoulet, bread and a carafe of Pinot Noir he felt better and more reassured. He drank his coffee slowly and waited for the departure of the night boat to Dover.

It was a wild night. Massive clouds scudded through the sky like a great trek of continents in search of a new world. Stars and a nearly full moon were visible now and then in the same sporadic rhythm as lit windows from a speeding night train. A gusty wind battered the wharf and Toivo was glad to be able to scruff in his, by comparison, immaculate clothes. But he didn't want to go aboard yet. He had a little time because the new shift of douaniers had been quick about it, eager to get back to their coffee and cards. Besides, a great deal less passports had walked through. The wind buffed his head and the sheen of chill it lay around his skull jelled his scrambled thoughts a bit. Harbor water slapped against the wall of the wharf with a slight growl, its soiled teeth grinning atop the short waves. The heavy mooring cables groaned and swayed along with the gangplank and the creaking hull.

The ferry was lit and the crew was hustling to make the crossing as pleasant as possible.

"Hey, you there, buddy, you Syystalvi?"

The voice pronounced the first syllable of his name as a hiss. Toivo turned to his left and saw a man in a coat coming toward him, carrying a round basket in his right hand.

"What do you want?"

Again he was weaponless, but this time he had had some warning. No one would dare shoot here and the man was already too close to risk a long shot. So it had to be body contact and he could use judo. How useless it had been when the guns started coming out. Always pinned at the center of the cross hairs waiting to be disintegrated by an unseen and distant force. The boat was now as far out of reach as the length of the gangplank. Toivo planted his feet firmly at a moderate distance from each other. He pushed his center of gravity forward toward the buckle of his belt and let his arms hang loose. His eyes were fixed on the eyes of the man and his peripheral vision picked up the other's motions as on a radar screen.

"Boy, it's cold, hey, bud? Relax, relax, it's just that we couldn't do anything about him anymore and you've got to take care of him yourself, see. Clever bastard, I tell you, slipped clean by us in Paree. Can't do anything about him here. But, as you can see, we take care of our buddies. 'Course you knew that all along, didn't you?"

"What the hell are you talking about?"

"I'll show him to you in a minute, okay? Here. Hold this for me for a minute, gotta blow my nose."

"No thanks."

"Jumpy, aren't you? That's not so good. He's first-rate, you know, so you better watch it. Then again you're on your toes, if you see what I mean. Anyhow, we've got a little friend to help you."

The man put the basket down in front of his feet and reached under his coat. Toivo calculated how to compensate for the basket to effect a clean sweep and maintain his balance on the salt cobbles. The man produced a handkerchief and blew his nose very carefully, examining it to make sure it had done the job and then dabbed at his sniffle, which was still draining.

He was lanky, which made him look taller than his nearly six feet. Unobtrusive clothes. His head was bald except for a rim of straight thin hair around the back of the skull. The shape of the head was conical and the features seemed molded out of the flesh. The thin mouth was of the same pink color as the skin so that it seemed as if the flesh merely opened itself into a slit. The ears were small and glued close to the skull, while the nose was short and thin and hardly noticeable in the poor lighting of the wharf. He had no noticeable chin: the face merely formed a base below his mouth which was broader than the tip of the smooth skull. Toivo would recognize him anywhere. After all, a man with a penile head is not easy to forget.

The man paid little attention to Toivo and picked up the basket again. A common, round lidded rattan basket with a leather latch. People were coming out of the customs shack and the man turned around to keep an eye on them.

"You see," he said over his shoulder to Toivo, "the guy you want will come through there in a moment and I'll point him out to you. First of all, he's stocky, about five-nine. Solid as a rock. Dark curly hair. Big ears. Brown eyes. Thick nose. Broken. Scar kinda like a big nick on his right cheek about on the same level as his ear lobe. He'll probably speak only French, but he understands English. Okay?"

"Sure. But would someone care to tell me what's going on? Don't you think it's a little weird standing here . . ."

"Not all all. Shut up and listen. We ain't got much time. I know my business and you know yours but I know mine a hell of a lot better than you ever could. So listen, okay, bud? Plaid overcoat. Brown suit with broad lapels. White shirt with mustard tie. Loafers with crepe soles. He's fast and he's armed. How the hell he's gonna get his gun through customs beats me. But he will, believe me. If he can't use a gun he'll probably either try to kill you with what the cops call a blunt instrument or with whatever else is handy. But no cutting. Knife wounds are difficult to make up as an accident. 'Course he might use his hands, try to break your neck or your spinal cord. Got that? Might use dope if he can swing it. Okay, step back here and take a good look. There he is."

The description walked rapidly up the gangplank and disappeared into the housing on deck.

"You better hope you saw him and recognize him because he sure as hell is gonna try to make you, or, let's say, unmake you."

The man chuckled at that.

"What in god's name is going on? Why don't you tell me what's happening? You people are driving me crazy."

"Hum, yes, his name, or what he's using for this trip, is Krantz. Now listen carefully, I've got to go. That guy now, he's tough. But all those guys got a weak spot, see. Except me, and my buddies of course. Anyway, his weak spot is his being scared shitless of snakes, if you get my meaning. You scared of snakes?"

The man was amused and the penile head was mocking him. Toivo shook his head.

"Good. Now you take a guy like that: tough, a professional, not afraid of the whole world plus a heap of guns. But show him a little snake and he'll go to pieces. We checked it thoroughly. He'll go nuts and if you do it properly it's as lethal as a bullet. That's what I brought you here, right in this basket. The little fellow is harmless. He might bite you but he's got no juice to spill. He's long too. Now if I was you I would chum it up with our Krantz friend, get him on deck and wrap the snake around his neck like a fancy tie, see what I mean? And you better because if you're not gonna get him he will get you for sure. No, don't interrupt, they're going for the plank already. You might look a little silly walking around with a basket but say that you're a weirdo with strange pets or something. Hell, as a writer you're entitled to nutty habits, correct me if I'm wrong. So long buddy and good luck. And don't you get squeamish on me now. We need you around hale and hearty, okay, pal? We goofed, I admit that much, but there's nothing to be done about it now. He's tough, sure, but he's not one of the top guys. He kinda popped up unexpected-like and we suspect he was a pinch hitter. I can't leave myself because it was too short notice and you've got to give your talk by tomorrow. Anyway, all of us are kinda stuck here. It's your life or his, remember that. And I am not fooling. I mean you remember some of those other little capers, don't you, and they weren't for show now, was they? Be seeing you, pal."

"Wait a minute. Who are you? What the fuck is this all

about?" Toivo stepped furiously forward toward the man, completely forgetting caution.

"You're missing your boat, buddy."

"What? Well, that's an idea. I'll miss the damn thing."

The man had stepped next to him. His snub-nosed revolver was aimed at Toivo's stomach.

"Just pick up the basket and get up there. No nonsense. You go or you're gonna have some very painful wounds, might even be maimed for life."

Toivo stooped for the basket with the barrel of the gun leaning against the back of his ear. Then he picked up his suitcase.

"That's a boy."

Toivo turned without looking at the man again and walked up into the ship. The man stayed a few minutes at the bottom of the gangplank as if he were saying farewell. Then the plank was hoisted, the cables tossed and the ferry shoved itself away from the quay hooting its loud sad siren.

17

Toivo had given his steward enough sterling paper to buy privacy. The man put the suitcase in Toivo's first-class cabin and made no further attempt to relieve him of the basket. After all, he thought, the man looks money. So let the balmy bloke walk around with his doped-up Siamese. As if I care, I've seen crazier things than that.

"When will you be retiring, sir?"

"I don't know. I like the sea and the fresh air. Besides I have not been sleeping well lately. A bit of nerves I think."

"As you like, sir. If you're worried about not feeling well, let me know. I know a thing or two."

"No, it's not that. I never get seasick."

"Well, sir, lots of people are going to be quite unhappy tonight."

"I'm hungry. Where can I get something to eat, and a drink?"

"Very good, sir. You just might have the entire buffet for yourself. Down the corridor, up the stairs and to your right. I'll be in that room there, sir, at the end there, if you need me. Just ring. And thank you, sir."

Toivo ate some sandwiches at a table in the lounge and then walked around to see how the ship was laid out. He had decided not to go down to his cabin until the contest was settled — one way or another. It was too easy for Krantz down there among groaning passengers where he could do what he liked with a silencer and experience as a sidekick. No, it had to be on deck. Couldn't be in the lounge either, which had too many people drinking, sleeping or talking all night long. They had to get outside, perhaps near the engine housing, or at the prow or by the lifeboats maybe. You could hardly knot a snake around somebody's neck in front of an audience. But, of course, Krantz couldn't do anything either. Let him give the cue. In the meantime stick with people and hold on to your basket. No wonder they kept Krantz up north. Fewer snakes. In southern latitudes he would be worthless. The man on the quay had said it was either him or Krantz and one of them would have to be dead before Dover blanched into sight. Toivo had to force himself to ignore his panic when it came to him that it could all be a joke, that Krantz would laugh at the snake and tickle its chin. But no, someone had been very busy trying to keep him alive.

He went back to the bar. You had to lean against it because there were no barstools. If you wanted to drink sitting down you had to take a table. Toivo stood there and drank Scotch.

"Haven't I seen you before somewhere?" a short pug-nosed brunette asked from his left.

It was what Toivo had been waiting for. His freshly minted fame had to be useful for something.

"Could be, but I don't recall meeting you. My name is Syystalvi, Toivo Syystalvi."

"American, right?"

"Right."

"Going to England?"

"Seems that way."

"How about a drink? The British haven't forgotten how to make Scotch."

"But they sure know how to make the Irish," she grumbled.

"What's your name?"

"Kathleen."

"Irish I gather."

"You gather correctly. What else?" And she laughed.

A nice, open laugh, uncommon in a woman. Her mouth was large with thick red lips. Gray eyes looked him over intelligently from under heavily arched eyebrows, trying to remember something. Short and stocky female with an impressive bust in an Irish sweater. Looked muscular and unyielding, but the eyes gave her humor. While her skin and hair added softness. Roan hair down the middle of her back: brown with strands of silver. A leather clasp pulled it together just below her shoulder blades.

"How about that drink? We might be companions for the evening."

"Okay. Hey," she said to the barkeep, "how about some Irish whiskey."

"Sorry, Mum, only Scotch."

"I should have known," she mumbled. "All right, on ice then. What's that?" she said turning to Toivo. "What's that about companions for the evening?"

Toivo looked around the tilting lounge, at the people holding on to their chairs and their innards.

"I just don't think there are going to be many people drinking here tonight, or doing anything else for that matter."

"Rough weather certainly can wreck a saltwater romance, can't it? Stomachs don't go for love."

Krantz had come in. He didn't indicate that he had seen his quarry but walked calmly to the far end of the bar and made his order understood after some linguistic banter. Toivo moved the basket between him and the girl with his foot and leaned his elbows on the bar so he was facing her.

"Going back to Ireland I bet."

The girl kept searching his face for her memory.

"That's right. I've got to help the poor country, the Limeys are bleeding it."

"You don't get seasick?"

"Never. I love boats, I love the undulating feeling as if you're in space."

"Or high."

She looked at him expressionlessly.

"I guess you would know."

Toivo laughed.

"I didn't mean anything by it. Yes, I might know. How about you?"

"Guess so, I've been in the States, you know."

"Doing what?"

"Studying political science and sociology. I was in the Movement and all that. I learned a lot but maybe I can do more in my own backyard than over there. I tell you I really got to know something about civil rights."

"How about another one?"

"Don't mind if I do. But watch it, friend, it might cost you a whole lot. I can drink anyone under the table, especially well-dressed elderly gentlemen on the make."

Toivo punched her arm lightly, laughed at her and got her another drink.

"First of all you're not that young, middle twenties I'd guess. Secondly, I'm not elderly, only in my midforties. And I am not on the make, I simply need someone to talk to for the night. I can't sleep in those crammed cabins, they give me claustrophobia. If anything I need protection. And I can't help liking good clothes, I like being well dressed. As a bachelor I have to pay some attention to myself because no one else will. As a matter of fact I've lived in different clothes quite often."

"Sure. I bet you don't wear jeans like I do."

"If necessary."

"They're good, you know: tough, cheap and they last and last. What do you do for a living? You must do something, don't tell me you're squandering an inheritance."

"No. I'm going to England on a lecture tour. I write for a living." Kathleen sighed. She was relieved, her face relaxed its intensity.

"That's it. I hate to forget things. Got to be on my toes, you know. Got to remember facts. Excuse me a sec."

She came back with a paperback copy of *Past Reason Hunted* and a ballpoint pen.

"Okay, smart guy, sign it for me, and if you put something nice in it I might even stick around."

But she was blushing ever so little and eagerly looked at the inscription.

"That's nice," she said. "You've just earned yourself female company for the rest of the night. Above board that is. And since you must have made some money from this book you can buy me some sandwiches. I am starving."

"I don't think people will stand for it seeing you eat," Toivo said while waiting for some three-deckers.

"This is true, since they're already sitting down. Say, what you got in that basket there? It's yours, isn't it?" She was already at it, but when the basket rustled her hand stopped and she looked at him with some fear.

"What is it?" she whispered.

"A dwarf dragon," Toivo whispered back, "a drugged leprechaun. I don't want anyone to touch him and light hurts his eyes, so why not leave him alone."

"What is it though?"

"Let's skip it."

The sandwiches took her mind off the rustling basket.

Do snakes get seasick? Of course they don't, their writhing immunizes them. If only he could order Krantz to plow a field invested with adders the way Ilmarinen had to in order to win the hand of the daughter of the Mistress of North Farm.

Kathleen had another drink, but the alcohol only made her skin freckle more and loosened her muscles and larynx a bit.

"Don't think I am a hedonist or one of your damned materialists," she said sternly after they had been silent for some time. "I have been working on my soul too. In the States, with an expansion team, soul expansion that is, and in France. I have been hitching all over the place to chalk up some experience before laying it on the line back home."

"How could you do that, the traveling I mean?"

"I won a British scholarship. I am quite brilliant, you know, but they didn't figure what I would use my brains for."

"You can hardly escape notice as a woman either."

She caught him looking at her breasts.

"Yup," she said morosely, "guess I can't. I wish I could reduce them, diet or something. They're in the way. A male body is so much more anonymous. Of course you wouldn't agree with that, would you? In your book you certainly don't."

"Did you like it?"

"Yes I did. You certainly know your way around death. That's what I've been concentrating on: death. I am scared to death of it and I have been training myself to overcome it, neutralize it as it were, making it as commonplace as peeling potatoes."

"How?"

"With yoga and transcendental meditation mostly. I've got to be over my fear when I go out into the streets and face bullies with rifles. You can't be brave when you're afraid of the price you might have to pay. Yoohoo, mister, you got any red beets? That's right, beets. I don't mind if they're out of a can. You don't. Well, another roast beef sandwich then."

"Beets?"

"They're good for my karma. But I am a realist too, a potato eater if you know what I mean. So I'll eat anything handy, drink when there's no dope around or fight when meditating gets you nowhere. Gotta be flexible."

"You're quite something. Have you ever been in love?"

She scowled and hid in the sandwich. Then she answered him still chewing.

"Yeah. None of your business. Love and sex are private affairs."

"They sure are."

"Okay, mister, stuff it." The gray eyes sparked flint and she drew her height up to his elbows. "You can joke about it all you like but I've got a few things which are not for grabs, see. Some things you just don't let hang out. Damnit, damn words. So I am not completely hip and I don't care if I am. That's my life and nobody had better scoff at it. And since you're so nosy, that's why I wear a bra: I like them. Besides, with my bust I'd be killing myself when I'd be running away from the cops. Practical, you see." She was laughing again.

Toivo was getting fond of her. Would be good to have her around in this mess: her hard-nosed realism just might scare off the mystery that was following him. Toivo reached inside his jacket and got out his notebook and ballpoint. He noticed a slight jerk of Krantz's left arm. The bastard is a little nervous perhaps, and he's left-handed. Toivo started writing down some of the things Kathleen had been saying, also some notes on the man on the quay and shorthand images of wind, weather and the sea air at night.

"What are you doing?"

"Nothing, just scribbling some thoughts down."

"I bet you'd do that anywhere no matter what the circumstances were. I guess writers are weird, but then you've got to be, don't you?" It had never occurred to him that he could do exactly that. In Amsterdam he had noted how the corpse looked, in Paris how the glass had shattered, now he was taking down details of a living person still breathing next to him.

The lounge was almost deserted by now except for a few sound or perhaps desperate sleepers. The floor swayed steadily, though not in a uniform motion: the channel's crosscurrent and the gusts of wind chopped the roll of the waves. The basket rustled between his feet and Toivo looked around for Krantz. The man was next to Kathleen and saying something in French.

"He says that it is a rough night and that we seem to be the only ones not minding it," Toivo translated for her.

"Well, cheers then, buddy," she said and clinked with the smiling Krantz.

He still wore the same clothes as in the description and Toivo's inexperience saw no telling bulges under the jacket. Krantz was smooth and charmed with ease. He had what looked like a souvenir pockmark on his forehead and a nick in his ear.

"He says that you're charming and gay and that he would like to buy you a drink and that the night may last as long as you are beautiful."

"O la la," mocked Kathleen, "a fancy pants. Sure I'll have a drink."

Krantz had ordered one for Toivo too before he could refuse, so he watched the journey of the glasses with bitter care, grabbing his before it could pass under Krantz's hands and drop something in it: a poison with a time fuse, a calculated delayed reaction with cramps and pains mimicking seasickness. No one would be the wiser until he landed dead on arrival.

"Hey, look, the foam is hitting the windows," Kathleen cried. "Let's go for a stroll, all of us. I bet it's delicious out."

"I think you're right," Toivo said, and politely translated for Krantz. The man agreed with a slight bow and the same smile that had been lubricating his face for the past hour or so.

"I also remember," Kathleen said confidentially in Toivo's ear with an alcohol-misted voice which threw just a pale of fog around her words, "that when I went downstairs to get my copy of your book, I saw another one lying around down there. I think I'll pinch it and have you sign it for a friend of mine. Jonathan. He's a book nut and an officer in the I.R.A."

The three had to link arms to keep from sliding slow motion back to the bar when the ship, like a shrugging whale, tipped broadside. It made for camaraderie and they careened toward the door with laughter and high spirits, the girl in the middle, Krantz on her left with his jacket buttoned up beyond the button of fashion and Toivo holding on to his basket, which was rustling again.

It was indeed a fine night. The moon faked phosphorescent foam on the waves which were bucking like shaggy ponies. The wind was strong and had been successful in running off most of the clouds and was now chasing little puffballs like a solitary ice hockey player. When they looked at the prow pistoning up and down with well-greased ease it appeared they were stationary. They passed a lit porthole to the garage down in the hold. Down there it would smell of gasoline and of the road still on the tires of cars. Soon they would be looking at England. Krantz had been a patient man. Toivo hooked himself loose from Kathleen's warmth and turned to her saying: "Why don't you go get that book now. It's getting a little chilly here, don't you think?"

"Okay. Besides, I also better have a look at the bathroom. I'll join you at the bar. See you."

Light fell on Krantz from behind Toivo's shoulders. The broad hull of the ship skidded through the sea and the adversary had to hold on to the iron structure for a moment. He smiled at Toivo.

"You have been very kind to translate for me, but I'll leave you two alone now. I don't think it will be necessary anymore."

I can't get him with the basket. Stay calm, use your ability to be objective. The man had become a problem to Toivo. Could he do it? It seems you'd better bone up on ruthlessness, my friend, you're not in the same class. Let it be surprise then.

"What can I do for you, Mr. Krantz?"

Funny how formal you become when the situation is extreme, the formality of duels and knights. Firearms kill good manners.

"Well, perhaps you'd smoke a cigarette with me here? It has been a pleasure drinking with you, but all good things must come to an end, don't you agree?"

He had unbuttoned his jacket without Toivo noticing it. The wind yapped at Krantz's hair in vain; the close curls lay fast on the skull while Toivo's hair was playing flags over his forehead. The moon was bright, smoothing its metal ice on the deck. Krantz was not smiling when he repeated his offer of a cigarette and his left hand went up to reach inside his jacket.

Toivo dropped the basket and leaned firmly on the slant of the ship and had the man on the deck with a foot sweep. With one hand on the man's right side, where he felt an unmistakable hard and long shape coming from under the armpit, Toivo ripped the flimsy leather latch from the basket and reached in. Krantz, the professional, was already halfway to a successful countermeasure when Toivo's hand appeared in front of his face with a frightened snake coiling stiffly from his wrist. It had bitten him but he had hardly noticed, gripping the brown and green slither for a direct aim at the man's face. Which was looking at the splayed head with the curving teeth and the cold lifeless eyes which were dark and slit like a gunner's turret. The man had gone rigid with a fear so consuming that nothing mattered but that jabbing head. A rasping howl tried to suck out of his throat while he clawed at Toivo's body. Toivo sat astride him and slung the snake up in the air and caught the bottom half in his left hand. Then he quickly slid it under the man's neck and tried to pull the snake tight and lay a rapid tie in the shining ripple. Man and snake heaved and coiled together for a moment with intense fury and than all was still. The snake skinned away like a liquid dart, a beam tossed like a trickle of moonmetal on the deck, its movement chopping it up in the night like a shattered droplet of mercury, and was gone. The corpse clawed at his neck and the muscles, locked in extremis, lifted the body a few inches from the deck with terror battened on its soaked face.

Toivo got up and tossed the silenced gun and the empty basket overboard.

18

"IF A MAN looks around him even in a perfunctory manner, he cannot write uplifting books. If he does so nevertheless, I suspect that he is either kneading bread with his typewriter or he's a facile moron. Cataracts are not only a disease of the elderly or the badly fed. I don't see how one can dress insanity up in gay flutters as if words were being fitted for a ball. Write misanthropic books: perhaps they are the last honest gesture left."

Toivo only rarely dared sweep the audience of deadpan eyes three feet above the chairs. Why not lethal x-ray vision, collapsible guns which could be assembled in the lap and fired by periscope. Blowguns are very effective in auditoriums. The lectern could be wired to explode when he put his full weight on it, or there could be a heat-sensitive device in the neon-tubed reading lamp vulturing on the edge of the lectern which would eject gas when his breath had heated it to the proper temperature. Gunshoes, sleeve throwers, razor toupees on the principle of boomerangs. But always silence, death in a silenced world. It's getting so bad I am wishing for the good old-fashioned flash and crack of a bullet rifle.

"Difficult you ask?"

They asked nothing, orator, and they won't. They're armed with silence. Perhaps they're thinking of the man with the snake tied around him on the boat. But the verdict was heart attack. Official forms proved it. Yet they will rise and hurl reptiles at me.

He finished his speech with great difficulty, the words rolling like pellets of dough shaped from a loaf of bread out of frustration. He had to stop this. He could not endure the strain of this public vulnerability any longer. When they actually rose and applauded, his instantaneous reaction was to a volley from the audience. It took him seconds to reassure himself that he was not gathering the bits and pieces of himself off the floor. Then he nodded, bowed, managed a smile.

At the reception afterward he was praised for his unusual talk, which had shed some "idiosyncratic light on the process of creation, given a memorable voice to much of modern literature," said something about his self. As a writer of course. Not as a hunted freak, a sprung fool who ran because the pack was on his heels. He signed his books by the dozen and smiled. Compliments and praise. The British public obviously cared for his work. He was surprised to see his audience was not exclusively young: he was reaching all age groups. But he also knew that when he got outside the building and the cognoscenti had drifted into the vast web of London, no one would recognize him anymore. Except the ones who knew wherever he was all the time, everywhere, at any hour. No more public appearances. He had first to find out what was trying to catch him. He had to know the caster behind the net which covered the globe, its purpose, how much it thought to draw in.

Toivo closed himself in a phone booth and started feeding coins into the slots. But when he reached the embassy and was supposed to push them in he hung up and stood there in silence. They would tell him, as they had done before, to go on with his other planned talks and readings in London, Oxford, Cambridge, Birmingham, Edinburgh and god knows were else. He was tired. He was scared. He was fed up with their scheduled unconcern. He had to find help. There had to be someone here in England whom Kall had known and who would help him for his father's sake. Then he realized that he was standing in a glass booth, a box of leaded panes, giving his enemy a perfect target, even squaring it for him. He slammed the door open and tried not to run for a bus. The underground he dared not take anymore. To be in a tunnel, rushing forward at great speed with a mass of people, choking him so severely that he had great trouble getting enough breath to climb the stairs back to space. The world was congested with bodies, a surfeit of humanity he wanted to cut through to open up room for himself.

Nor could he return to Hyde Park. No longer could he stroll along the Serpentine as he had done that morning before his lecture. Two shots had been fired at him from Kensington Gardens. One had rushed past his nose, the other had gone right through the space where his head had been before he dropped to the sward. Both bullets had ripped into a tree and shaken summer leaves down. No one had noticed with all the heavy traffic. The tree trunk had ruptured open, showing rough butter needles. It had angered him for a moment to see the wound in the tree.

Toivo wandered aimlessly through the heart of London, dodging into shops on Oxford Street whenever he felt his shadow close enough to count neckhairs. Surely no one had ever been assassinated in a shop, a sacrilege in a nation of shopkeepers. That day he saw all the ingenious devices man hides himself in, all the things he fills his living space with, all the words he spews out to feed his intellect. He bought a copy of *The Kalevala* and when he was finally too exhausted to control his feet he sat in a restaurant and browsed through the familiar verse while he listlessly drank coffee and munched a baked sweet.

But his professional interest still flickered from time to time and half an hour before the shops closed he noticed a book of memoirs written by a man who had been in intelligence during the war. Kall Syystalvi was mentioned with honor on several pages, though the text hid more than it revealed. The blurb said that the author, Delmer Higgins, had known wartime intelligence from personal experience, having been an agent for the British in his own country while ostensibly spying for the Germans. He lived at present in northern England. The company that had published the book was closed by the time Toivo reached its offices. Somehow he had to get through the night before he might obtain his address and go to the man for help. It was his only chance. If that didn't work he had no idea what else he could do.

Once before he had been similarly alone, despairing and

afraid. But now it was worse. Then it had been an absence, now it was the presence of something unseen. Invisible death.

He could no longer face hotel rooms where every opening door was the final scene of a play he had been prevented from seeing, where he heard clear footsteps in the carpeted corridors and his bed was made only for the deaths of strangers. Lie in bed in a dark room with the lights of city streets hunting over the ceiling, every architectural fault a scream and the blankets made of lead. He would start seeing doubles and kill them. He would have to go to bed fully clothed. And the luxury of ordering snacks in his room was soured since each prepared tidbit or opened bottle might have been seasoned with poison. In caf-eterias at least, with their assembly-line food, there was safety in mass production. He thought of himself as a paranoid with an incurable passion for gathering mushrooms who sees in every edible fungus a deadly *Amanita verna*.

Safer at night to wander through Soho. The dead of night has a homeopathic cure for fear. Amusement areas with their calico illuminations create an illusory dark. For who is to tell whether night exists there by virtue of artificial light or light because of darkness? Obscurity loans beauty to people. Pleasure people noising it down the sidewalks, suited for fun, perhaps even gay enough to take a stranger in tow. Democratic night who gives equal rights to crazies and to louts heavy with cash.

Toivo went in and out of expensive bars and clubs and dingy dives and strip joints. Whores, with the discretion cultivated by law, asked him for a light, offered him a place to sleep, a place to exercise, a massage, offered to take exotic photographs, offered artistic poses, called him handsome and a gentleman.

In the middle of a small square a pop-art pigeon ruffled by neon lights slogged around with a slice of bread hanging around its neck like an empty window frame, a garish clown bumping around the piste with his head sticking out of his oversized collar. It finally flew sluggishly off like an overloaded bomber with the slice still around its neck.

But even the night crew grows tired, doors are locked, and take is counted, registers are totaled and emptied, bartenders tote up what's left in bottles, entertainers wearily remove formal clothing, costumes and make-up and slouch home. Finally there was nothing left but the neon lights and silence. The few stragglers didn't stroll but strode with rapid pace to a definite destination. And in the wee hours when there was nobody left and Toivo sat on a chair outside a closed bar (why it was there he couldn't figure out) and was lighting yet another of the cigarettes which by now tasted like pencil lead, a soft, smooth sound came down the street.

It was a well-dressed man in a blue suit, starched shirt and modish tie, motoring himself down the sidewalk in an electric wheelchair. His highly polished shoes caught the lights of the streetlamps. Paying absolutely no heed to Toivo he very slowly rustled by the display windows of strip joints where neon frames cast a flat light over the nearly nude girls. One of his hands was in leather and the other in a velvet glove. The hands clawed around the armrests and he would look very slowly and carefully and then hum on to the next joint. Expressionless. But every so often his head would droop forward and he would stare in his lap, down his palsied legs, as if he were checking his face in the mirrors of his shoes. Then very slowly, with great effort, he would get his head back on his shoulders again and stare. It took him almost an hour before he hummed around a corner and was gone.

Slopped in the corner of a window seat, Toivo waited for the train to leave Euston Station for the north. He didn't feel like or look fit for a first-class apartment, but he wanted privacy. With grained eyes and a night stubble, his clothes crumpled and with a motionlessly melancholy face he looked like an unemployed clown. He was too tired to let the flickers of his fear be coaxed into a brand: he wouldn't have been able to defend himself against so much as a killer flea. At the railway station he had sent a telegram to Mr. Higgins stating that he hoped the man would help him for the sake of his father.

Slowly the train moved away from the platform. As it had done steaming through the Cotswolds, Cheltenham, Broadway, Mickleton, through Warwickshire, Leicestershire, Northumberland. By car it was. Or truck, bicycle, barge or foot. Huge yawns forced tears from his eyes which faded under their drooping lids or stared mesmerized at the compartment wall or at the scenery flowing backward without recognition.

In that mesosomnic state where reality is fluid and irreality is photographic, independent of the will, he never noticed to whom he gave his ticket but the punched hole he saw as clearly as a crater's edge. Metal was jabbing his side and he wondered why anyone would do business on public transportation with a large gun with an octagonal barrel. It was merely the metal corner of the fold-out table, which he knew, of course, but still wondered about. And he looked blindly out of the window where his eyes were striped by telephone poles which asked whether it might not perhaps be a good age to die. Or should he wait for old age? Now he might get a six-inch obituary but at eighty only two. Is it more heroic not to cling to humanity so long or would he want to be eulogized for breathing back the enemy for eight decades? What is the proper age to die? Did the world of trouble canonize a Patroclean death fit for ballads, or did the very fact of toil and suffering insist on a Job, noble in his endurance? Does it matter when you compose back into molecules dervishing it around nature? Molecules aren't sered with time or fresh with youth. Fame doesn't faze them; anonymity is their hallmark. Molecular democracy! I am a table a leaf a cat a bear a mug a train. I am glass. And they can see through me and know the lay of my mind. Someone knocked. Can't you see that I already had my ticket checked? I know, sir, but perhaps you'd care for lunch in the restaurant car. Yes, thank you. Last call, the voice intoned down the corridor. Toivo rubbed his eyes like a child. He had slept longer than he'd been aware of. He had to change at Penrith.

When he finally arrived at Windermere he was a mechanism which assumed that effect followed cause. When he had missed his connection at Penrith it had not bothered him. You wait for the next train and when you wait you sit no matter how long a time it takes to struggle through the aspic of inactivity. The curtness of clerks is normal. Jostling by crowds is part of the fare. Not knowing where Higgins lives can be remedied by asking. He walked around the small lake town certain someone would show up. And with a car too and who gladly took him to Higgins' house situated outside the town on the slope of a hill. Then you wait in the vestibule to be verified by the master of the house. It is to be expected that a strange man will come at you with an eager outstretched hand and a face glowing with pleasure and the obvious remark that you are much older now than when you were a boy.

19

"BLIMEY, YOU LOOK BUSHED. You ran here all the way from London?"

Toivo nodded and spoke for a few minutes.

"In trouble, aye, that's all right. I am good at trouble. Sidney," Higgins said to the man standing behind Toivo, "take this gentleman upstairs and help him to a bath. Give him some comfortable night apparel, a robe, slippers, and bring him back down again. To the study. And tell Bridget to brew us some strong coffee and uncork a bottle of my good brandy. Fine. I'll be waiting for you," he said to Toivo, and turned on his heels and marched back into a large room.

A fire of big hardwood logs was blazing in the study. Higgins had sequestered him in an elephantine easy chair from which Toivo could see only the hearth, his host and a teak table with his coffee and brandy.

"Hope you don't mind the fire; houses like these get chilly on summer nights and my bones have lost some of the heat they used to have. Call me Short 'n' Happy or whatever you like: Short, Happy or Higgins. But not Delmer. Can't stand the name."

Higgins was a powerfully built man of nearly five feet six, with shoulders squared to his hips and with what had once been a proportionally narrow waist but which now, with the fattening of age, was beginning to level with his ribcage. Large hands with fingers squared at the tips and small feet in expensive Italian shoes. He wore a woolen business suit, a white shirt and placid tie. The skin of his neck turkeyed over his collar but the rest of his face was smooth and taut with freckles everywhere. Higgins sat solidly in his chair like a hard-boiled speckled egg. Eyebrows like bleached furry awnings shaded a pair of intelligent, blue and canty eyes. His large ears with tufts growing from them were covered by a curly red mat of hair, the kind of hair that never grows white and never falls out. His teeth showed when he smiled, natural teeth stained brown from the cigars he had been smoking since he was sixteen.

"I've the kind of hair that makes the coppers happy. I seldom dyed it. If I got caught because of my hair it meant I hadn't done the job properly."

The prosperous little man buoyed confidence and strength so that Toivo talked freely. The hot bath and clean clothes, the warm fire and the brandy had converted his almost pathological exhaustion into a snuggling up with his tired body.

"Yes, I see what you mean," Higgins said thoughtfully. He poured Toivo some more of the strong Brazilian coffee and made him drink it.

"Just a few questions, pal, and then you go to bed and get your gear in working order again. I've got to have you with a fresh mind and a body ready for action. This slumpy bag of thrashed corn is no good to me. Or to you for that matter."

He sat down again and bunched his upper lip into chicken fannies with his thumb and index finger, pulled out and let it snap back. He got up, still silent, and threw the butt of the squashed cigar in the fire, took a fresh one from a large sandalwood box, bit the tip off with the sound of dry leaves crunching under a boot heel and lit it with a large silver lighter. He puffed smoke to the ceiling which was twice his height above him and then let his eyes roam around the walls of books.

"Do you know that I have read most of these," he finally said, grinning proudly at Toivo.

"But you wouldn't think an old rogue like me was literate, would you now. Yes, sir, I am the man who keeps people like you in business. Won't be long though with the telly and stuff. But I admit to prejudice — I want you to notice that I know my two-syllable words as well as the next bloke — I read mostly spy fiction."

He stroked his hand as gently as a feather duster along rows of bindings.

"Got 'em all. Conrad, Buchan, Childers, Household, Greene, Ambler, Fleming, Deighton, Le Carré, Hall. And all the books by the experts like Dulles and Masterman, and the real stuff about Philby, Burgess, Maclean, Blake. Everything, including my favorite spy book, *Hamlet.* See, there's yours. Not properly the same thing but then Shakespeare or Conrad aren't quite on the level either, are they?"

Higgins was the picture of a proud man standing there like a safari hunter boasting over a large horned kill.

"But," he said, imperceptibly tightening his body, "I am not just a fellow who knows things from books. That came later. I know this business. I am proud of my learning, see, but I have known the original rough stuff too. How did you think I got myself this house here?"

He spread his arms out and did a demipivot as smoothly as a retired ballet dancer.

"Plus ten acres of the most beautifully kept green you'll ever see. And a pond, a brook and peacocks. Terraces too and a greenhouse. Well, what do you think?"

He poked his cigar at Toivo's face and snickered.

"Give up, right? With money, that's how. I've been lucky. Before the war I was in shady business, stealing here and forging checks there. One of the best safecrackers in the business. I had the eyes, my friend. Just look, I still don't need glasses and I am sixty. Surprised, you say? And careful — boy, was I careful. The Yard was on to me though but they couldn't prove anything and then the war broke out. The Jerries had some stuff on me: a pal of mine squealed on me because the bastards had different methods than the Yard of course. So the Jerries blackmailed me, calling it a proposition. Dirty games is the word I believe. Love to keep up on the lingo of the profession. I accepted. Got large sums out of them and promptly went to our side, the Dons you know, and doubled, crossed over, call it what you like. It was fun. I was something like an illegal legal or a legal illegal. His Majesty paid me handsomely too so that by the end of the war I was sitting pretty. I had saved almost everything, the authorities let me keep the Jerry loot and filed all their records they had on me under 'dust' not to be opened until old Winnie walks again or something like that. By that time I had also gotten my hooks in the Yanks, made a few good deals and got married to a wealthy woman. But that's another story.

"I've always lived on the fringes you might say, seriously now for a moment, but then I've never cared for the center of the rug. But neither did I want to be swept under the carpet. I wanted money and some fun doing it and I did it. I am glad I can brag about myself. Not too many people can say the same thing."

He was up again and went over to put his hands on Toivo's shoulders.

"Look, all I meant with all this is simply that I know a few people who know people who know a few things. I still got some irons in the fire and, also, money can always get a little information. I am going to make a few calls while you're sleeping your misery off. It's just like a wicked drunk, that's all, believe me. You don't look like a wet blanket to me, that's for sure. From appearances I'd say that I'd hate to fool with you. And if you're a writer you got brains. Fine. Rest them up. The best of hunting dogs gotta have their sleep, you know."

"You understand what's going on then?" Toivo asked listlessly, not believing it could be possible.

Higgins looked at him steadily, his eyes gone flat as slate and all the antics wiped from his face. Then he grinned, broke into laughter and the freckles danced on his face. He straightened up and stroked his sucked-in stomach.

"Yes I do. It isn't easy to fool me and I knew your father. You've obviously forgotten that you've met me once, in this very same town as a matter of fact. But then I was living in a rented cottage. I liked Kall. I said so in my book. Did you read it yet? Had no time? Well, you should, you know, and you can tell me if it's stylish and such. Let me see now. You're a famous writer on a lecture tour in Europe. Suddenly you find yourself being shot at and getting gifts of corpses wherever you go. That's it, right? Sounds utterly insane to you, doesn't it. Perhaps so. But there's always an explanation. With some facts you can start moving. Some things about all this ring a bell somewhere. Well, even a couple of calls will make a little more sense out of it. You came to the right place, my boy. If I can't figure it out no one can except the fellows who are putting it to you."

When Toivo was almost across the doorsill on his way to bed Higgins stopped him once more. Toivo leaned against the door like a privileged child who has been kept up past his interest in fun.

"Sorry I kept you so long. I talk a bit much perhaps but it gets lonesome here sometimes. But don't be mistaken. I might be sixty but I can handle more of these spooks than you'd believe. Years make a man cagey and you cut down on risks to make sure of a dead-certain shot. Okay. Sleep well, pal. See you tomorrow."

In the bright sun of the early afternoon kept brisk by a wind from the lake, Snarker Hall looked splendid indeed. A square, brick building with countless windows and a slate roof, it had the solid luxury of nineteenth-century architecture. The top floor above the room Toivo had slept in was not in use, but it seemed to have the same high-ceilinged rooms, parquet floors and oaken doors. The wood in the house was dark and polished and gave warmth to its basic stone. The bedstead he had slept in was wide and it creaked, but the mattress could have been sliced to service at least three modern beds. The staircase was broad and the labored breathing of its wood was muffled by thick gray and blue carpeting. The sweeping curve of the banister presented a marble hall which had been kept just within the proportions of domesticity. Off to the right was a dining room large enough to seat an exclusive convention, and to the left was a sitting room with couches almost as wide and soft as the bed he had slept in. Deep pile Persian and Chinese rugs cloistered every step and Toivo noticed that they were the lightest color one could find, with designs as simple as arabesques allow. It was a perfect choice to keep the darkly polished wainscoting of the huge spaces as ungloomy as possible. A dwelling that could only house harmony.

Around him swept rolling green horizoned by thick forest. Near the house formal gardens had been laid out with an abundance of flowers, shrubs and vines to cheer the gloom even from Persephone returning from that nameless land. A color guard of peacocks as disdainfully tame as courtiers paraded on the gravel paths. Not a single pergola showed its latticed skeleton since they were abundantly fleshed with clinging vines and sprinkled with blooms as thick as the pearls on the robes of Elizabeth I. Fruit was ripening on clusters of trees and a vibrant peace decked the scene like shimmering glass. Only the calls of birds laced the silence and every now and then a peacock opened his tail into the sun.

Toivo was finishing his breakfast on the terrace. It had been brought by Bridget, the cook, a local farmer's daughter, because Sidney the butler only served up dinner. Higgins had taken his clothes for size early that morning and had bought him some new shirts, a soft leather jacket, corduroy pants and a pair of soft leather lace-boots the height of those worn by hikers. Then he had destroyed the clothes Toivo had arrived in. Cleaned, shaven, barbered by Sidney (who also did Higgins' hair because the latter mistrusted barbers) and in new clothes which were only slightly too large and therefore comfortable, Toivo was beginning to recoup his confidence. Finally he had managed to find a haven, almost an Eden, immune to violence. The gravel on the circular driveway in front of the house grated under the wheels of an automobile and Higgins came to take him away.

"Not bad, 'ey," Higgins said with ill-concealed pride. "I left it pretty much the way I bought it. All I have to do is keep it up, though that costs plenty. But you just can't set up a place like this anymore in our day and age. But to business. You said that you aren't going to do those lectures anymore, am I right?"

"That's right. And I am not telling the embassy. Let them figure it out."

"Good. That's one line of information cut off. At least they won't be sitting in the balcony waiting for you to open your mouth. We're trying to make it difficult for them. Now the clothes I bought you won't do much in the way of disguise, but then they weren't meant to. You simply would look very obvious around these parts in a suit and tie. I got you good-looking durable stuff."

"I'll pay you back. I've got money."

"That's good. In town you'll give me some of those traveler's checks and I'll cash them. They know me. Good thing you got some money because I've got quite an overhead."

"Where are we going?"

"I am giving you the lay of the land around here so you have some notion where you are. Besides, it's safer talking in a car."

They were driving along Lake Windermere with its water barely cockled by the breeze from the trees and hills lining its shores. The stoop of the rushes gave the wind away, otherwise the blue sky was pure steady summer.

"You say they didn't tip you, that is, recruit you?"

"No."

"You have never done anything for intelligence?"

"No."

"This business doesn't smell criminal to me and yet there's nothing I can see which would make anyone so determined to kill you, can you?"

"No."

"Okay. Now wherever you went they were always there before you or, at the very least, knew where you were. That has me worried a bit. You're an amateur to be sure, but that can be an advantage too. I'll hope to make use of it. But damnit, it takes quite an operation to follow you that closely around a continent. Now the only thing you were asked to do was to look up that scientist, right?"

"By Blaise Donner."

"Donner. Yes. I sure would like to have a talk with him. He would have this thing figured out in an afternoon, just sitting behind his desk pushing a few buttons here and there. But I can't imagine him fooling around with small fry."

When the light softens the Lake District unrolls parallel to the Irish Sea like a fragile Chinese scroll — contouring mountains, fells clasping tarns, dales fleeced with fog held by the indubious brushstroke of ink.

"But you were never hurt. Someone else always got to them. So one bunch was after the other. Maybe you were bait. Yes, of course. Why not. Bait! I'd say that's how it is. But the why has got me stumped."

20

HIGGINS INSISTED that Toivo go about armed. He owned a large collection of firearms, which he kept in his study. The handguns were preserved on velvet in compartmentalized drawers under the shelves of books. His rifles and shotguns stood in a tall cupboard with glass doors. All the weapons were ready for use. They were well oiled and constantly fussed over by either Higgins or Sidney. Knowing that firearms are illegal in Great Britain, Higgins was taking a big chance giving Toivo a revolver: a Smith & Wesson .38 special airweight. Along with the weapon he supplied fifty rounds of ammunition, not jacketed but lead with a cross carved on the nose. And if Toivo were ever to go traveling again before the mystery was solved Higgins had promised to give him a 7.65 mm Mauser for distance work.

Higgins had a large variety of other models more modern in design and claims. But personally he preferred to go to battle with an old Smith & Wesson .38 he had bartered during the war for a case of champagne, or with a Colt .45 automatic pistol.

"Mind you, I want those weapons back," he said while showing Toivo how to operate and draw the Smith & Wesson. "You can't get out of the country with them on you and if the coppers are after you you'd better ditch them. I am not a fool, of course. The serials have been tampered with. The authorities simply don't know how many guns I actually have, even though I have a permit for the lot. I am doing this because you've been walking around too long like a pacifist clay pigeon. They know that now and they don't expect you to get back at them with lead.

You see, my boy, your judo doesn't do you much good at ten yards, now does it? Get out there in the back and practice. No, not with those lead bullets. Here, take the regular stuff, they're cheaper."

There were two man-sized targets, made out of unpainted knotty pine between a couple of stout oaks. Higgins made Toivo go for a brown knot the size of a British penny about where the heart would be.

"I don't want you to shoot in terms of colored circles. You'd be surprised how dumfounded fellows get when a man simply refuses to wear them."

Higgins loved firearms, ingenious tools which still depend on human mastery and intelligence for their effectiveness. Anyone can do a hundred in a modern automobile, he felt, but to kill a man required skill, practice, a native flair and mental preparation. The finest-tooled weapon is useless in the paw of a moron.

At the first shots the peacocks scattered, the birds fell silent and the smell of cordite bludgeoned the perfume of roses. As if he had put a stopper back in the flacon.

"You're okay. You said Kall taught you as a boy? Well, he knew his business. There is no time to make a crack out of you. I mean you can try and wing the guy but I would concentrate on a kill. Those fellows will not be missed where they came from so aim to kill and maybe you'll at least incapacitate them. That's a boy. Very good. You might make it yet. Remember that amateurs never make the grade because they don't care to kill. That's the thing, you see. Drawing fast is for idiots, it's not that important. The moment your hand goes for that butt you're out to kill. If that's your state of mind you can win from the most pompous gun toter with the fanciest gun all dolled up with god knows what contraptions. He'll hesitate. By that time he'll never do so again — ever. That's all you want. If you don't intend to get him you'd better run for cover.

"The best place to carry it is in your waistband. But it would bulge when you had your jacket on. The one I got you still isn't large enough. So keep it in your trouser pocket. Not on the hip, that's too far to reach. I had my housekeeper sew a chamois pocket in your pants so the damn thing won't fall out when you're taking a leak in a public john. Now don't be afraid of the weapon. It's short, only a two-inch barrel, and it's not too heavy. It won't jam on you or go off accidentally even if you drop it on concrete. It's as good as any automatic, and let no one tell you different."

The weight was a comfort and Toivo felt a rare attraction to the weapon. Not since the Suomi automatic in Finland had he held a weapon so close to him and he never had had one on his body. The Parisian Luger had been an accident. He had seldom had steel on him, not even a wristwatch. He would have to get used to it.

There was a perverse thrill in tearing the green membrane off the summer afternoon. His shot had been good and the white gladiola smashed in half, spraying a pulp of blooms and stalk, the rooted stump oozing a liquid green.

"Don't kid yourself, pal," Higgins said evenly. "You've got it down there somewhere. That's just dandy. After all, you can't kill them with words."

But Toivo wasn't happy with the praise. The enormous sound was grotesque in the stilled garden. And can you splint a flower? Can you kill a ghost?

"Of course you think they had silencers. Amateurs usually do. Except for that auditorium job, which was probably done with a silenced .22. A guess, mind you, nothing more than that. Except for that one I bet you ten guineas that the others were plain old shooting. People get the idea that a shot is instantly noticed. But how many of them really know what it sounds like? In this noisy world, who needs the help of silence? I ask you, why should a professional louse up his aim and make his weapon unreliable with a clumsy tube when he can do just as well without it? I bet I could finish a whole clip in a hotel and by the time somebody got wise to it I'd be drinking coffee at the Ritz. No, my boy, that fellow in Paris was shot pure and simple. Were there any cars in the street? Right. With traffic around who needs silencers?"

Toivo had hired a boat to think in for a few shillings an hour. He had rowed some distance from the pier crowded with fathers and mothers collecting their offspring and was now drifting with the current. He was lying down so that he saw nothing else but the blue sky and some threads of clouds evaporating like streaks of water on a hot skillet. He had left the revolver at Snarker Hall. He wasn't used to the weight yet.

He had always been a light traveler and during his tour he had been stripped more and more only to be reequipped again now. Admit your fascination for the easy prowess the weapon gives. But it's ridiculous, a step down. That's because you haven't been shaped to the new form yet. Higgins' world has shape and if it's a shambles he pries and acts until it has a structure he recognizes and can deal with. Higgins' world is known to you, you've visited it at night over your typewriter: a switch of realities. I can't act the way he wants me to. I am not a soldier. All this time you have had things happen to you: violence visited you unannounced and you served it tea and cookies and took notes. It's that blank side of yours, as hidden as the other side of the moon. A photosensitive blank which would put an injunction on action for interfering with its registration. But you're afraid that that world you've momentarily retired from is real and you wouldn't know what to do with it. What bothered you at target practice was the realization that bullets explode it into reality. I've got to have details; it's been a tenantless space, thin obstacles that hindered me like cobwebs. But in your recollection that space was defined as walls that spit at you. I want to fight like Väinämöinen. Sing down my enemies, enchant my enchanters, defeat them with the magic of materials that will load them down and sink them out of sight. "Sing shoes of stone onto his feet, wooden pants onto his hips, a stone weight onto his chest, a chunk of rock onto his shoulders, stone mittens onto his hands, onto his head a hat of rock."

Toivo managed to light a cigarette and watched the smoke laze off over the edges of the boat. On shore they'd be wondering whether there was anyone in the drifting boat floating toward the sun, pulled on by the moon, down the creeks, down the rivers, with the relentless listlessness of a tired sadness until it would slip into the sea and haul itself from horizon to horizon until the bottom had been worn down to the grain, woven into the marine fiber of sea and sky. The wind sent midget buccaneers to board the vessel: marines with feathers for swords. His cigarette was already a butt, sucked away before he'd had a mouthful. Caught between two realities like a fly between two sheets of plexiglass. And not illusion and reality. It never was. Between reality and reality. The way it had been when after a night of writing he'd had to restrain himself from annoyed astonishment at the existence of textbooks and grammars, assignments and students asking about grades on a curve or straight. Or when he'd had to walk from desert heat to Barb's bedroom to get her the Vicks for a raw nose in the flu season. Concepts are real and so is a Smith & Wesson .38. Philosophers make very good assassins.

Kall would have had none of this sense. Higgins had told him some, but his farewell father remained as aoristic as before. Code name Vak because he had been indeed the only hole cut in the ice of Russian intelligence. The only agent liaisoned with Russia, England and America. A lonesome spook, Kall, one who didn't want to be part of any machine and so a machine was built around him. He needed no regrooming in the north — only in England was he conspicuous when he spoke. Like a spider he hunted alone and to Toivo it was like a crib of Higgins' words that Kall had done so from aphilanthropy, a silent, bitter man playing off lives in a chess match because the pieces don't touch the nerves. But even in the cold up north a spook like Kall was not alone. They had given him information that suited their purposes and after some time Kall was caught in a web not of his making. The most detailed bit of information Higgins had been able to give him was that Kall had known a Soviet colonel whom he had met as a fellow cadet at the military academy in St. Petersburg. The colonel leaked him battle information which was to be used by the officers' underground in Germany to help them plan their assassination of Hitler. In return Kall supplied him with Allied secrets. But these secrets were sent to Kall via London. There his superiors carefully laundered what they sent on to him, gave him only innocuous facts, and they never let on that they were double-crossing him. Against his better judgment, Kall was forced to put a man on the colonel's staff who had been sent to him by Blaise. He was a Finn whose family had emigrated to Fitchburg, Massachusetts. Kall didn't know that the man had been encouraged to hate both the Germans and the Russians. Behind Kall's back the Finn, following orders from London, began to recruit agents on his own and even approached Russian military defectors. The colonel, for whom the Finn was ostensibly working, was tipped off by a member of his own staff who had been approached by the zealous Finn. The colonel confronted Kall, who had no idea that this had been going on. To save his own neck, Kall blackmailed his former ally with the very association which had been so profitable to Kall's own cause. Kall knew all too well that even an iota of the truth would put the colonel in a camp for the rest of his life. Unable to find a solution, the colonel committed suicide. But Kall had begun to realize that he was being used as a marionette by controllers and beyond them section chiefs and beyond them cosmopoliticians. In retaliation he began exposing the small number of the Finn's recruits and when the Finn cried foul, Kall was recalled to London. Kall only went, said Higgins, because they told him that his son was in danger from a Russian-controlled Central European column of illegals. After much confusion, Kall was sent back to Russia, newly assigned as the controller of the Finn. Higgins said Blaise had sworn that that was true. But Kall was never heard from again. Vak had made the hole and an icebreaker had gone in and smashed a channel to keep the traffic flowing. At the end of the war Blaise was in sole control of every operation in Russia, Scandinavia and Germany. His personal stamp on the network was his use of agents from mutually hostile nationalities to ensure distrust. His career was made. The yellow tea roses the Finnish florist sent abroad, even when Toivo had been staying with him, were part of an ingenious code Kall had devised, based on the number of flowers in each shipment, the number of thorns and the length of each stalk. This code was never cracked.

Toivo didn't know much with all that. As in learning a foreign language, many of the rules of espionage resisted coherency of comprehension. Thin hindrances he could not penetrate, a whirl of Democritus' atoms, two realities with ill-fitting doors. He got

the oars out and began to row. Action stills thought. Tom Thumb
in seven-league boots. The Snark was a boogum you see. A
revenge from a quarter century ago? Was Higgins Mikko? You
are rowing on Lake Windermere, the longest lake in England.
Boating it in vacationing Britain. You've taken your mind for a
ride. Severed horseheads bobbed in the placid water, the oars
stirred up debris. Bombs kill kittens. Landscapes are declared
offensive and individuals be damned. He was safe here except
that Higgins had insinuated his armed origins into his consciousness again. Light, I want to be light. Shrapnel trafficked through
him. Fiction a stained-glass window. Rowing a slicing motion.
But the realities meet, you said to de Bruce. Boxes. Am I still
boxed in? That's all you're likely to get. And if there's more it's
either madness or a lie, since nothing gives of itself for nothing.
But you've got that country they'll never know, an inscape
absolutely yours. It is free, it has no laws, *it's of no use,* it never
will be a utility to them. How free you are! They're iron-booted
by a reality of consensus but you've got one walking your head
that no one knows about unless you send out messages. A quarter
of a million Russians and eighteen thousand Finns died in five
months of battle. The Finns had fought for their lives. But what
had the Russians died for? Now strike those oars in the water
harp. Interlace your fingers with those of the singer and sing out
loud. Sing out and rock slowly the rhythm:

> Old Väinämöinen then got angry, then got angry and felt ashamed.
> He began to sing, got to reciting.
> He didn't sing children's songs, children's songs, women's jokes,
> but sang those of the bearded man, which not all children can
> nor half the boys indeed, not one bachelor in three
> in this dreadful time, in this fleeting final age.
> Old Väinämöinen sang. Lakes splashed over, the earth shook,
> copper mountains trembled, solid slabs of rock split,
> crags flew apart, stones cracked on the shore.

Toivo jumped on the wooden pier that fingered the lake and the
rental man came up to him and asked for an extra hour's fee.
Toivo felt in his left pocket. It was empty and of a different
material. The chamois pocket where the gun was to be. His
money was on his hip.

"I ain't got change for a fiver, sir, unless you'd care to have five pounds of coin."

"Keep it, keep it."

Toivo wiped his face and it was all right when its moisture smelled of the sun. He wanted to get back to the hall and watch the peacocks spread their tails. Just like that. For no reason at all.

21

THE TRUNKLINES to London were overburdened by brokers gorging on a monetary crisis. Higgins was also handicapped by Lazard, his man in London, who had been compromised by yet another boy he had acquired for a lump of opium. Mr. Lazard had had to take a week off on the Continent but would be back. And Lazard would find out, Lazard always did. Lazard was as essential to the underworld of London as scales are to fish. Higgins had loaned him an Austin Healey and told him to tour the Lake District for a day. He motored along the upper shore of Lake Windermere, along Rydalwater where in spring the daffodils dance along the shore like yellow little trumpets of cherubim. To Grasmere, where he visited the simple grave of Wordsworth, the poet of the inwit of things, who admired nature enough to try to glimpse its immutable core and leave it be. Up along Lake Thrilmere to Keswick where Coleridge and Southey lived, then down along Derwentwater, through Borrowdale, through the Honister Pass and the Buttermere Fell, to the village of Buttermere surrounded by mountains.

There were few people on the road even though it was a high summer's day as much beyond reproach as the robe of the Stella Maris. He drove with the top down so the sun could scent his hair. Toivo felt good: that morning the cheval glass in his bedroom had shown him trim, tanned and in high spirits. He was traveling through nature's tone ladder: from long green dales with rivers, brooks and creeks, along lakes, up to fells, past mountains with heather slopes, crags flashing the mirrors of tarns, past swooping mountain slopes with the stretchmarks of primeval glaciers. Boulders, stones and waterfalls, streams and stone-walled pastures.

He got out of the car and climbed a steep slope to the top, high enough to see the road mapsize, high enough to plant your feet and yell and roll with the echo of your laughter and have the wind whip you and nothing but hugeness all around. Huge but not vague. The parabola of the slope across from his misted with purple erica down to an irregular cincture of boulders like the floats of a seine. Below him, next to the road, a stream with a fence through it and cows grazing like horned Saint Bernards. Gnarled trees, bracken and, under his feet, grass. Changes from specific form to specific form but no stiff structures, an endless double helix with no finality. You could become a monk of detail here, amassing an encyclopedia of forms and have covered a foot at your death. He lifted his arm from the ground and the patient grass bent upward again. Just there, in that elbow of green, he peered into a multitude of forms and structures civilization would never exhaust. A cathedral of grass. Grassmass. Green blades mutely gay. Gay mutes nicking the wind. Fucoid forests traveled by hundreds of thousands of insects hunted by spiders at 64,000 per single meadow acre. A heather thrush sang over his head. The wind threw his hair over his face and a strand nicked the sclera of his left eye and caused his vision to close.

In Cockermouth he had high tea of scones, fresh butter, jams and an apple butter which the sun had melted into jars. He was just as surprised as the other customers when an embarrassed waitress paged him. They were not used to receiving phone calls for strangers. The voice told him to go to a telephone booth which stood on the crossroads of Lorton and Cockermouth. It was urgent, Higgins had something to tell him. Everybody in the tearoom stared at him under cover of politeness and Toivo hastily paid up and left.

In the middle of acres upon acres of fields and meadows with no house or shed visible on the flat land, a phone booth stood by the road, a few feet from a tridirectional signpost pointing to Cockermouth, Low Lorton and High Lorton. It shouldn't have been there, that weird cubicle with the crowned post horn painted over the door. A freshly mowed field smelled of green butter and it was so still he could hear the sun. The official box rattled. The phone was ringing — an unbelievably loud clatter of metal on metal and Toivo felt the angry fields watching him. The booth kept on ringing and he finally went up to it and jerked the door open and stepped into the cacophony. He lifted the receiver and said: "Yes?"

There was no answer. Fear choked him and when he stepped outside to run a bullet crashed through the box and Toivo stood there stupified with the instrument dangling from his hand. A second shot tore up the dust in front of him and he was running for the car. Insensate terror pumped his legs and if the pebbles hadn't gnashed under his shoes he wouldn't have known he was there. He vaulted over the trunk and crouched behind the vehicle. In the distance a figure came through the barley holding a rifle high. He shouldered the rifle and Toivo heard himself scream. Then the figure stopped and leaned forward into the barley and was swallowed there. The sharp crack of a rifle shot shocked over the land and crows flapped up, black splinters hurled by the yellow into an indigo sky. Silence lowered again as tight as a hoop around a barrel. Off to his left Toivo saw another figure standing. It stood and leaned a rifle to its side and lit a cigarette. Waved a hand toward him, turned and walked away.

"Strip," Higgins ordered him. "Damnit, get those clothes off, fast." While Toivo mechanically undressed, placing his clothes carefully on a chair, Higgins kept on mumbling behind his teeth. His face was white and the freckles crawled over his skin like angry flies.

"Using my name, the fuckin' bastard. I'll show them yet, those fuckin' sons of bitches."

Toivo stood naked in the middle of the study while the short, red-haired man pulled his hands free from his sleeves and flexed his fingers. Toivo looked impassively over Higgins' head to the rows of books.

"They've got you bugged, and how. Not in your clothes, I bought those myself. Sidney took your suitcase apart. Nothing in there. It's got to be on you. The bug's got to be on your body, the cocksucking bloody, filthy double-crossing bastards."

He blew on his fingertips and flexed his fingers some more.

"Hell, I've opened some of the toughest safes in the business, so I sure as god's shitting hell can crack your code, buddy. Stand still and answer my questions."

Toivo felt the fingertips walk the length of his flesh. The man on his knees in front of him could just as well have been working on a vault.

"Okay, so they're clever. That's what they think," Higgins said after he had frisked him quickly but thoroughly.

"But don't worry, friend, I'll crack your combination." And he scowled at Toivo and plucked at the tufts of hair in his ears.

"Now just answer yes or no. Been to the dentist lately? Okay. Doctor then? Anything at all. Think. You remember anything having to do with your body in the past few months?"

"Yes," Toivo said slowly.

Higgins jabbed at Toivo's stomach and slapped his face.

"Snap out of it, you big lug. Remember. Just let it come out. You don't want them to win all the time, do you? My reputation is at stake here."

"Boston. It was in Boston."

"Boston? I don't care, Cairo is fine with me too. What about Boston?"

"I came out of the Auditorium with Barb, my ex-wife, and got hit over the head and robbed."

"Excellent, that's good. You remember anything at all, any details?"

"A pain in my leg before I went out or something."

"All right, that don't matter. Where in your leg?"

"My thigh, the inside of my left thigh."

The fingers were probing there already and Higgins was grunting happily. Then he whistled when he pressed down hard and Toivo jerked back.

"That's it. I got it. Okay, you can sit down now for a moment in that chair there. This business is getting into shape, it's getting clearer and also a hell of a lot more complicated. Lazard's got to get his teeth into this. Anything else you remember in connection with that leg?"

"It was painful for a while and then it itched. I had a Band-Aid over it when I came home that night. I thought that the police doctor had put it on, that I had hit it on something when I fell. People get mugged all the time in America. There was nothing unusual about it. Blaise also noticed it and . . . What do you think, Higgins? It isn't a . . . can't be . . ."

Higgins lit him a cigarette and Toivo hung back in the chair staring at the spot on his thigh.

"Well, my boy, they have been listening to you. They got one of their ears inside of you if I may say so. A microtransmitter. Nowadays they can make them no bigger than an aspirin. You've been bugged all this time, they had you under audio-surveillance and knew exactly where you were within an hour, at the most, from your last transmission. They've been taking good care of you."

They planted a mechanical bug, a piece of machinery in my body. Plugged my brain too? Why not paint the inside of my arteries with phosphorescent paint so I glow in the dark. Recode my DNA/RNA. Human use of human beings. They tampered with me. His brain had been redyed and then sneaked back in its casing while he took a nap. His bones had been radioactivated and Geiger counters crackled on his footsteps like plodding lobsters. They had tooled him, made a remote-controlled device out of him. Knew what he did, because he beamed it to them. Gotten under his skin. Made an implement out of him. He began pounding his body as if he were trying to box out a fire or a stirred-up hornet's nest sewn under his skin. Punched himself methodically until Higgins grabbed him by his arms and when Toivo got up out of the chair to break him too Higgins yelled for Sidney. Together they wrestled him back down again. Sweat poured from his face and it tasted metallic.

"Okay, I am all right now."

Sidney handed him his clothes and Toivo got dressed. Higgins shoved a tumbler of whiskey at him and Toivo drank it down. The little man patted him and soothed.

"We're not through yet, my boy. This time we've got them. Now you and I are going to a doctor friend of mine and we're gonna remove this little bugger. Then a little fooling around with vehicles and hospitals and without their little friend they've been thrown for a loop. Let's go. Sidney, you drive. And bring a gun. I am not taking any more chances."

Toivo lay out of sight in the limousine. Sidney had his clothes on and he was wearing Sidney's. The doctor took an x-ray and confirmed Higgins' skill. A local anesthetic and a brief operation. Then the tiny metal device lay there like a silver leech and Higgins smashed it with the hammer the doctor usually tapped his patients with to check reflexes.

Then Toivo was very visibly brought to a private hospital in an ambulance with Sidney in a doctor's coat and Higgins driving the doctor's car. He was wheeled into the place, brought into an emergency room and then walked out a back door into another ambulance. For a week a patient who was in a coma and under strict supervision was registered under Toivo's name.

The ambulance took him quite a distance, along all sorts of country roads, and finally stopped in Lancaster, a town south of Windermere. There Toivo dressed in a rest room of the railroad station in clothes Higgins had bought and put on the sunglasses he had gotten in Paris. It was the first time since then. Now he was wearing a woolen, open-necked shirt under a corduroy jacket slightly too large for him, a pair of khaki pants made from a good grade of cotton and brown half boots with crepe soles. Tucked in his waistband, under the buttoned jacket, was the Smith & Wesson .38 special airweight.

Sidney brought him back under cover of darkness. That night in Snarker Hall Toivo tried to get drunk while Higgins told him what he was going to do.

22

"YOU KNOW how to fall, don't you?"

"I'm good at it. In judo it's the first thing you learn; otherwise you're not allowed to fight."

"Good, then you're all set for your short holiday as a clown."

The two men were sitting on a rock on the shoulder of the road to Grasmere. Behind them a wind-seared apple tree dangled a few seedless fruits between leaves as tough as leather. An outcast from orchards, it had no right to be in the domain of tall poplars, yet it stood there bent into the wind like an old man stubbornly climbing a steep mountain.

Both men had sunglasses on and were peering down the road for dust. There were revolvers in their waistbands.

"Why don't they stay in the bigger cities," Toivo said. "It's certainly more profitable than working the little towns."

"Well, they're handicapped by newfangled innovations such as television, radio and the motion pictures, you know."

"Are they good?"

"I wouldn't say that. Most of them are rejects from the large shows on the Continent. Like Barnum and Bailey with three rings and a tempo that makes it impossible for you to follow anything. I like this troupe, they're stubborn. That's because they know nothing else."

"What's your connection with circuses?"

"Childhood and to pester the ghost of my wife. As a child there was nothing for me like the circus. Perhaps that's where I got my first taste of con artistry and of intelligence. I don't know. But it kept me spellbound, literally tied up my tongue. My parents could have sneaked away and left me there and I wouldn't have noticed until the lights went out."

Higgins shrugged, nosed his dark glasses and squirmed on the rock: the gun was muzzling his genitals.

"Becky, my wife, was the daughter of a vaudeville couple. Born in a trunk as they used to say in the States. She was a lousy hoofer but had the body of a knockout. Her tits kept her onstage long enough to get from the States to England. Yes, didn't I tell you, my wife was a Yank. And because the woman talked so much, well let's not call it that, because she yelled constantly all day long — even her dreams had sirens in them — I picked up Yankee slang because it rubbed off whether I liked it or not. She had learned only one acrobatic trick, a back flip, and with a sonsy body like hers with all them tits it was somethin' to see. I fell for her. I had the clothes, the car and the money and she married me. Then she wanted to become respectable. The old story: from tramp to Tiffany's sort of thing. And wouldn't you know it, her mother, back in the States, hooked an old codger who just so happened to be sitting on an oil well he didn't even know was bubbling under him. That woman could smell money if it was hidden in a sewage plant. She made the guy bubble it up and he died on her a very rich man and she a very rich widow and Becky a very rich heiress. It's too funny for words really. And Becky had to leave all of it to me because there was no one else around. That's what the law said. Here I had done all sorts of things to get rich: risked my neck, my life and my health. And there sat that dumb broad on her fat useless cunt and the money just dropped in her lap like it was raining. Wouldn't do any work around the house 'cause she was an artiste, that's what she said, even when we were living from my pickin's. I washed the dishes and vacuumed the joint, almost between heists as it were. My wartime capers she found 'thrilling' and she got fuckin' goose bumps like any old horsehair-stuffed baroness. So I took her to the circus because she hated to be reminded of the smell, which I liked, or of the little skits of the clowns which were so obviously about us when the big one would kick the little one around until the little one would stab a huge needle in the seat of the big one and all the hot air would stream out with a horrendous squeak.

Would even steam, that's how hot that air was, and the biggy'd collapse. Fine stuff. And she hated it. When she died, a year after the war, I put some of her loot in a circus. I had warned her not to gab while she was eating but she couldn't stop and one day she choked to death on a piece of steak."

The heat made a mirror of the road and the rock was getting hot.

"See anything yet?" Higgins asked, looking down the road.

"No."

"They couldn't be far."

"Depends on where they're coming from."

"From a fair in Lancaster. At least that's what Colby told me. He's the boss. He's incoherent over the phone, says that circuses don't know nothing about phones."

"You own the outfit?"

"No. Colby wouldn't go for that, besides too expensive. Even little secondhand flea shows cost too much to own. No, I'm the only backer they could find when they were down and out in the fifties. Only in Europe there seems to be some life in it yet, but here in England the telly has killed it or you've got to have one of those big affairs like Barnum and Bailey and fill Piccadilly Circus. And even then it's a gamble. No, only country fairs these days. Anyway, I've given them plenty to keep them afloat and Colby once in a while tries to pay some of the money back when the take has been good for that year. But I don't care. It's absurd, you know, to have money to support a hobby, not even a hobby, a childhood memory. It still works on me. My one weakness you might say. Hell, they owe me and that's why they're gonna hole you up for a week as a spare clown. No one notices an extra one when the pack of them fall into the ring. Besides, I could hardly get you in as a lion tamer, could I? 'Course the lions they've got wouldn't chomp through the gums of an old lady. I need a week, seven days, one fourth of a month, my friend, and between Lazard and myself and my connections high and low, add to that my old cronies from the war who also know a few things, we'll figure the whole thing out for you. All you have to do then is put in the pluses and the minuses. Just keep your flaps well down, friend, and Short 'n' Happy here will fix things for you."

"Thanks and thanks so much, that's . . ."

"Well, when you're on the run with fear you're lucky to find someone to help you. I dreamed of it when I was in your position and I sure as hell hoped for some stranger to step up and say I'll help you, what do you need. It happens sometimes, you know, but not often. Boy, do you need it when the whole world is reaching for you."

"You've done a lot . . ."

"Skip it. Thanks is difficult. There they come. Poor slobs, they're getting slower and slower."

They stood up under the old apple tree and when Toivo leaned against it two sterile apples let go and rubbered in the grass.

A Chinese dragon of dust swirled over the road with the sound of old engines somewhere inside it. A caravan of consumptive trucks and trailers rattled by and he could hear the tree cough from the dust. Higgins jumped on the road like a highwayman and the lead truck wheezed to a stop. Idling engines shook the bodies' painted metal; the flourished letters and colors that needed to be gay were dull from bad-weather traveling. Faces hung out of the windows and trailer doors. The animals in the barred wagons didn't even bother to stir. The caravan looked like a panting old monster recently escaped from a secondhand lot.

A tall, white-haired man so thin he seemed to have lived on dust all his life climbed with difficulty out of the truck's cabin in front of Higgins. His movements had the puppet precision of an arthritic for whom activity is a series of mechanical problems solved only by pain. His hair was white and bushy and stood on his head like a load of lather. A white handlebar mustache pushed his lips down and his eyes were too far into their sockets to show any color. He had on a checkered cutaway over a white shirt with a cravat which he had tried to adjust into a boast. Long gray pants doubled at the cuffs over patent leather shoes with spats. A long, red scarf was wrapped around his neck and fell down his back so that he had to lift it to get a handkerchief out of his hip pocket. He shook it out and mopped his forehead, which had not squeezed out a drop of sweat for a decade, then wiped his palms.

"Hot," he said, "it's very hot this time of year."

He folded the handkerchief into a square packet and placed it back under his tails. He shook hands with Higgins and looked Toivo over.

"Meet Colby, ringmaster and owner of COLBY'S CAMELOTE, with an "e" at the end. You're meeting a perfectionist of the old school, a rear-guard action of show business, isn't that how you put it?"

"I did."

"Colby here will take you in. Mind you don't work him too hard, he's only an amateur, you know. But he can fall. He can fall real good he says."

"That's all you need to know for an apprentice clown. To make an artist out of him would take years. I'll go get the books so you can examine them while we're here."

"No, that's all right, Colby, some other time. I'm off on some business. Just remember that Toivo here is a guest of mine and that he has to hide for a few days. No one is to know. If he suddenly tells you that he has to leave you, let him go, all right?"

"I'm used to that, Mr. Higgins."

"Well, that's it then. Give 'em hell, Colby. You better get going or your troupe will die of thirst here. A traveling show is a safe house, Toivo. Until I call you then."

"You there, sir, you will go down to the third wagon and ride with Messerschmidt. You'll get your instructions this afternoon, tonight and tomorrow morning. We have a show to put on. And make sure you stumble when you fall."

The convoy puffed on.

Colby's troupe had come to Grasmere to entertain at the festival of the Rushbearing Ceremony. A celebration from the days when floors of houses and churches were decked with straw, rushes and sweet-smelling herbs for the church aisles.

They hoisted the tent that afternoon, the entire group, cursing and groaning at the cables in a heat that just wouldn't give up. As soon as the tent was a man's height off the ground, Colby stood in its center and slugged out commands to set the pace. He had an astonishingly deep bass. That's what he was, a voice box, a ringmaster trimmed down to his essence.

The tent had rattled to its top and domed out, anchored on its thick cables, to shield the ring. Everybody sprawled on the grass panting and passing bottles of soda pop while Colby strode around the tent to check its anchorage. Some of the troupe swore out loud and vowed never to work for such a dump again. They'd hire themselves out to an outfit that could afford to rent a hall and all you had to do was put up your equipment. This was ancient, ball-busting stuff and if the man wanted a tent he could blow it up himself.

Groups of children walked in procession through the town with their arms full of flowers and flowering herbs and rushes, with the local band behind them. The copper and brass echoed off the houses and the children laughed and threw flowers at each other. It was a festival fair and after the church service there had to be plenty to do with plenty of fun.

The children in the church sang of thanks and the elders joined in. Then everybody amen'd some more and left a field carpet on the flagstones of the church aisles. Local people and tourists milled in the streets while some boys ran off to the circus to make a little money for an illegal pint by feeding the wild animals.

No one was up to showing Toivo his tricks and that evening it rained hard and the performers stayed in their trailers.

Messerschmidt was a human cannonball who was misfired one time. He shared his cabin with Dora, a kind plump female who had once been the Spider Woman rushing up and down a web of steel cables as if Newton had never been born but who, after a long illness which changed her metabolism, was grounded by chronic obesity.

Then there was Striker, an erstwhile black belt in judo who had been finished for competition by shell shock on the Normandy beaches and had sublimated his fear with the obsession of teaching a bear the sport well enough to have him qualify for a brown belt. It was an offbeat act, with the tall man in his judo gi and spasmodic muscles circling around Butterball, a black bear bought cheaply from a company that had run out of gas near Hamburg, trying to get a grip on the animal's fur for a throw. The pudgy bear waddled amiably around the cage with him, rolling his tongue in and out, and got thrown a few times. Striker couldn't understand why Butterball, who had been gelded, declawed and unteethed, never learned to get a proper grip on his gi. He dreamed of a telegram from the Imperial Judo Academy in Tokyo inviting him to train a squad of Malayan sun bears for the Olympics.

Most of the troupe consisted of castoffs from bigger and better circuses on the continent and embittered artists who had lost their touch and no longer dared fool death. But every season there would be a star attraction who had to leave the brighter lights because of some scandal and take cover in the second-rate. This season it was a high-wire artiste who had murdered her partner because he had gotten her pregnant. After a debilitating abortion she had stirred a sugar cube of LSD into his coffee before he went on and the man had fallen to his death. A perfect crime since there was no trace of foul play on or in his body. But she had thought it better to "retire" for a season and get away from an unbalancing fear of revenge. She still drank only what she made herself and ate after her toy poodle had sampled the food.

Besides the bear act, the only other animal attractions were two lions and two tigers who jumped through hoops with the aplomb of those who want to underline their boredom. They acted and looked more like crotchety retired colonels from the British Colonial army than the ferocious beasts with cavernous jaws and slashing claws they were advertised to be on the cheaply printed handbills. The lions were kin to the Metro-Goldwyn-Mayer lug. No elephants, no elaborate equestrian act, nothing to give Barnum cause for alarm.

Of necessity then, Colby had fallen back on a second line of defense, the more traditional fare of touring shows: clowns, jugglers, tumblers, knife throwers, fire-eaters and midgets. Colby's Camelote was really the clowns' show. An old-timer of sawdust and tinsel days with horse-drawn caravans and monkeys, Colby loved the waning glory of itinerant buffoons, mountebanks, cock lorels and lorettes, the artifice of those who in French are called the saltimbanques. Secretly he was happy with the pecuniosity which forced him to build his sideshow around the saltimbanques. He was good at it and he had no ambition to master the flashier acts, and hoped to be able to keep his secretive world alive until he died. Three-ring circuses he despised because they befuddled the audience with excess and degraded the performers, turning them from artists into hustling competitors.

"They've made it a stock market of art, taken the dignity away from the individual. An artist cannot develop his act with grace and attention — with *gravity,* remember, gentlemen, yours is a grave art — to allow the audience to catch on to his wit. Those bombastic baboons on the Continent and in the States of America, where I'll never hope to go, have made a television show out of it, a spectacular where more is better, where production is the secret, where your individual styles are drowned. With us you have the opportunity to develop your art at leisure and with skill. But I demand skill, gentlemen, skill. There's a grace to falling."

His standard speech before every grand opening in no matter how small a hamlet. And his charges knew he meant it, which was why they stuck with him, even those who had had the fluke of a chance to go three-ring or nightclub. Yet the more perspicacious member of the troupe realized that there was a shrewdness also in the way The Voice (as they called him behind his back) structured the show.

He knew that in the backwaters of a nation there still linger memories of traveling shows which displayed more magic than machinery. As long as you bring out the clowns and jugglers, he reasoned, you've got a show. People bring their children to the circus for the clowns, not for Lippizaner stallions mimicking a Viennese waltz. So he emphasized illusion, introduced himself as a master of mirages, left the word "circus" out of the show's title and welcomed his artless audiences to Colby's Camelote.

It was a brave show built by ingenuity from a poverty of materials which mined the secret of the clown: his caducity. So Colby hired a tightrope walker who refused to retire and masked his frailty in the suit of a white grotesque and his teetering on the wire became comic and the audience none the wiser. A knife thrower of dubious aim was helped by strong magnets hidden in the wooden target while his beautiful victim writhed horribly within the safety of the illusion of death. A strong man reduced to being merely big was taught to mimic a craving for lit torches. But before he could plunge one of them down his throat a midget would steal it from him, douse it in a bucket of water and put it back on the stand until the giant finally had only extinguished torches left and, out of despair, would drink the belatedly discovered bucket, indicating to the audience that he thought he was imbibing the fire he desired. While he drank the dwarf would run around the ring handing out foot-long lit matches to the people, bouncing with glee. And so The Voice made clowns of them all and made a living.

"O yes," Dora said to Toivo, "you've got to admit that he's good at it. It's amazing how he can dress up disaster into an act. And the ones beyond repair, he lets them stay on as hands just for room and board. The rest of us don't mind, that's all we've got when you get right down to it, and they take some of the nastier chores away from us like selling programs and peanuts and hoisting up the tent. We don't mind. We've got no other place to go. None of these characters here are fit to live a normal life and they grumble and moan but they know it and they love the old fox for squeezing the last drop of talent out of them for some bread and butter."

Toivo was looking at a lanky man with his crew-cut head bowed, staring somberly at a large ball in front of his feet. He was sitting on an upturned crate in just a pair of short pants and a singlet.

"Now Brush there," Dora said, "is a different story. He's even got The Voice stumped. But Colby likes him and keeps him around. Brush, we didn't know what else to call him, Brush is touched upstairs, if you know what I mean. Nobody knows exactly what his story is but he seems to have been an acrobat once and says he's a Gypsy. It doesn't matter. He's convinced he's a figure in a painting and not just any old painting either. He thinks he was the model for those clown paintings Picasso did."

"Really?"

"You're surprised, aren't you? Don't worry, all of us know it because the crazy fool goes around showing everybody re-productions of the paintings and asks us what else he's got to do to look more like them. He goes to libraries and steals the things from art books. The ones of harlequins with tricorn hats. I patched him up an old costume once and made a tricorn out of an old felt hat of Messerschmidt's here so he would look even more like the pictures that had harlequins. What can you do with that? Nothing. Now he's trying to make one of the few kids we have balance on that large ball in front of him. There's a picture you see . . . And, damnit, the crazy bastard is making it. More and more he looks like those people in the paintings and he's begging to convince us that he really was the model and that Picasso pulled a fast one on him and didn't share any of his glory with poor old Brush here. Brush was a pretty big guy once, but now he is down to just over a hundred pounds. He's starving himself to death trying to fit the size of those skinny harlequins by that Frenchman."

"Picasso was Spanish."

"I don't care. He could be Bulgarian for all I know. Well, Brush there, he scared the hell out of us after I had made that harlequin's costume for him. That's what I do for a living here, I am the show's seamstress and I also clown around a bit. One day we didn't get an answer from his cabin, it's really a small space in the equipment truck, and when we went in there he was lying on his bed with his hands folded like this on his stomach like a praying corpse and his face all white like the clowns paint it. And by god if there isn't a picture of a harlequin lying just like that, and if it isn't meant to be a corpse. Colby forbid him to do that again. So he sits around trying to fit himself into the pictures and asks us how he's getting along and he's mad that he can't find any women or children to help him complete the rest of the scene. Even wanted horses and monkeys next to him or walking in the distance the way they do in the pictures, you know, they always got some sort of animal with them, but Colby won't allow it, he's afraid he'd lose them. You can't blame him, can you?"

"He doesn't do anything but that? Colby surprises me more and more."

"Well, friend, Colby kinda looks on him as a mascot. True, everybody pulls his weight around here except Brush. But he's so weird with that silence of his and looking at his picture all the time that most of us don't bother him. And Brush don't bother anyone else, so why worry?"

"Tell me, Dora, when I was practicing this afternoon with Booboo — it's Booboo right and not Bobo?"

"That's right, like what a little kid says when he's hurt."

"I see. Well, Booboo and the other clowns seemed sort of depressed to me, as if they were scared of the townspeople watching them. There weren't many, mostly boys, but I could sense that they didn't like it. The clowns finally chased the kids away."

Dora looked down at her sewing. She was mending the glimmering bodice of Greta, the high-wire artiste with crime on her mind. She looked at Messerschmidt and the man shrugged his shoulders and nodded.

"Well, I don't know if I should, we don't like to talk about death. It's bad luck in our business. But all right, you're a stranger and you won't be with us for long. We had a clown, an old fellow, by the name of Emil Jung. This past June, in Liverpool, he was beaten to death by an addict with the nozzle of a firehose in a hotel room. They caught the killer. How'd the papers put it, Messerschmidt?"

"A bludgeon slaying and the killer was trying to get money from Emil because the man was out of work and needed a fix. The murderer was a junkie, see."

"Right. And on top of that, in July, kids threw rocks at Bozo. Got to have a Bozo, right. In a thing we do at real small-town fairs. Bozo sits on a wooden face of a clown over a tub of water. The wooden face has hinges and can be knocked from under him with soft balls, and then he falls in the drink and it's big laughs. People always used to aim at the target and never at the clown himself, but that time some boys aimed at Bozo and not only that, they used rocks wrapped in white socks. They hit him in the head and he was in the hospital with a concussion. The clowns are angry and scared. It never used to happen and Colby is down in the ears because he thinks that our time is up. That's what he told us. Said that people have no respect for clowns and performers anymore because of the telly and all the violence and that when people hurt or kill clowns we might as well write the end to civilization. That's what he said, didn't he, Messerschmidt?"

Messerschmidt nodded and said: "The old guy talks too much. He's always in the ring. 'Course he's right, you know. It sure as hell isn't like the old days when a horse girl could marry a millionaire."

"Ah, Schmidt, you're crazy. That never happened. But all the same we can't go around armed, now can we? You better watch it, friend, or Colby will make you the bodyguard for the clowns. Don't look so dumb. Schmidt and I saw that gun you've got. But we won't tell anybody. If you're a friend of Mr. Higgins' you're all right. That man now, he loves circuses. Owns a piece of us. Crazy guy doing that. Of course millionaires are always peculiar, aren't they, Messerschmidt?"

The Voice entered the ring in a shower of light. The six-piece band, all brass and drums, struck up a disjointed march and the people applauded perfunctorily. Colby cracked his long whip and slowly looked around the tiers of people and the arena sputtered into silence. When it was quiet the tall figure in a cutaway lifted his hat, swept the sawdust with it and with slow motion placed it back on his head. Then his voice filled the space and Toivo understood Colby's nickname. Costumed sound stood disembodied in the light almost as if it were coming from its center, while other spots strummed the audience and kept their eyes from focusing as the show was introduced.

As soon as Colby was through the band struck up again and the clowns, pierrots, augustes and midgets filled the ring. Toivo flatfooted it among them, his large soles flapping, his baggy pants held up by enormous suspenders over a loud checkered shirt. Bozo had painted arrows on his whiteface, drawing the left kohled eye down and the right one up, and had attached a red nose as large as a light bulb and drawn gigantic lips and an arrow pointing down to his chin. It gave him a mathematical face which was offset by the empty ice bag on his wig. All he had to do was to be one in a crowd, fall, stumble, get kicked in the pants. When his timing was off the other clowns skillfully covered up for him or the midgets would stand there, slap their thighs and roar laughter without sound while they pointed at him.

In performance it became even clearer how much the show belonged to the saltimbanques and that the other acts were skillfully inserted, to recapture the attention of the easily bored customers. Colby also alternated loud and bustling acts with tension, silence and fear. And there was an even subtler interchange between similar-looking acts. A clown would lumber up to a tightrope six feet off the ground and demonstrate his sorry equilibristic skill. Always falling, teetering, tottering, losing garments and retrieving them just in time, mimicking fear, making his arrival at the other end a feat of will over skill, while the midgets and clowns applauded and mocked him from below like an audience within an audience. Shortly thereafter the wire would be stretched twice that height and the true tightrope walker would come out and perform his art with an ease and smoothness which, in contrast to the sustained incoherence of the clown's attempts, made it look easier, if not easy. His arrival at the end of the rope was predestined and plausible while the caricature had made triumphant achievement out of faltering dilettantism. So too midgets aped lions and tried to swallow clowns three times their size, and when the animal trainer gingerly thrust his head into the lion's maw the audience remembered the clown's exaggerated pantomime.

Greta redeemed her paranoid aloofness in her act. A pretty female of normal size she stepped into the limelight clad in the glittering bodice Dora had repaired. It fitted her appealing curves tightly, accentuating the sensuality of her body, creating a dream of nudity. Her hair was long and blond and fell free down her back. Barefoot, curtsying and smiling prettily, she was all feminine charm and seduction. But as soon as she grabbed the rope and coiled up to the swaying platform, the spotlight following her and limning the ripple and swell of muscle, she was male.

Her unorthodox act combined the high wire, the trapeze and acrobatic contortions suspended by hair or teeth high above the piste. She worked without drum rolls and without a net. Up there near the nook of the tent her grace and agility became as sharp as the edge of a knife and her flesh dematerialized, her body mocked the gravity-bound hunks below straining to gape, she apostrophized herself into a symbol of implausible movement. The light made the wire disappear and the acropedestrian strolled in the air with the elegant step of a dancer, doing a headstand or wheeling around an invisible hub for no apparent reason except perhaps sheer exuberance. Then she'd shoot herself from trapeze to trapeze like a shimmering explosion as if to show that there was no necessity in walking the invisible wire. She'd perform arabesques around the suspended bar as if cutting lit stencils in the dark — a telautograph of pure motion. It was both a relief and a brutish descent into reality when she fastened the gear under her hair and hurled herself down, stopped at the last moment by her head, which should have come off but remained faithful to her body which she then telescoped in and out, seemingly oblivious to common pain. But this was a bodily feat and therefore reassuring after the inhuman art up above. That was no female body whirling there, nor was it male in its smooth sinuosity. When Greta slashed down the rope to the ground again she was, despite the evidence of her body and smile and pretty curtsy, beyond the sexes. They had been abstracted into a shape sinister in its transgression of normality in the miraculous passage from the human to the divine. Toivo could hardly believe the sweat on her skin.

The clowns came in again and Greta seemed to have charged their license to fool. Jugglers, a dog act, balancers and tumblers. Then again silence and an empty ring.

Booboo came out. His face was painted a somber mask above unwieldy clothes and under a bowler several sizes too small. He carried a dustpan and a broom and in the semidarkness he solemnly pursued a circle of light around the ring, determined to sweep it into the pan. Nothing could stop him, not the silent laughter of his confreres, not when the disc was on a face (he'd sweep it), on an animal (he'd sweep it), on a prop (he'd sweep it), on himself (he'd sweep it), under his shoes (he'd sweep it). Nothing could distract him and when the audience laughed he would look up at them with his sad face and silently ask them why they were laughing at a task which had to be fulfilled even though night after night he failed. Climbed up the ladder to sweep after the circle, sweep along the tightrope, sweep in the air thrown from body to body by acrobats, sweep after the circle while he was hoisted up to the trapeze platform. And at the end this beggar kin of Odysseus tramped after the spot of light for the last time all the way around and then out of the ring, down the exits, behind the curtains, out of the tent, the town, around the countryside, down alleys and avenues, up and down hotels and through apartment houses, in trolleys and buses, airplanes and submarines, always surprised that people reacted with mirth to his eternal search and always saddened that they did not understand his sweeping.

23

"WHERE HAVE YOU BEEN all your life? You don't believe such things are still going on? Sure, a lot is done with machines: computers, special telephones, data banks and the lot. But you can't control everything that way, you know. There are human angles to this business, you just can't lick by pushing buttons. Like death, for example. Get the point? God, some of you people. You think that everything is done with credit cards these days."

Higgins leaned out of his chair and dragged his fingers through the air, trying to draw the bartender's attention. But the pub, Ye Olde Lyon Rampant, was full of afterwork drinkers and the publican had his hands full. Toivo got up and went to the bar. He ordered another double Scotch on the rocks for himself and another "snowball," a repulsive mixture of bourbon and lemonade, for Higgins. Toivo wondered how Higgins managed to keep them down. The small, dimpled Tudor panes — part of the pub's remodeling to cash in on the lucrative nostalgia fad — concaved drops of rain. With dusk coming on, the wet streets would soon join the sky and London in its natural gray.

"I'm sorry, pal, it's just that when I see people fall into the trap the agencies want you to fall into I get a little mad. More and more is being done by pushing paper around. But all the satellites in the world can't solve the problem of how to eliminate somebody."

"I have killed at least five men, you say?"

Toivo had just wandered into what he thought to be a pub only to find the last act of a play where the players accuse him of being all wrong. Then, just when he had convinced himself it was a play, they turned on him with all too real a malice and all too lethal a violence and it was no longer a play but a scene of life with elements of both dream and play and frighteningly real.

"That's what's doing the rounds among the opposition. As I told you at Snarker, I was right by the way, you were used as a scapegoat, but I'll say as a peculiar one, you were released into the field when they, your friends, had one of the enemy cornered. Your side, let's say that to keep things clearer, played up that scientist in Amsterdam to be of importance. The opposition fell for it and staked him out. You come into the picture, spend a lot of time with the man and one of the opposition tells his people you are getting that man to come back to the States. Now the scientist had accepted money from the opposition, had met one of their top dogs, but all without his knowledge: he thought he had been favored by an obscure foundation. So when the opposition thought you were dragging him back to the States they were steaming as hot as piss in winter. Get me another one of these snowjobs, will you. A great combination."

"I just can't believe that de Bruce was collaborating with them," Toivo said after he had brought a fresh round. "He simply couldn't care."

"Perhaps that's why he used their money, just for kicks. How the hell do I know. Anyway, your side killed the scientist so suspicion would fall on you, but they put the lid on the police. Then the game was on."

"It's almost funny."

"Because it worked, my friend. If it hadn't you'd be very dead by now. It worked as a plan and I must say it's damned clever. It worked because of the men behind you, your shadows I guess I'd call them, and there must be more than one because one operative can't have held on to you for this long over such long distances, and those shadows behind you were very damned good. That's why it's almost funny."

"They had it all figured out."

"Of course they had. This sort of deception you don't do at the spur of the moment. Once you know it it's perfectly simple, but I wonder who dreamed it up."

"I've got an idea."

"You walked out into the light, in full view, as your side's brand-new dealer in executive action. They'd never seen you before so it was plausible. Proof number one was your supposed killing of the scientist. You also had the most perfect cover: famous author abroad on a lecture tour sponsored by the U.S. Information Agency. Always with crowds and in the news so it was difficult for the other side to get you alone. That way they had to prepare more carefully to stage your killing and this in turn gave your shadows time to pick off the opposition."

"But why not one of their own men, a specialist, an expert? Why me?"

"The complete reason I'll never know, but one thing is that there's nothing like an innocent abroad who's manipulated without his knowledge, by remote control, let's say. Dilettantes can be very useful."

"So it was all to get rid of some assassins?"

"That's right. And if you don't think they still exist let me remind you that, for example, the GRU still trains terrorists and assassins in its Fifth Directorate. Anyway, I am leaving. I have been in touch with Lazard and asked him to be of service to you. I gave him some money. Now if you're smart and give him some more without letting on that you know I paid him he'll be even more cooperative. He's my last trump card, the last station of the line. If he can't satisfy you the only other thing to do is join the Service itself and sabotage."

Higgins smiled and bottomed his glass.

"Look, you've got to act for yourself at a certain point. Maybe you're lucky and the operation is over and you can go home and write a book about it. I know how you feel. Kinda like a ball being bounced around on a basketball court. It's up to you whether you'd care to make the ball have a set of teeth and bite back or roll off the court and let it be. Lazard might have more. Don't thank me, it's quite all right. Keep the Smith and Wesson. It might be handy or it might already be a souvenir. I'm going to leave now and you won't see me again. All good controllers try to keep contact down to a minimum and longevity is not part of that relationship. It's raining. Good. Fewer people about. Make sure you're not tailed. Have fun with Lazard. He's an educated man and don't let his attitudes and the way he lives fool you. He knows what's what. Goodby then."

Higgins shook hands and left.

Toivo didn't have a raincoat, so when he picked up his suitcase by the coatrack he stole one, put it on and walked out of the pub. The rain was steady and soon his hair was soaked.

It seemed that his tour had also been part of the plan. Boxed in there too. Maybe they'd let him choose the ribbon at least. The pistol was butting into his stomach and he had to shift it. If only with one shot he could get his adversary and that would be the end of it. One of his worst fears had always been premeditated harm. When Toivo realized he was getting scared he tried to draw the rain closer around him. Hide in a meteorological blind and watch the game go by.

He had taken two buses at random and then a number of taxis to arbitrary stops. Because of the rain most cabs were occupied and it took him a long time to get to Bond Street, where Lazard lived. The houses were dirty and covered with a soot that came off on your hands. The banister of the staircase was slick from lack of cleaning and the runner had long given up trying to impress anyone.

Toivo's knock was answered by a tall man who looked and smelled of sour dissipation. His filthy apartment only made that dissipation ostentatious, while the man wore profligacy lightly, mockingly aware of the impression he made, as used to it as to his skin, used to the reaction he always elicited and amused by it.

His leprechaun ears were very prominent under the shortish brown hair. The face was full and, like the rest of his flesh, taut and shiny. A rather sharp nose peaked over his pursed mouth as if he would mince words, which he didn't; his voice was surprisingly deep and warm. His heavy eyebrows hung like thick circumflexes over lime green intelligent eyes which were never dull, always ridiculing what went on around him. He had not shaved for quite some time and his face was oily, with traces of powder in the pores. His open-necked shirt was grimy at the collar and his pants could have made an honorable attempt at standing up bodiless.

"Sorry everything is such a mess. Can't stand to clean nor can

I endure a bustling woman around me. But do come in and sit down. You are a most impassive man, but even impassivity must rest. Have a drink." Toivo would have liked to clean the glass first but he figured alcohol kills germs, though these were probably of the Herculean variety.

"Well, well, so this is what a rich and famous American author looks like. I could quote you some lines from the Tragedians on fame but I won't because it might undermine your education. I was once the best Greek scholar at Oxford, so adept that I could hold a conversation in it on any topic you please. Hasn't been of much use except to impress old classmates and editors. I am a bit of a writer myself, a journalist of sorts. I regale readers with notes from the authentic London underground, the true steaming brew of debauchery and venery. It takes. Cock-cheese and mental butter keeps a smelly stew simmering that people pull their noses at but can't resist devouring. Of sorts, I said, I am as much a sorts writer as anything else I do. But I am good at the sorts bit, if it pays. I like money, boys and excitement — not necessarily in that order. You'll take Scotch, won't you? That's good, I have nothing else."

No matter what was brought up in the course of the evening Lazard spoke of it with disdain and intrepid scorn. It had made him a reputation of being utterly without morals, scruples or manners, though this did not prevent him from being as charming as a courtier and without conceit when his private code commanded it. Lazard drank fast and in great quantities and was soon drunk. It did not seem to impair his diction or his thinking. It only sharpened his appetite, which he satisfied with whatever came to his mind and happened to be around the apartment.

"Anyway," Lazard said, "let's also enumerate the positive aspects of your position. Maybe we can cheer you up a bit. Feel sorry for yourself? Well, that can't be helped, though a man with all the money you must have shouldn't be so morose."

"I'll pay you, if you can help me."

"I can see Higgins told you about me and you think of course that all I want is money. Which is very true of course. Let's say I won't promise anything but I'll accept a retainer of, well now, let's see, I am in need of about three hundred dollars right now. I have come to believe that money is the only thing that doesn't smell."

Toivo signed over three hundred dollars worth of traveler's checks.

"Some good opium has come in from Indochina. I was getting fed up with tincture, not strong enough, but I didn't have the money to buy any of this shipment of my favorite stoker. Of course they don't stoke coke anymore these days on ships, which is a pity, it appeals to my imagination to have shiny wet men laboring down there in the bowels of the ship and forgetting their misery with bamboo pipes on their narrow cots. Ah, the days of the lascars with real suffering that could kill you and you could nurse. Nowadays it's all so maudlin. It's difficult to be a devil these days. No, they don't stoke coke anymore . . . With the money you have so generously entrusted to me I can get myself a headful of snow and have some to spare for trade on the meat market. The nice little lambs they have these days, succulent, with blond wool on top and on their flat little bellies, the dears.

"Sorry about that. I said positive. *Bon.* Given the nature of the game, you are now several steps ahead of them. They don't know where you are which gives you the useful element of surprise. I believe in surprise, very much so, and in audacity. It'll get you a lot and into almost any salon you feel like crashing. Did I tell you how I wrecked the party of the Countess of . . . well, let that be. You're out of their control for the moment. Debugged as it were and loose. That must worry them. No more lectures so that they have no definite time plan to go by and, since you're an amateur, they don't know how to predict your movements. That's good. You see now what I mean by positive? Now, you see, you can sniff them out and be on the receiving end for a change. Also you're armed and Higgins tells me you're pretty good. Which is fine: when in doubt it gives a man courage to hold on to a gun. I don't use them myself, only for passionate emergencies."

"Who do you work for?"

Lazard was silent for a moment and peered over his glass at his visitor.

"Anyone. By keeping it that way everyone employs me for the dirty stuff on everybody else. And dirt gets you a hell of a lot more than going through channels. Don't be bothered by those voices. I've got whores all around in this building and other, even more indecorous neighbors. It helps me stay anonymous in terms of my movements and visitors. I never did understand people who keep secrecy behind propriety. It's so easily shot full of holes, so very much more vulnerable."

Toivo said relatively little all evening but the man seemed to guess his unvoiced questions.

"Your shadows are three. No one can tell me if they're regular agents, but they certainly work for your side, chum. They're the best, that must be obvious, even to you. The objective of this operation in which you are kingpin, so to speak, was to eliminate a squad of the opposition's very best assassins. Reason: they couldn't be caught. Too good. And their bagging was formidable. Our side, god bless it, was never able to keep anyone it turned."

"Yes. Higgins said to ask you about that. I still find it hard to believe that sort of thing goes on anymore."

"Intelligence is a farcical comedy. But we have to keep it nasty or no one will believe it anymore. There are still men who decide what is important and what is not. And when someone gets too hot according to their rules then that person has to be silenced. Now, you can go and tell him, ask him to keep his mouth shut, buy him off or kill him. The last possibility is obviously the most germane and the most conclusive. We know Moscow, for one, will eliminate agents who aren't needed anymore, or who are turning or if they know too much about something than is good for them. Our Slavic friends are still somewhat Byzantine."

"The Fifth Directorate?"

"Oh, yes, it exists. They most assuredly do train saboteurs and terrorists, and assassinations do occur, take my word for it. Think of it this way. There are the most unsettling statistics showing that every country has a large percentage of unsolved murders. A number of these are people you never will hear about, insignificant little creatures like cracks in the sidewalk: you step on them, they squeak a bit. How many of them were rubbed out, as I believe you Americans put it, for intelligence purposes? A term, by the way, which has little to do with that capacity which makes us the paragon of animals. Your friends have been bothered for over a year now by gaps and holes in their networks. No one stayed alive long enough to give information. Without information the intelligence service is dead; just imagine if there were no secrecy in the world anymore. See, the poor slobs would have to start inventing some. And no information, well, my boy, what do you propose you could shore up their budgets with? No, no doubt about it, those nasty little fellows had to be put out of commission. They can't be bought very easily, besides, who wants them. They don't *know* very much you see, they just *do* a lot. You know what they did, you know who controls them, but you don't know when they will strike again. You eliminate eliminators by eliminating them. Rule number two: you don't use your own best men. They're the best and you'd like to keep them that way for as long as possible. You don't waste them on something nasty where they're liable to get killed, so you use a decoy, like you, for instance, let him run and hope you'll be able to pick off the game when it gets close."

"You mean that I am less important to our side, as you put it, than one of their own men?"

"Precisely."

Toivo went to the bathroom.

The apartment was unbelievably filthy. Nothing, absolutely not one thing was clean. Cigarette burns were on everything from tables to lampshades. Dust or grease covered most things and the furniture was loaded down with clothes, odds and ends, magazines, newspapers, dirty dishes and blankets and sheets on the sofa where Lazard had slept. On a console stood a birdcage whose bottom was lined with pages torn from an edition of Milton. Lazard maintained that this gave the canary a grave delivery.

The bathroom looked like a public convenience. The tap of the sink had to be turned with a pair of pliers, if you could find them, and the plug had been gouged out of a rubber doll. The plug for the bath was part of an undershirt wrapped around a golf ball. The mirror was covered with messages and telephone numbers scrawled in anything that will stick to a surface. As Toivo was zipping himself up Lazard appeared in the doorway with a confidential air.

"I must do something about this place, wouldn't you say? By the way, I can get you descriptions of those three men behind you, if you want. For a little, just a little extra. Now what more do you want to know? I have a date."

"Who set this whole thing up?"

"Wowee, that's a tall order. American vernacular is all right. But I bet you can figure that one out better than I could. If anybody ever can. Once you know all I've told you it's so absurdly simple. Someone who knew how to use your natural cover, which, by the way, will be blown for you: they'll simply tell the losers in this game that you really are a famous writer on a tour and they'll realize they've been taken for a ride. There's satisfaction in that. To find out who set this all up you've got to remember that a good case officer must know how each agent he controls thinks and lives. This job was set up by a patient and very cool man who has knowledge not only of our present disease, organization, but also of the blood and guts stuff from the war. You see, if there were no slips in the intelligence machinery the world would be ruled by a nameless, faceless, very efficient bureaucracy devoted to snooping. But there are always leaks, there's human failure, there is sordidness and sex. And the bigger the organization the more absurd things happen. Like those children here in London who found eighty pages of confidential defense telephone numbers. And that wasn't the first time either. In nineteen sixty-seven the *Saturday Evening Post* published the address of MI-5 and the telephone number of MI-6. It's good such things happen, I always make sure that they do from time to time. Without them we'd be lost. Your country is already relying more and more on machines, but they're neutral and have only mechanical faults. You can't write a memo saying 'Bang, you're dead' and expect it to work. An old hand at wet stuff, as the Ruskies say, set this thing up."

"And he would know why I was chosen and for how long this has been going on?"

"Right."

"I am tired. Have any suggestions where I could sleep?"

"Right upstairs, old boy. I took the liberty of leasing the place for a few days from the tenant who's off to Scotland peddling body paint. Now if I were you I would get myself a woman, but since I am not I am going to bait myself a boy. Didn't you say that they told you you could use the facilities of the embassies? Well, audacity, my friend. Simply walk in and use one of their hush-hush spermariums, as I call them. I'm told they are fancy brothels staffed by professionals on the government's payroll. They are used by officials who might have urges to go to the wrong swallows."

"Swallows?"

"Birdies, my friend. Girls. Snatch. What would you call them. All American embassies across the world have these wonderful little subbasements so they can reduce the risk of their official and not so official personnel being blackmailed. Efficient, of course, as usual. Very secret too. Hell, if I were you I'd use them. They owe you as much. They'll choke on their fat cigars when you simply walk in and demand to have a go at the relief station. That's what they're called for bookkeeping. You do what you must and walk out again. It'll kill them. And while you're at it you might as well demand a telephone conversation with the chief of the Company in Langley, Virginia, and you know what, they just might put you through. Of course he has nothing to do with this. Anyway, the flat upstairs has a phone and here is the number. When you leave, that number doesn't exist anymore. I don't mind this a bit, I've been involved in sillier things. Besides, I'm in England, the Yanks can't touch me. You tell me in the next twenty-four hours what you're up to. You've been most generous and I'll try to reciprocate. *Ciao* now. Have a good fuck."

24

TOIVO HAD BLUSTERED his way into the embassy and while rules and regulations were blabbered by secretaries and other underlings close to cardiac arrest, Toivo stolidly insisted on using the relief station, on seeing the ambassador and on placing a call to Donner in Washington.

Any moment he expected the marines to storm in and drag him away from the horrified clerks. But the absence of force only emphasized his conviction he was right. It was a matter of sticking it out. Any piece of unpliable substance in a machine will finally grind it to a halt or be demolished. Toivo figured he was finally grinding them to a stalemate.

"Very well, you win. You are right in that you have the same privileges as any other official who's cleared for Tech Six."

"What?"

"That's the code name for the subbasement."

"The relief station, you mean?"

"If you care to call it that."

"And my phone call?"

"We've had to wake the ambassador for that. He was extremely annoyed."

"So am I. I'm annoyed that he was annoyed at having to do his job."

"We are working on the call. We have no idea really if Mr. Donner will consent to . . ."

"He will. Just tell him I think he's a killer and a liar and a coward and that I will report this whole business to the press."

In half an hour they had issued him his card which gave him

entrance to the subbasement. It was an American Express card of perfect likeness except that two digits had been added to the normal cipher. It was checked against a ledger by an attendant, put under an ink roller, and Toivo had to sign an authorization slip with his name and address and number inked on it, just like buying gas on credit. Then the leather-padded door sighed closed behind him and he was in a windowless, air-conditioned room, narrow and low-ceilinged like a submarine. There was a small bar, a coffee table, some chairs and obtrusive indirect lighting. There were two doors across from him in the far wall. One went to a bathroom and the other to a dressing room. A woman closed the latter behind her, came up to him and said her name was Ludia.

A diaphanous cloud of watered silk bore her forward barely touching the carpet, wafted on by the tender breath of a mighty god. Specks of gold showered with motionless movement toward her lap in a never-ending stream like particles of dust in a beam of light. Unshod, her feet rose with grace into ankles as sparse as her wrists. Clear lacquer mirrored all her nails — tiny shields casting her liquid reflection twenty-fold. She had the kind of legs sheer stockings were invented for, through she wore none. Her convexo-concave thighs met her torso at the triangle capped by a frizzle so blond it must have been spun from flesh. The pelvis was a reverent rhomboid with a curve of such bare suggestion it must have been thought. The living plane modulated about the navel with astonished omphaloskepsis. For, gazing up to the unaided orbs crowning their curve in aureoles of golden brown pinched into sweet pink buttons, what else could her body do but ponder the normal necessity of parturition and call her navel a still point of peace? Her torso curved like a fluted vase, or did its perfection adorn space into forming grace? No contour here but a tremor of outline never settled to affirm. The arms coiled like the necks of swans, anchored to the shoulders in round arches bending tenderly over the hollows where no hair shadowed, another simple progression of pumiced marble planes. Sloped up into the fragile column with faintly beating vascular trees delicate as fans supporting an artfully untouched face. A face all liquid blue eyes, which made the other features surprises, caped by honeyed gold.

An emerald necklace divided head from torso, the stones glowed with an energy so delicate it could only be fueled by her flesh. And when she smiled she showed faultless teeth as bright as pips in oranges, as if her tongue dropped pearls from that evergreen fruit. Gods had brushed her into the air as fragile as a water color. Gods had fashioned her for their own delight in beauty and no one had ever thought to brain her. It would have been a blemish. Nor could she bear issue since such tooled quintessence can only worship of itself. Eros is Venus' abstraction, not her flesh, nor can we bear to hear her philosophize. She was terminal like death. She had been recruited in Topeka, Kansas.

Ludia mixed a drink for Toivo at the bar, swaying with the canned music, and told her charge about her profession. Love for her was not committed by chance but with the smooth assurance of practice based on objective data. Like her sisters, she had been tooled in laboratories of sex where all response and solicitation had been geared to further objective knowledge of coital pleasure. It had been a training rigorously and scrupulously scientific in eliciting the maximum in application from the male subjects, thereby increasing mutual pleasure. If anything, she intoned, she was a technical assistant.

"That's fine," muttered the ailing Toivo, crumbling under the weight of her perfection, "that's most becoming, but can you fuck?"

Ludia expressed shock and begged him not to use such language in her presence. Crude elixirs like that were not necessary here to induce tumescence. She represented labor for the public good and such a level of service could only be reached through intimate knowledge of the mechanism of love. It had the delicate precision of clockwork and if one erased outmoded prejudices and phallacies one could attain maximum efficiency in somatic pleasure. While she thus recited Ludia helped Toivo remove his clothes, put them on hangers and accompanied him to the broad couch which was covered with a soft synthetic fiber that could be removed and dry-cleaned. Ludia got down to business.

All through the four phases of love she told him softly in her voluptuously trained lisp what procedures were to be followed whenever Toivo showed precipitous lapses of instinct. While applying manual stimulation to his extragenital zones she directed his attention to her target organs to achieve a mutual initiation into the excitement phase. Psychogenic stimulation had been provided by the environment in the station so that all attention could be concentrated on somatogenic inducements to orgasmic fulfillment. Since the physiology of the sexual response is remarkably similar in the two sexes she knew what the cycle would demonstrate in him as well as in her.

The first indication of satisfactory manipulation was the erection of the nipples, although their tumescence in the male was less remarkable than in the female where it achieved an erective response of nearly 1.0 cm. Nor has the male the increased definition of the venous pattern of the breasts which, in the female, also increased in size due to vasocongestive reaction. Beginning late in the excitement phase and progressing increasingly throughout the four phases the sex flush spread over both bodies, originating over the epigastrium and extending to the anterior chest wall, gradually involving the lower abdomen, thighs and arms, unto the buttocks. Both were achieving tachycardia and their systolic and diastolic rates elevated. Corresponding to the male's penile erection the female underwent vaginal lubrication and the same vasocongestive reaction caused the scrotum to thicken and resulted in testicular elevation while in the nulliparous female the major labia elevated and the minor labia increased twice in size.

In the plateau phase the maculopapular rash became markedly more defined and the supine female adopted a patulous position. Her nipple erection was almost swallowed by areolar engorgement and with her superior manipulative techniques she evinced carpopedal spasms in both participants. The female's vaginal outlet had distended and removed the normal anatomical protection. A vaginal barrel was formed and extended to accommodate the penis. Both secreted a mucoid material from, respectively, the male Cowper's glands and the female Battholin's gland. The rising preorgasmic tension level evidenced mild discoloration of the male's penile corona but pronounced a clear reddening of the female's minor labia.

Proceeding into the orgasmic phase the female entrusted the fully engorged penile shaft to the vaginal barrel, which was now fully extended to accommodate intromission. Penile containment and thrusting provided the stimuli which increased the orgasmic response in both participants. With the increasing coital activity of the male the female's vagina began to contract with increasingly shortened intervals up to ten contractions. Since she was not desirous of conception she reached for the orgasmic experience, though this considerably lessened the chance for the seminal pool to attain contact with the cervical os. Before the onset of the ejaculatory process the male was momentarily hampered by a psychosensory haitus when it came to him that he might ejaculate dust and he saw the image of a senile phoenix rise. But instinctual response answered to the procioceptive and exteroceptive stimulus of the receptor organs. Tachycardic rates reached orgasmic intensity, the elevation of blood pressure peaked and myotonia became involuntary, occasionally developing into spasms. Expulsive contractions had started in the male and were now irrevocable, and the expulsive force reached a level of propulsion sufficient to deposit the ejaculate almost ten inches within the vaginal barrel.

After the female had experienced her longer orgasmic plateau the resolution phase set in for both with rapid decrease of vasocongestion, detumescence, return to normal coloration, disappearance of the maculopapular rash in reverse order, return to normal heart rate and blood pressure and normalization of breathing. Both experienced their relative propensities for perspiratory reaction and gradually lapsed into postcoital weariness.

The canned music returned to Toivo's ears and the indirect lighting was kindly mute. Ludia offered him a cigarette and they smoked in silence. She didn't billow as much when she shrouded herself in the sheer fabric again since sweat held it down to her body. Nor were her steps as elevated as before and her body printed her feet in the wall-to-wall carpet on her way to the toilet. Toivo did not hear her flush. That accommodation was probably soundproofed, he figured, to increase discretion. He left before Ludia could ask him to participate in the customary debriefing session.

He scowled his way past the skeleton night staff and wearily set about losing all potential tails. He was depressed and angry. The spermarium had failed to relieve him.

Only Lazard could have left the sort of note on the door of the apartment where Toivo was to sleep. It said: "Re: T.S. B.D. most definitely implicated. Have located Π, M and ϵ. How's applied venery these days?"

Toivo tore the note up and flushed it down the toilet. The phone was on the floor in the living room. He had told the embassy people the number Lazard had given him, and they had assured him that the Washington call would come directly there. He sat down in front of the phone and while he was waiting he cleaned and loaded the revolver, loaded it with the double-crossed lead bullets Higgins had given him.

25

THE VOICE rustled over the thousands of miles, crackled and snapped with the interference, yet always managed to get its prints in his ear. Occasional asides from other voices about business, travel or about pain. Incomprehensible operators apologized for the connection every so often, adding to the atmosphere of a Babylonian conference in an aquarium.

— true son, I used you — I thought you wouldn't — give you staples for fiction — render — look — am an old man with final caper to top — career — no one knew how to handle them — I had the war mentality and could cut — bureaucracy — safe at all times — risks — calculated — had some of my best men after you like guardian angels — where are you — damnit — operator — in London — of course — no not a liar or coward — all carefully planned a beautiful operation — damned operator — no I didn't mean you — other — okay — well where was I — no need to get mad I gave you a fiction to work on — believe me no more than that because no one would believe it to be true — way before that I had planned it — you — one perfect — itinerant genius — limelight — unknown — not one of us — and then a sudden killer — perfect —

Nightoil pouring from the larynx as metallic as his smooth fat. Could talk bullets back into the chamber. Should be tested.

— maybe this will go a little better for a while — okay here we are again — your father loused up an organization because of his

pigheadedness you also got enough of that — I grant you his
work made me in a sense and I wasn't about to let him destroy
my chances — I looked ahead beyond the war and a firmly
established pipeline — keep this line open operator this is official
business — official yes — Washington — government — fine — I
disliked him for his refusal to fit to join in always on his own no
matter how many carefully created networks he might be destroying — that's dangerous in my line of business — still there?
— you too are a son of — look I am used to hysteria — not — if
you like — irked me obstructed me angered me — almost ruined
my prospects — had to be taken care of — no — you said that — I
— if you like — you seem to have been talking to ghosts —
sensed that — all the time — time — yes all — hate — years — I
brought you up and gave you everything — wouldn't forget how
son — father — anyway I don't waste men my own perfectly
good men on such a business — I finish things clean and orderly
and shaped to perfection including my career — no one will stop
me from that — would you prevent a retiring man from
compiling a catalogue of rove beetles — Staphylinidae — I'll tell
you — common — almost 3000 species — everywhere — flowers
and carrion — about to sting — don't — bite easily — predators
on kind — it's work — right — no — life —

He had been catalogued as if he were part of Donner's hobby.

— rich — what? — good — yes right I'm an entomologist you're
an etymologist — look a good operator knows his agents as if
they were kin I knew you better than anyone else and I put you
in a position of use — USE — I created you and don't you forget it
— I gave reality to your talent — surprise you? — not —
understand — hold on let's get this clearer so you — what I did
for you okay hold it — twisted the arm of that vice president at
Pembroke — my needs — nothing would have happened with
your writing if I hadn't forced it — I had some political dirt on
him and forced him to make you — advertising that's what —
what else makes an artist if he has the talent you could have gone
unnoticed for the rest of your life — it worked — his massive
campaign of advertising finally brought you to the attention of
the public and you were finally recognized — perfect cover for

194

the main piece of my operation — what? — WHAT? — if you like
— okay I'll say it louder — UTILITARIAN — I don't care how —
yes your success was programmed if you like — course intrinsic
value — but — why shouldn't art be utilitarian — common good
— you're not? — well that's too bad — like father like — don't go
romantic on me — hard tough world — without my meddling
you'd still — and ever — precisely — if that's the heart the core
of you I have only made it come to light — deserved — course I
do — nonsense — to live not kill — you're crazy — done more
often than you think — he's happy — president of Pembroke
now — you brought him luck — never talk — success can be very
discreet — nor me either you crazy man —

Metal stroking metal strikes a spark.

— like now I'll always be at a large distance from you — can
never touch me and you know it — be realistic — care to dig at
yourself — not — father nor you really — set it up before your
success of course — am responsible for that and it was programmed yes from my point — not bad swap — fame for a little
tension and several books from this — she? no she did it for the
money and never from whom or why — beggar mine — had to
make sure you wouldn't smell anything — vice presidents are
sometimes troubled but believe me presidents never are — no
reason to take it like that — I have been honest with you it
doesn't harm me nor has this harmed you — I have tried to make
good to you what I might have MIGHT have mind you done
wrong to your father — I have steered you in a full and rich life
while having made a little profit out of it for myself — that's not
so — occurred to me — you must take chances — calculated —
but few — those three are special — unusual but perfectly
adapted to their job — why I chose — sure always are expend-
able — dangerous professionals that's why — from your reaction
I can tell you're no match for them — you think too much — in a
sense you're right — if you say so — what's that — well — bye —
don't think — never — always — out — accept — happy —

Click! Dry drone in the plastic ear. Electric whir. Toivo cocked the hammer all the way back and pulled the trigger. The five cartridges from the cylinder tore through the instrument and through the nearby chair, spitting fragments all over the room. As he ejected the shells debris settled down slowly on the floor. Cordite fumes swirled lazily over the wreckage and the noise only gradually allowed his ears to register the persistent ringing of the telephone. He gathered it up and had to put the revolver down to listen properly. There was much static on the line. Then a voice came through over a long distance.

"Donner here. Toivo? Good. Well. You said you wanted to talk to me?"

III

26

THE TRAVELING CLOCK set off its alarm, recharged itself, and the little jackhammer went to work on sleep once more. Slowly the sound insisted that the mind answer its call and life crept into several sections of the body. The sleeper struggled against the covers, shoved his torso up against the headboard and had begun to get his legs over the edge of the bed when the alarm clock began its automatic excavation job for the third time. The man fumbled for the switch and silenced the little machine. Then he motioned through the room like someone trying to recall the rationale for habitual automatism.

Drawing the curtains did not help much because the morning was as gray as the shadows in the room and he had to switch the light on in order to see. He was a large man with a penile head and the room was really too small for a frame of his size to fumble around in. So he bumped into things and left a trail of dislodged objects behind him while he aimlessly moved around the apartment, uncertain what his actions should be.

He lit a cigarette while an electric coil heated water in a cup and the taste of burning tobacco helped him clear his head with its foulness. He scratched his jaw and looked out the window over a steady sea of rooftops. He mixed some instant coffee in the furious water and drank it. The phone rang. He slouched toward it and grunted into the mouthpiece. He grunted several more times in agreement and then grunted some doubt about whether he would agree to meet with his caller. He gave a number and said to reach him there later on. He slammed the receiver down, swore when it hurt his knuckles and went to the bathroom down the hall.

Back in his room he dressed, except for his jacket, and mixed himself another cup of artificial coffee. There was doubt on his face when he checked the mechanism of the pistol that had been under his pillow. He could not carry it in his waistband or back pocket because it would have made telling bulge. He strapped a shoulder holster under his left arm and placed the automatic gently behind the spring. Then he put on his jacket and his overcoat. There was puzzlement on his face when he left the room. He had forgotten to switch off the light.

Mu would not resolve his apprehension that day, nor would he notice that he had left the light on. Details had kept him from charting his day according to the zodiac and that too had been foreseen in his daily horoscope. Nothing in his life had ever been done without the stars. Even his profession as a killer had been implicit in his natal chart.

Algol on midheaven means a career marked by violence. A white, binary and variable star $(25° \propto 3^i)$, Algol indicates the Medusa's head in the hand of Perseus. Medusa, the only mortal of the three Gorgon sisters, who lay with Poseidon in the spring grass, whose face turned men to stone and who was killed by a ruse devised by Athena, the goddess of wisdom. Mu had cast his lot with his astral fate and since Algol, this most malefic of stars, is a harbinger of murderous tendencies and a life of violence, he had made it into a living.

Pluto in Cancer in the 12th House asks for assassination, and with Uranus in Aries in the 8th House death will come through a head injury. Uranus squaring Pluto again speaks of death and catastrophes.

Since his life was shaped by the constellations Mu refused to do anything without consultation, and this made him obnoxious to any organization which operates by dint of reason and efficiency, so he had to go free-lance. Blaise used him frequently because he knew Mu performed without moral hesitation.

But on that day, when Lazard told him in a pub that Toivo would be coming up to see him at six o'clock, Mu was fooled by his professional pride and by not reading his horoscope for that day until he was in the elevator on his way up to his rooms. On that day Saturn and Mars were conjunct to Algol, setting off the Pluto-

Uranus square by midpoint and semisquare. Saturn and Mars conjunct means a steady violence set off by the moon occulting Uranus and affirming the double semisquare to his Pluto-Uranus square. Which was ominous. But he could not accept violence coming from the amateur he had been following so closely all that time and whom he knew to be anything but dangerous.

Astrology had taught him to be punctual and at three minutes past six that evening Mu opened the doors of the self-service elevator and saw Toivo standing close to the wall opposite him. Mu smiled slightly at his charge and had to exert strength to keep the doors open with his left hand, which also held a rolled-up astrology magazine. Trucks roared by on the busy street in front of the building. His face an impassive blank, Toivo took one step forward, jerked his arm up and shot the man twice in the head. One bullet went through the left eye, the other smashed through the bridge of the nose. The lower half of the corpse held the doors of the elevator open. The expression on the face was no longer one of puzzlement. Toivo took the stairs and walked off stiffly down the street.

Epsilon almost failed completing his magna cum laude education because the paper he typed his doctoral dissertation on had cried out in mute pain. Duty to his mother and the scholarly heritage of his family of rabbis had willed him to finish it, though the torture had left him forever unable to read. Every printed page was language stretched on the rack and its pain brought on a migraine of such ferocity that modern psychiatry and associated medicine were unable to cure it. And so he became the most educated illiterate Jew of his community.

It had started early. As a child he could not bear stroking kittens or puppies; shaking hands was a squeezing of tormented souls in Hell; later even the kissing of the Sacred Scroll was too much for him to bear and he was excused from that duty according to the Law which declared him an *istanis:* a person too troubled, too delicate and sensitive to be forced to abide by Scripture. His sensitivity to suffering even in its most subtle manifestation — toasting bread, darning a sock or having intercourse with a woman — became so chronic that his friends feared for his mental well-being. Medicine was helpless and comforters of the soul were equally unable to cope with such formidable *istanis,* so Epsilon was reduced to his own resources.

Now Epsilon was a man of great courage, will power and intelligence. His courage can be seen in that he managed, despite the severity of his delicacy, to reach manhood; his intelligence was evident in his learning and in his knowledge of the Law; his will power was exhibited, for example, in the fact that he ate. The latter activity, though excruciating, he consented to because otherwise he would have starved to death. And to take one's own life was to go against the Law, hence he had to eat. It took him a great deal of time to convince his mother not to subject him to elaborate meals of steaming hot dishes and to allow him to satisfy his body with food compressed into tablets which he washed down with rainwater. Since rain must fall and be sucked up by the earth anyway it might as well be sucked up by organic tissue.

One can imagine the suffering such a monstrous delicacy endured among the race of men. The day was not long enough to exhaust the pain of life. He tried shutting himself up in a dark room. But he knew his mother was sitting outside the door, trying to stifle her sobs so he wouldn't hear her, but also refusing to budge until her child was well again. There was no job which absolved him from contact with animate beings and for Epsilon, the scholar, language (and its reflection, thought) were equally subject to torment. It was a relief when one day he discovered that he had a greater tolerance to steel, and to mechanisms tooled out of steel, than he had expected. Financed by his perplexed father, Epsilon bought a gigantic boiler from an old steamer, welded sheet metal into furniture and began to collect guns. With the same dedication and perseverance he had once applied to his formal studies he now taught himself to become a marksman of superlative ability. Epsilon soon became a professional killer of genius.

Killing was not violence but an act of mercy for the subject as well as for the executor. Between his monstrous delicacy and the surfeit of pain in society he had no chance to extricate himself from his dilemma except through insanity or by taking his own life — two forms of suicide, and one's own life comes first in the eye of the Law. One day he had to go to the city morgue to identify the body of a young man he knew who had been shot in a political demonstration. It was nothing short of a revelation when Epsilon realized that corpses show no pain, nay, cannot suffer pain since they are inanimate, suspended in a state of declining familiarity. He visited other morgues as well as the basements of undertakers and concluded that three out of every four corpses distinctly smile, or if they don't, could be made to do so with a proportionally small exertion of force — proportional, that is, to the bliss they were to show in their finished state.

Hence killing relieved his catastrophic delicacy and brought individuals sooner to the blessed state of nonbeing. The implements of death were rifle or pistol, steel mechanisms which gave him little pain and even, when he had tested his cure on a marked stool pigeon, a feeling of joy no other movable object had ever granted him. Given the state of the world, he would eventually be forced into taking his own life — which would be against the Law so that, since killing prevented him from doing so, this *istanis* to the nth abrogated the Sixth Commandment. Epsilon did not kill but practiced moral euthanasia; those he dispatched would have thanked him for his expertise. For he, so eager to insensitize pain, would not pull the trigger until he was certain his shot was true and death instantaneous.

Such perfection is rare and Epsilon was much in demand, but Blaise had little trouble recruiting him for his threefold shadow when he explained the nature of the assassins Epsilon was to eliminate and their crude bungling which sometimes made their victims die in great pain.

When the doorknob turned Toivo was lying prone on the floor of Epsilon's room partially shielded by a large overstuffed easy chair. He had taken the shade of the standing lamp and had bent the flexible neck with the bare bulb at the end of it toward the middle of the room. Toivo's right hand was on the plug, ready to shove it down into the wall socket. No emotion troubled him. He just wanted to shoot and leave. He recognized the man who had waved at him in the fields in the Lake District. Lazard had told him that Epsilon aimed long and carefully to make sure his shot would be true, no matter what the circumstances were. This gave Toivo a chance.

The man closed the door behind him and was turning for the

light switch. He had not yet seen the visitor who was supposed to come and talk to him. Lazard had leaked him this information and had also insinuated that he'd better be careful because the visitor seemed to have something to do with the sudden death of Mu. Toivo whistled once and the man turned and his eyes were caught in the light of the naked bulb. Toivo shot him in the stomach and chest. He got up off the floor and stepped over the writhing body. Lazard had left a bicycle for him against the wall of the house and he unlocked it and pedaled away, straining against the wind, which made the machine difficult to operate.

Toivo lay burrowed in the snow lying in wait for the last of his three shadows. It had been difficult for him and Lazard to steer Pi to Finland. But Toivo had insisted because he felt spooked by rooms and buildings and he didn't know nature's open spaces in the rest of Europe as well as he did in Finland. Not being familiar with a rifle and not trusting a revolver in the open, Toivo had acquired a Suomi automatic pistol, which could both squeeze off single rounds as well as produce bursts of automatic fire. Acting on Lazard's information he had finally stung Pi into motion by sending him a crushed stone through the mail. The man had left that night for Helsinki to avenge this outrage.

Pi knew himself not as a man but as a stone. He conceived of no border between the animate and the inanimate so that he saw no contradiction in being an animated mineral resembling a man. Pi therefore felt no scruples in killing people because they were not of his kind: pain could only be ascribed to inanimate things. He had been born and brought up at the edge of a desert of stone where he heard the minerals contract and expand with the changes in temperature and since this hurt him he knew he was feeling sorrow for his kin. Skeletal remains of travelers in that wilderness only reminded him of foolish jokes. Their very presence was a mute stupidity. And besides, what is pain?

We assign it somewhat dictatorially to that which resembles us. But when we writhe in agony from a wound in the leg, does the limb hurt or does the body or do we, that is, our soul? Furthermore, if we say that the man next to us feels pain in his leg is that pain similar to ours or do we merely approximate the concept of that pain which is in reality completely his? In other words, pain is a totally subjective experience, and a lonely one. My pain cannot be shared, or, if it can, it is fake. No one can feel my pain the way I can, so no one can really relieve it unless I can do so first. Pain is relative suffering and therefore need not be restricted to that organic pile called man. Nor is movement a prerequisite for the expression of pain. A seemingly immobile pebble can be suffering unaccountable terrors. All we can say of the other is that we imagine him to have a pain similar to ours, but that is not an identification because we do not feel it. One could say our sympathetic imagining is something like a cruel fiction.

Pi was therefore neither right nor wrong. And he felt closer to stone than to man since he had heard stone cry out in the freezing night of the desert and felt it as an expression of his own suffering. When he saw people in agony he indignantly dismissed this as a poor copy of that which a rock quarry endures, and he felt no compunction whatsoever in destroying the life we have tried to sanctify without much success.

Blaise found him out and recruited him. Donner had a keen sense of the extraordinary when it suited his machinations — would subscribe to fictions if they were useful for his particular purposes. So the man who knew he was a stone joined him who was ruled by the stars and him who was excused from the Law by adhering to it as the trio shadowing Toivo across a continent.

Insensed by the crushed stone sent him in the mail, Pi had allowed Lazard to guide him all the way to Finland, never realizing that Toivo was traveling with him in order to know where he was going. Toivo was about two hours ahead of Pi when he had chosen a spot in the deep snow, in the tree line, overlooking a clearing, about ten minutes beyond the cabin Pi thought he was hiding in. Toivo had left a clear and fresh trail away from the empty dwelling and had erased his trek for the last few yards so that he seemed either to have taken wing or to have leaped into the frozen forest of sered, encrusted shapes.

Zipped into a white coverall over a thick parka Toivo lay burrowed in the snow, white on white, like an armed snow hare waiting to trap a wolf. A slight movement in the petrified scene made him ease the safety of his weapon and he grinned when he saw the stranger fumble into the clearing on snowshoes awkward to his gait, a rifle slung diagonally over his back. The light was graying into the long darkness and there would not be moon enough to kill in the night. The pursuer stopped where the tracks ended and was looking around as if the gelid silence could give a clue. His breath clouded in front of him and such evidence of life made him pathetic in the monotony of white encrusted with silence. Toivo laughed and the man heard him. Hampered by the layers of clothing and unsure of his footing it took a lot of time to get his rifle off and ready for action.

Toivo aimed very carefully, balancing the weapon by its drum on a stump. He shot the man in the chest. But the other would not concede death and kept on coming toward him despite the foray of bullets, kept on walking, stumbling, falling, crouching, crawling toward him until Toivo, horrified at such persistent movement, put burst after burst of automatic fire into the shape until it had been smashed into a heap of fragments barely held together by a riddled sack. Toivo had already reloaded with a new magazine when he saw that there was no more movement anywhere. He got out of the snow and put his skis back on and went over to the kill and suddenly felt a terrifying pity for the limp shards in front of him.

Flattened between the low sky and earth shoved upward by the pressure of winter he tried to shoot some breath for himself in the atmosphere compressed as tight as inside an insane skull. The bullets merely ripped up the snow on the ground and shattered the ice casing off the trees and frozen patterns from the branches of pines until the mechanism was empty and silent and there was nothing else to be done.

BRINE ICE covered the steel cables like a stiff fur, hung swords from the railing and made the deck treacherous as a polished shield. The ice added tense sounds to the normal creaking of the hull and the blows of the waves — a threat of imminence. The wind kept the air many degrees colder than the thermometer read and the sun had not been in the sky for a long time; it seemed incapable of thrusting through the low sky as solid and menacing as the heads of a stampeding continent of cattle. The sea slapped huge sheets of pliable slate against the hull and splinters of foam darted through pea jackets or knifed down a boot. The crew only came on deck when absolutely necessary and communication was reduced to bare essentials.

This is what Ragnarök is to be: the end of the world preceded by three years of winter until the giants cross the sea in their ship made from the uncut nails of the dead, cross the rainbow bridge and storm Asgard, home of the gods. Both giants and gods will be destroyed and the earth will drown. When everything has been annihilated the earth will rise again in green splendor from the sea and the past will be less than the stirring of a nightmare. But spring was an impossibility to Toivo, lashed to a boom at the stern, no more than a wish in a dream. Sheets of heavy linen had been rigged all around him to give him cover from the bite of the wind and a large slab of ice had been fastened to a spar directly in front of him so that the two figures stared at each other with transparent blankness. It was a good place to be.

During his retreat from the Finnish wood Toivo had realized how the violence around him had absorbed him into the activity of killing. The deaths of the three men could not even be called revenge, they were merely the result of organic reflexes triggered by his intellect so that his consciousness had been extraverted and frozen rigid in the mechanical duty of the kill. Violence brooks no insubordination; its dictatorial power renders behavior precise for that one function through a series of corrective registrations. Ignited at last when he saw that his art had been made a decoy, his being, possessed by anger, had mechanized him as efficiently as a fully automated robot. He had become a tool subject to the limitations of its function.

In Copenhagen his recollection of having once been unconfined was accompanied by a severe breakdown, followed by a gradual repossessing of his former self as if he were boarding a very brave man-of-war. Released from the municipal hospital, he liquidated all his possessions by wireless, had all his assets transferred to Denmark and bought, after much patient bargaining, enough holdings in the refrigeration ship *The Hoelnir* to dictate his wishes to the owners and crew.

When he boarded the ship for the first time, all that was left of his original luggage was his collection of stones. Luckily he had carried them on his person so that they did not disappear as his luggage had, lost in transit between Finland and Denmark.

The Hoelnir was a medium-sized refrigeration ship that traveled between Greenland and Denmark all year long, transporting large chunks of ice cut from the glaciers in Greenland which were then cubed and sold in plastic bags in the supermarkets of Copenhagen for those whimsical drinkers for whom normally manufactured ice was too mundane and uninspiring. It was a good business and very steady, threatened only by the unlikely event that the tropics would move up to Scandinavia. Toivo never left the ship, even when it was moored in Copenhagen, except to restock the few personal necessities he still required. He lived an ocean exile bordered by Greenland and Denmark, places which were for him no more than points of destination on the map of the ship's navigator. The crew had become used to him and after years of perfect runs the superstitious seamen had elected him their good omen and made sure that nothing would happen to him. He was no more trouble than any normal perpetual passenger. The materials he needed for his art became part of the routine of loading in Greenland — really no more bother than stowing a few extra victuals.

In Greenland two extra chunks of ice, each about six feet tall, were added to the cargo, of which one was fastened to a spar on the stern deck and the other lowered into the ship for cold storage. Toivo worked on the first piece of ice on his way over to Denmark and the second on his way back to Greenland. And since it took him about the time of the journey to finish his work he never went without.

Toivo no longer wrote. His agent in America dealt with the few business matters still left after his years of silence. His holdings in *The Hoelnir* took care of all essentials and a Danish bank cared for the modest sum he had deposited there to speculate with. He did not write another word after *Past Reason Hunted* since he spent all of his time sculpting the same figure out of the hunk of ice the deck crew fastened in front of him so it wouldn't slide away. Loosely tied to a boom so that he did not have to use his hands for balance, Toivo spent his days on deck carving his figure out of ice with a pick and a torch.

It was a pietà with the head of a clown, holding nothing. The larger outlines he hammered out with the pick and the details with a cold chisel. But what he enjoyed the most was trying to attain the smoothness of the folds in the robe and the curve of dejection in the shoulders. He worked at this with the torch, heating the ice with a rolling motion until the flame had melted the ice into the hard translucent satin he desired. When the ship moored he would not look at his creation anymore. The higher temperature of the harbor would melt the sculpture into a formless block and if it hadn't dissolved by the time the ship cast off again, the crew tossed it overboard and, when they were out at sea, lashed a new block down so Toivo could resume his work.

Since it was a medium he was not accustomed to he had to grope his way from primitive approximations through the sureness of craftsmanship to the simplicity of perfection. Whether he would ever reach that final stage was a moot point. Since the history of his achievement had melted away, the only comparison which could possibly be made was with the stills in his mind. But these, of course, had never been reproduced.